Mr.

A Pride and Prejudice Variation
Elaine Owen

Text Copyright 2014

Dedication

Dedication

To my friend Cyndi and to my high school English teacher, Nancy Vocature Thank you for teaching me to love writing. This book is dedicated to you.

Table of Contents

PROLOGUE

Mr. Darcy came toward her in an agitated manner, and thus began, "In vain I have struggled. It will not do. My feelings will not be repressed. You must allow me to tell you how ardently I admire and love you."

Elizabeth's astonishment was beyond expression, but she could not be insensible to the compliment of such a man's affection. She tried to compose herself to answer him with patience.

"In such cases as this, it is, I believe, the established mode to express a sense of obligation for the sentiments avowed, however unequally they may be returned. I am sorry to have occasioned pain to anyone. It has been most unconsciously done, however, and I hope will be of short duration. I must, with all possible gratitude and appreciation for the favor of your application for my hand, nevertheless decline."

Mr. Darcy, who was leaning against the mantelpiece with his eyes fixed on her face, seemed to gather her words with no less resentment than surprise. The pause was to Elizabeth's feelings dreadful, as she waited to see what her unwelcome suitor would say or do next.

CHAPTER ONE

At length Mr. Darcy turned and strode toward the far side of the room, then turned abruptly back to her. Elizabeth could see the struggle between his native pride and the humiliation of his current rejection reflected in his face. "Forgive my forwardness, madam," he said in a voice not at all like his usual haughty tones. "I have no desire to be the cause of any unpleasantness to you; and I hope in the future we shall both be able to forget this interview as quickly as possible, for both our sakes. But I must ask. Was I so mistaken in my estimation of you to think that you had perhaps come to have some regard for me?"

Elizabeth's surprise was even greater now, if possible. To think that Mr. Darcy had believed she had come to care for him! How could he possibly have overlooked her teasing tone, her piercing remarks toward him, and her avoidance of his company? Certainly she had never desired his good opinion!

But he was waiting for her answer, and she must give him an answer that would be honest yet not compromise her own peace of mind. She was not obligated to list every objection she had to his person. Indeed, she dared not mention Jane or Bingley. She did not know how much Darcy confided in his friend, yet it was reasonable to suppose that any words about Jane might make it to Bingley's ears, and she would not invade Jane's privacy. Could she tell him that she knew about his treatment of Wickham? No, Darcy was a powerful man, with friends in many places. Elizabeth would be sorry to be the instrument by which Wickham was punished once again.

She need not give him any reason at all for her refusal. A simple, "No" ought to be enough. But there was a look, an expression on his face as he gazed at her which required an explanation from her. The disappearance of his haughty mien had unexpectedly revealed a man who would be deeply hurt by any refusal she gave, and she had no wish to be cruel. She chose, instead, to raise the one instance that involved her own feelings only, without involving anybody else's story.

"Mr. Darcy, at almost the beginning of our acquaintance, even before the formation of it, I was painfully aware of your opinion of me. I had no reason to believe your opinion altered, and my own regard for you never had a chance to form after that."

Darcy looked at her with incredulity. "The beginning of our acquaintance, madam?"

"At the very first ball you attended in our county, with Mr. Bingley. Surely you recall?"

He continued to regard her with puzzlement.

"Mr. Darcy, at your first assembly in Meryton, you said that I was not handsome enough to tempt you."

Darcy's face paled and he sat abruptly down, with his hand to his mouth, staring out the front window. After a moment he said with some difficulty, "I must beg your pardon. It has been many months now since I have believed you to be the handsomest woman of my acquaintance."

Elizabeth looked away, too embarrassed to say a word. She hoped, she prayed that the Collinses might abruptly return and put an end to this painful interview, even as Mr. Darcy asked in a gentle tone, "Is there any chance that I might be able to undo that poor first impression? A mere apology for such an unkind statement, made in a moment of pique, could never be enough. Tell me what I may do, anything that might make it possible to change your estimation of me. Perhaps with time the memory of my poor manners might fade, and your present inclination might be reversed."

"Mr. Darcy, I do not even know you, and you do not know me. We have scarcely had half a dozen conversations between the two of us, and those conversations have been marked by more pauses and silences than any exchange of ideas. Indeed, there could scarcely be two people who have had less to say to each other than we have, until now. I repeat, sir, that although my manners may have been at fault, I have never intended to engage your affections, and it was done most unconsciously. Please allow me to express my gratitude for your offer, but I must decline the honor of your proposal."

"Forgive me, then, for my intrusion upon your peace of mind," Mr. Darcy replied formally, hardly knowing where to look. "I believed I had made my intentions toward you clear, and that you were, in fact, anticipating my address. The fault has been mine; please do not distress yourself with any recriminations. Please accept my sincere wishes for all possible future happiness." He stood, bowed, and made his exit, leaving Elizabeth in a high state of agitation.

∞

Mr. Darcy in love with her! And so much in love as to defy the expectations of his family, to disregard her fortune and connections, and make his proposals in the very shadow of a relative who would not but disapprove, and that most vigorously. Could she be so dear to him? Could his affections truly have overcome such obstacles? His manners were at fault, surely. He had dwelt on the inferiority of her connections in a way destined to be offensive to her, yet still he had declared himself, and with a surprising directness that spoke of the strength of his feelings. Her rejection must have been painful, exceedingly so, yet the manner of his leave-taking was charity itself.

How had Darcy come to believe that she cared for him? She could think only of the morning walks, three of them, where he had joined her. The first time they had walked together had been truly by accident, at least on her part. She had not welcomed Darcy's company when he suddenly appeared but she could hardly have turned him away without awkwardness. The other two times had been in the same grove at the same time of day. He must have thought that she had appeared there again in the hopes of meeting with him again! How unfortunate that she had not perceived his intentions before, and that now he must think she had been willfully deceiving him.

She was glad that she had mastered herself and not shown anger at the manner of his proposal. If she had given vent to the indignity she felt at some of his statements, she would not have heard the unvoiced passion behind every word. Then too, her indignation on Jane's behalf threatened to raise its head, and that alone could have caused her to say things she might have regretted later. Even her knowledge of how he had hurt Wickham could have come to the fore if she had given full vent to everything she truly thought about him. She congratulated herself on her self-control and her narrow escape from exposure of her own passions.

So much had happened that she felt a headache coming on, and the indisposition she had previously pleaded now became true. Feeling unequal to Charlotte's perceptive gaze, she retired for the night, but sleep came only hours later.

∞

Darcy left the parsonage in a daze, hardly knowing where his feet were heading, hoping that they would somehow carry him to Rosings of their own accord. His heart was urging him to turn around and go back to the parsonage, to Elizabeth, to plead his case with her; and controlling that urge took most of his conscious energy. The rest of his mental energy was being used to recall all of his interactions with Elizabeth from November until the current day.

How could he have misread her so badly? He had spoken only the truth--he thought Elizabeth to be patiently awaiting his addresses, recognizing the struggles he had faced as he overcame his own arguments against a union with her.

No doubt she was conscious of those arguments without him having to point them out--her lack of fortune, her poor connections, the lack of propriety in her family. She had to have known them. All women were aware of their advantages and disadvantages in marriage from the time they first entered society. She would have been more so, being one of five daughters from an entailed estate; knowing the reasons why Jane, for all her loveliness, had yet to receive any offers. Even Bingley could not, should not, overlook those reasons against offering for Jane.

Darcy stopped dead in his tracks, a new thought entering his mind. Did Elizabeth know? Did she suspect that he had played a role in separating Bingley from her sister? He stood still, the April breeze blowing on his face, as he replayed their conversation in his head. What reasons had she given for declining his offer? She had said that she had heard his horrible statement about her last fall, that her dislike of him had been fixed at that time, and that she had not cared to know him since. No. She did not know about Bingley. Had she known she no doubt would have been merciless to him, caring for her sister as she did

He resumed his quick stride. Elizabeth was right. She did not know him, and her first impression of him had been that ill-fated statement at their first assembly, a statement made only to prevent further conversation when he was uncomfortable in the new setting. He would have to explain that to her, explain why he said it and then apologize profusely. Surely she would let him plead his case, if he could just speak to her again.

Deep in thought, he entered Rosings by the back entrance, thus avoiding his aunt's notice, and went directly to the suite he shared with his cousin.

He must begin again with Elizabeth, go more slowly this time, and lessen her ill opinion of him. Hopefully her reluctance was based simply on the affront he had caused her that one time. Elizabeth was generous, kind to others, and possessed a forgiving nature, as he had seen for himself. She had withstood attacks from Miss Bingley and

Mrs. Hurst many times without the least ire, and she had maintained a friendship with Charlotte Lucas even after Charlotte had accepted the proposal of Mr. Collins, a proposal that rightly should have been made to one of her sisters. Thank heavens Mr. Collins had not proposed to Elizabeth herself! Mrs. Bennet would hardly have allowed her daughter to decline such an offer, with Jane already as good as spoken for and the other sisters still so young.

Yes, Darcy thought, he just needed time to make amends for his thoughtless remark. Elizabeth would forgive him, he would renew his addresses, and all would be well. He sat on the edge of his bed and allowed his valet to begin undoing his tall boots.

Darcy let his gaze drift to the oak writing desk opposite the bed. Perhaps he should start by writing Elizabeth a letter? He was fluent and articulate in writing, much more so than in the spoken word. He could write Elizabeth a letter tonight and put it into her hands tomorrow morning in the grove where she liked to walk. She would read his words of remorse, her heart would soften, and he could continue to court her.

But he discarded this thought almost immediately. A note would be difficult for her to explain to others if she were caught with it. Propriety dictated that an exchange of letters would not take place between a couple that was not engaged. The lady's reputation could be damaged. She could even be forced to marry the gentleman if her reputation suffered enough, a circumstance that Darcy did not find appealing. Heaven forbid that odious parson should discover Elizabeth with a note from Darcy!

No, he would find time to speak with her alone, and then pursue her again with all possible decorum. This time she could not claim to be ignorant of his interest in her. With this determination in his mind he finally let himself rest for the night.

CHAPTER TWO

The next morning Elizabeth rose later than usual, having lost much sleep the night before. Her headache had abated but not disappeared by the time she appeared at breakfast, and Charlotte looked at her with concern.

"Truly, Lizzy, I had hoped that an evening of rest at home would help you feel better, not worse. You look more peaked today than last night. Shall I call the apothecary?"

"No, I thank you, Charlotte. I believe a bit of fresh air will help cure whatever ails me, and I plan to take my usual walk this morning. Perhaps you would care to join me?" Elizabeth hoped her friend would agree to accompany her so that she would be certain of not running into Darcy again by herself.

"I am afraid not. Lady Catherine has asked Mr. Collins to produce the household books this afternoon for her perusal, and I must review them for him this morning. I shall accompany you tomorrow, perhaps."

Elizabeth rather doubted that Darcy would want to see her again, but when she set out she took the precaution of striking out into a new path, one which she had not yet explored. Her thoughts were still occupied with the scene she had passed through the night before, and the beauties of the greening trees and emerging flower buds were barely noticed.

Darcy had certainly presented his suit in the most unforgivable way. Never had she heard of a man who pointed out all the shortcomings of his potential bride to the potential bride herself! Never, except perhaps for Mr. Collins in his proposal to her. But then Mr. Collins was a particular and unique case. Her mouth twitched as she imagined Darcy's indignation at being compared to Mr. Collins.

Yet upon reflection she realized that it was possible that Darcy's words about her low connections were meant as a sort of confidence, an acknowledgement of the difficulties he felt in looking for a union with her, and not meant to disparage her. Perhaps he spoke freely out of a mistaken belief that by listing the objections he had had to overcome, he was complimenting her with the strength of his attachment to her. A rational scheme, to be sure, and one that might explain his manners to her if she knew him better, if she were more familiar with his ways of thinking. Still, his chance remark about her lack of beauty stung her pride even now, and she could not overlook his role in Jane's life and in Wickham's life. She had no desire to know Darcy any better than she already did.

She was unfamiliar with the part of the park in which she now walked, a charming copse with a small brook wending its way slowly through. The path she was on cleared the brook with a low footbridge, and then rounded a tree abruptly as it turned back towards Rosings. The trees suddenly behind her, Elizabeth recognized that she had entered her favorite grove from another angle. There stood the gate separating the parsonage from the great house, the palings shining white in the morning sun; and there stood Darcy facing away from her, looking earnestly at the pathway from where she usually entered. Obviously he had been waiting for her again.

She started with confusion and abruptly turned away, but he heard her footstep and approached her immediately. "Miss Bennet, I have been walking the park for some time in the hope of meeting you. Will you allow me to walk with you?"

She had much rather not walk with Darcy at all, not after their conversation of the previous night, but she could think of no way to politely decline. Darcy took her silence for assent and fell in beside her as they proceeded forward, offering her his arm as he did so. Elizabeth, embarrassed, took it, but did not dare to meet his eye. They proceeded for a minute or two without saying a word. Elizabeth was determined not to break the silence and Darcy obliged her by beginning the conversation.

"I feel, Miss Bennet, that I owe you an apology after our conversation of last night. I put you in a difficult, even humiliating, position, and you deserve a full explanation." He paused to look down at her, his brows furrowing in concern.

"You owe me nothing, Mr. Darcy, nor I you. We misunderstood each other's actions and words, which led to your proposal and my refusal, and that is the end of the matter. There is no need to belabor the point."

Darcy shook his head. "That, too, was uncomfortable, but I am not speaking of my offer to you. I refer to my unguarded words about you at the assembly last autumn."

Elizabeth looked at him archly. "Where you found me not

handsome enough to tempt you?" She still felt uncomfortable speaking to him so freely after his startling proposal but she could not resist the chance to tease him.

Darcy flushed. "I did not actually mean those words."

"Clearly not, or you would not have been tempted to propose last evening."

He pressed on. "When Bingley and I first entered the assembly I could not help but be aware of the attention that we attracted in such a small gathering. Where the society is larger, such as in town, our appearance is of little interest; but in country society we are sure of being pointed out and watched. Every move we make is monitored, every step we take commented upon. Every time we ask for the favor of a dance, tongues wag to determine the date of the upcoming marriage with the lady in question. Our fortunes are brought up, discussed, weighed in the balances, and measured for their relative value."

Elizabeth gazed steadfastly forward, her face revealing nothing, but she silently acknowledged the truth of his statement. It was true. Before Darcy and Bingley had been half an hour at the assembly every person there knew their names, family situations, and fortunes.

"Meryton, of course, is much the same as any other country assembly. I dislike being the object of such scrutiny, and taking my turn on the dance floor invites even more. When Bingley approached me I was already fatigued from the evening's activities and had no desire to invite more attention, yet he persisted in his efforts. I could think of no other way of discouraging him than saying that nobody there was tempting enough for me. In that way, he gave over his attempts to entice me to participate, and I knew that nobody there would then desire me to join them."

"Mr. Darcy, I am sure I do not believe you. All you had to do was say that you did not care to dance, or plead fatigue. There was no need to insult me or any other young lady." She looked directly at him for the first time, wanting him to know that she did not accept his flimsy excuse.

He inclined his head in acknowledgement. "You are correct. All of the reasons I have just stated do not excuse my behavior that night. Though my objections were true and valid, the fact remains that I insulted you. And the main reason I could not bring myself to simply state that I was fatigued or that I did not care to dance was because of my abominable pride and temper. Both get the better of me at times, and I let them do so that evening. I did not behave in a gentlemanly way, and for that I must beg your pardon."

Elizabeth hardly knew how to answer. Darcy had at once confirmed and contradicted every previous impression of himself. She had always believed him to be an ill-tempered, unpleasant sort of man, and now he had confirmed his ill- temper and pride. Yet he had also humbled himself enough to apologize to her for an offense long past, and on a day when his pride must surely have been propelling him to run as far away as possible from the woman who had humiliated him most by rejecting his proposal. Contrary to every expectation, he was showing a new side of himself.

She said nothing, her face concentrated in confusion as she tried to take in this new information. Darcy regarded her earnestly. "Please, Miss Bennet, tell me that you will accept my apology. I offer it most sincerely."

"You perplex me exceedingly, Mr. Darcy," Elizabeth finally answered, neatly avoiding a direct answer.

"In what way, Miss Bennet?"

"I am trying to understand your character, and am failing quite impressively. I cannot make it out at all. You have made an offer, I have refused, and I would expect you to decamp from my disgraceful company at your earliest opportunity. There is no need to press your apology upon me again."

"My honor demands that I do all in my power to make amends where possible. There is nothing further to understand."

"Am I to understand that, if I give you this forgiveness, you will then regard yourself as having redeemed your honor? And having thus cleared your conscience, will you then feel no further obligation to pursue my company?"

"If it is your wish, then of course I will importune you no further." He hesitated. "However, I have another purpose in speaking to you this morning. As you said last night, you and I do not know each other. I presumed too much in making you an offer upon an acquaintance that was, in your eyes, inadequate for such a purpose. If it is agreeable I would like to further our acquaintance."

"You wish to court me?" Elizabeth asked with a feeling of disbelief. Would this man never go away?

"I do. When you come to know me, you will find that I am persistent in pursuing something of value to me. I am not easily put off by encountering obstacles. But of course the choice is entirely yours. Should you tell me not to persist you need not worry that I will impose myself on you ever again. I merely ask for the opportunity to start anew with you, as I should have started long ago."

They had reached the end of the palings that separated the parsonage from the park and by mutual accord they stopped and faced each other. Elizabeth studied the ground, earnestly wishing that her tongue, usually given to fluency, would not pick this moment to become immobile. She had too many things that she wished to say to him, yet did not think it wise to voice any of them. The affection of such a man was flattering, to be sure; but she still remembered his failings of character--his interference with Jane and Bingley, and his heinous treatment of Wickham. If she allowed his courtship, these were topics she must and would raise. And yet now she wondered about her own conclusions of his character. Teasing, teasing man! Would she ever be able to understand him, and did she even want to try?

The silence, to Darcy's ears, was unbearable. "Miss Bennet?" he inquired anxiously, inclining his head to look into her face.

Elizabeth finally raised her head. "Mr. Darcy, I gladly give you my pardon for your remark at the Meryton assembly. I believe, as you said, that you succumbed to a momentary fit of mood that controlled your temper, and that you would not say again what you said then. As for courtship--" her brow wrinkled, "I believe that I must ask--"

"Capital day, cousin!" came the colonel's interrupting voice. "I trust I am not interrupting your ramble with Miss Bennet?"

Elizabeth and Darcy recollected their circumstances and greeted the colonel with as much courtesy as they could under the circumstances. His smiling face and genial manner did not indicate that he noticed any awkwardness in their circumstances. While Elizabeth was relieved that her interview with the gentleman was at an end, Darcy felt all the frustration possible in such a moment of interruption. He was anxious to converse privately with Elizabeth again and hear her response to his question, but was instead forced to join his cousin as they walked Elizabeth back to the parsonage. Their conversation would have to wait until another time.

CHAPTER THREE

For the next two days Darcy applied himself to his aunt's estate matters with a thoroughness it did not usually command.

He had previously fixed it with Colonel Fitzwilliam that they would quit Rosings the next morning, but until he had a clear answer from Elizabeth he was unwilling to take his leave. He must find a way to communicate with her again, and he must ascertain if there were any other obstacles he must overcome in order to win her affection. His whole attention was focused, whenever possible, on guessing what Elizabeth would have said next if they had not been interrupted.

Lady Catherine and Colonel Fitzwilliam were both surprised when Darcy told them there were unresolved issues with several tenant farms and that he would be unable to return to town for at least several days. He rose earlier than usual each morning and walked in the park hoping to meet Elizabeth, but he did not encounter her again. He did not know whether to attribute her absence to a wish to avoid his presence, or to the fact that each morning had been unusually chilly and with a light rain.

On the third evening his patience was finally rewarded by seeing the Collins party arrive at Rosings for a pre-arranged gathering. They arrived shortly after dinner was cleared and Darcy escorted Mrs. Collins into the drawing room, followed by the colonel escorting Elizabeth. As they sat, Elizabeth looked towards Darcy with an expression that seemed to indicate her willingness to speak with him, but there was no room near her for him to sit and so he remained where he was in silent frustration.

Lady Catherine and Mr. Collins started the evening's entertainment. "If it pleases your ladyship, I have prepared the revision of the message I will deliver on Sunday and am prepared to submit it for your approval at this time," Mr. Collins stated.

Lady Catherine inclined her head in acknowledgement. "I will review it at my leisure tomorrow or the next day, and will have it returned to you so that you may practice its delivery adequately. I trust you made the changes I suggested."

"Your ladyship is all condescension and affability, as usual. I did indeed make the changes you recommended, and I added some few comments of my own to the remarks you made."

"Do you normally submit your sermons to her ladyship ahead of time?" asked Elizabeth, curious.

"Indeed I do, at her kind request. She is gracious enough to give me guidance on what message should be delivered and even, at times, indicates exactly what is to be said. "

"What is the subject of this week's sermon?"

Mr. Collins smiled brightly at her interest. "The homily will be from St. Luke, the story of the Good Samaritan. As the sermon was first written, the main point was going to be the utter irresponsibility of traveling so far a distance as Jerusalem to Jericho without a suitable escort to provide security and to protect against the sort of mischievous persons as one sometimes encounters on the road."

Elizabeth smothered a smile. "I imagine that is a point of the parable that not many of your parishioners will have encountered," she said solemnly. "Indeed, it is difficult to see how one could improve upon that lesson from the text."

"Oh, but indeed it could be improved! Lady Catherine, upon reviewing it, pointed out that the real lesson of the story, the real moral, lies in the fact that the Good Samaritan was obviously a person of some means, culture, and high refinement to so generously provide for someone so far beneath his station. And while we may all aspire to such superior character, such charitable impulses are best left to those of genteel station and rank, who can easily determine who is most deserving of their efforts."

"I am sure your parishioners will agree, once they have had a chance to hear your thoughts and to learn the source of such insight."

"Miss Bennet is wise beyond her years to accept the guidance of those above her station," commented Lady Catherine. "She might make a good governess one day if she is unable to contract a suitable marriage. Miss Bennet, I believe you had one eligible offer of marriage already," here Mr. Collins bowed, "which you saw fit to decline. It worked out well for Mrs. Collins, who might never have found a husband otherwise, but it did not speak well for your future prospects. Have you never had any other more eligible offers?"

Elizabeth's color changed and she gave an involuntary glance towards Darcy, who looked earnestly at her. Until now he had not heard that Mr. Collins had ever made an offer for Elizabeth, and his whole mind remained fixed on that possibility, which in his estimation must have been most repulsive to her. He was almost immobilized with horror at the very thought.

Lady Catherine did not notice and continued uninterrupted. "Your older sister, too, is unmarried still. Most extraordinary! But perhaps not so unusual when there is no fortune to be had. I am told she is quite lovely, but gentlemen must have more to live off than a pretty face. Were I her mother I should never have allowed her to remain single so long. I would have most strenuously insisted that some suitable match be arranged, no matter how distasteful to those involved, so that the prospects of the younger sisters might not be materially diminished."

Mrs. Collins demonstrated her own good breeding at that point by asking Elizabeth if she would favor them all with a song on the pianoforte. Lady Catherine looked vexed at the interruption but allowed it to go forward, and Darcy recovered enough to accompany Elizabeth to the instrument, hoping he might now speak to her privately.

He stood near and turned pages as she played her first selection, which was well received. As she started her second song, a glance at the rest of the room showed that the others were absorbed in their own conversations. As there was no chance of being overheard now, he took a risk and said, "I had not realized that you had an offer of marriage from Mr. Collins at one point."

Elizabeth kept her eyes fixed on her music, but she arched one eyebrow. "I did receive such an offer, and I must say he was most reluctant to accept my rejection!"

"And after that he turned his attentions to your friend?"

"It was no loss to me, and it made a providential match for her." She glanced up at him. "I do find it amusing that you and Mr. Collins have something so unexpectedly in common."

Darcy was taken aback by the comparison to his aunt's parson and did not speak for a moment. Finally he said, "I hope that I am more successful in my suit than he was in his. Please tell me that you will permit my attentions further. You are too fair to reject something, or someone, you do not know."

"My sister Jane was in town these three months past," she answered, seeming not to hear him. "Did you happen to see her there at all?"

"I did not have that pleasure," he answered with some confusion. "She was staying with her aunt and uncle, I presume?" Darcy pondered inwardly why she had abruptly asked that question.

Why did she ask if he had seen Jane instead of answering whether he could court her? She had already asked him that exact same question not many days before, had she not? He was certain that she had.

"Of what are you speaking?" Lady Catherine's strident voice interrupted. "I would have my share of the conversation! If it is music you are discussing I insist on taking part."

"We were discussing some of the intricacies of this piece, your ladyship. I was telling Mr. Darcy that certain passages have defied my attempts at mastery, and he was encouraging me to persist in understanding them better. He believes that with time and familiarity I may come to appreciate this music more." She looked at Darcy significantly.

"Indeed that was my statement," Darcy concurred, hardly knowing what he was saying. "Time, familiarity, and constant exposure to the difficult measures will invariably make them easier to understand, and greater understanding leads to appreciation and enjoyment."

"I believe the composer may have made a mistake in this particular passage," Elizabeth continued smoothly, indicating a line on the second page. "He wrote the melody in such a way as to sound as though it would resolve at this point; but then the melody moves up instead of down, and it does not resolve at all. It leaves one with an unsatisfied feeling."

"Perhaps," Darcy said slowly, "at the time he wrote it, the composer felt that the resolution was fair and just; but now he realizes that corrections are needed."

"Then let us hope he realizes where he went astray and makes the needed corrections as soon as possible," Elizabeth finished brightly. "Until then I will play it no more. Miss Lucas, will you not favor us with your playing?" She vacated the instrument, leaving Darcy to turn pages for Maria Lucas until Colonel Fitzwilliam took his place.

Darcy determined from this conversation that Elizabeth had answered his question in an indirect way. In speaking of music she was referring to his pursuit of her. He, Darcy, was the composer who thought his efforts to claim her hand would be resolved easily. Instead, her own feelings were unresolved, and she needed to come to know him better before accepting him. The explanation for this coded message was easily determined in this manner.

Yet although this explanation suited well, he himself also had an unsatisfied feeling with the conversation. Some element was missing; some further meaning eluded him, and he struggled to understand what it might be. She had spoken of needed corrections, not of time needed. Indeed, he realized that he had been the one to bring up needing time, not Elizabeth. Then too, she also spoke of resolution. What resolution did she seek? In his mind, the resolution would be reached when she accepted his hand, but that did not appear to be her meaning.

Darcy had also noted that although Elizabeth spoke with a smile and without obvious censure, there had been a strong emotion in her face when she spoke to him. The expression in her fine eyes had hinted of reprimand or reproof hidden just under the surface. She was not pleased with him for some reason; and he longed to know what that reason might be, or if his own anxiety was making him imagine things.

Elizabeth, for her part, was well satisfied with the evening so far. She had hoped for some way to express her reservations to Darcy in a way that would not attract the attention of the others, and in this she had succeeded. Darcy appeared to have understood her hidden statement, that there were unresolved matters between them before she could consider a courtship; and his serious look in response to her statement told her that he would consider well what those matters might be. Her question about Jane would, hopefully, guide him to the right answer.

Lady Catherine eventually called the group to play cards with her and they all gathered around the table except for Miss de Bourgh and her nurse, Mrs. Jenkins. Miss de Bourgh was occupied in watching and listening to the others while Mrs. Jenkins nurse pulled her blankets more closely around her and asked insistently if the room were too cool or the lights too bright. Mr. Collins took the opportunity to state that he was most happy to play cards if his noble patroness so desired, as he saw nothing about the pastime that was incompatible with the profession of a clergyman.

As they played, Lady Catherine asked Mr. Darcy about estate matters. "I am told, Darcy, that you spent an uncommon amount of time in the stables today with the grooms. Tell me what commanded such attention, for I believe all the little matters there, which usually take up so much time, are well in hand."

"Generally speaking, they are," he answered, "but yesterday afternoon I observed a yearling with a curious habit which I wished to investigate further. This animal was in the habit of approaching any doorway only from the left side, when given an opportunity; and would become quite agitated when someone approached him on the left side of his body. He would also fix the doorway with a stare from his right eye. I began to fear that the vision in his left eye was impaired."

"I would have told you, had you asked," Lady Catherine rejoined. "John told me about that animal two weeks ago and we had the best farrier in the country examine him. The horse had a cyst in the left eye, but it is healing well and he will be much improved shortly."

"He may have had a cyst; I do not know about that. But I saw no cyst today. What I did observe was a mare in the small paddock, a mare that would approach the gate of the paddock in a similar manner as this yearling, always from the left to the right. I inquired and found that the yearling was the offspring of this mare, that she had been injured in an accident with a gate years ago, and that ever since she has approached gates only by using the vision in her remaining uninjured eye. The foal merely learned the behavior from his mother."

"It is curious, is it not," Colonel Fitzwilliam offered, "that offspring can learn such behaviors from their parents. A behavior that is healthy and sensible in one person may be observed, absorbed, and then imitated in a nonsensical way in the next generation."

"I suppose," said Charlotte, "that if we could look upon our own parents and family with true objectivity there might be many behaviors that we would see as objectionable in others, but find perfectly normal among those we love. Familiarity often dulls our sensitivity unless we see the behaviors again with fresh eyes, and we tolerate in familiars what we would never tolerate in strangers."

"I agree," concurred Elizabeth. "Scarcely a family exists but would have some cause for embarrassment in it somewhere, when viewed in a dispassionate way."

"That is certainly not the case with my family!" Lady Catherine cried. "The de Bourghs have never stooped to the low manners of those around them, but instead have set the standard for all public behaviors. My own manners have always been celebrated famously wherever I go."

"It is a blessing to have family members for whom there is no cause to blush." Elizabeth caught Darcy's eye as she said this and was pleased to note that the corners of his mouth twitched as he glanced involuntarily at his aunt. "Tell me, Mr. Darcy, how did the grooms respond to your assessment of the yearling's behavior? Will they work on training him and correcting the fault?"

"The grooms expressed their appreciation of my knowledge of husbandry," Darcy rejoined, "a knowledge I hope to expand upon in the future." He observed Elizabeth gravely as he said this, and she was forced to admit to herself that she must once again revise her opinion of him, as she fought to hide a private smile.

∞

"Darcy, I have never seen you so taken by a woman," declared Colonel Fitzwilliam in their private suite later that night. They sat in the small study, each sipping a final brandy before retiring.

"I hope my interest was not obvious."

"I don't believe so. I only knew about it because you told me. Rest assured our aunt is unaware, or you and the lovely Miss Bennet would be dismissed forthwith!"

"A fearsome thought indeed. I should not wish to cause Miss Bennet any discomfort or subject her to Lady Catherine's abuse."

"Then you had best dismiss yourself forthwith, before she discovers your interest for herself. You were so demonstrative tonight it's a wonder she hasn't realized your real interest in 'estate matters.' Certainly you should decamp before announcing your engagement. When will that be?"

"I do not know."

"Generally an engagement follows immediately on the heels of the proposal, so when will that be?"

"You misunderstand the situation, Edward. I made her an offer three nights ago, and she refused." Darcy stared into the fire moodily.

"Good God! You cannot be serious!" Edward stared in absolute surprise. "Has she already had another offer that she may not decline?"

"Not at all. I believe her reasons were much more personal."

"And what were they? Or do I dare too much by asking?"

Darcy shook his head. "You may ask, but I cannot tell you, for I do not know. She mentioned an insulting statement which I made last autumn within her hearing. I apologized and she has accepted the apology; yet I believe she still has something against me. She as much as told me tonight that she will not accept a courtship until I correct whatever the matter is."

"However did you have this conversation, Darcy, under Lady Catherine's very nose? Without her awareness?"

Darcy briefly related the substance of Elizabeth's conversation at the pianoforte, leaving out the curious change of subject.

"I applaud your taste, Darcy. What a mistress she will make for Pemberley, if she will accept you! I practically told Miss Elizabeth several days ago that had I the means to marry where I wished, she would not be safe from me."

"You were speaking of marriage with Miss Elizabeth?" Darcy wondered how many men had intentions towards Elizabeth besides him, and then considered that it was surprising there were not more suitors for her hand.

"Last week sometime, in a general way; it was nothing serious. We spoke of you more than of me, truthfully. I must say she did not seem well pleased with you at the time."

Darcy regarded his cousin with an incredulous look. "You spoke of me? And she did not approve of me?"

"She questioned your interference with your friend last autumn."

Now Darcy absolutely started and could not look away. "How did she know about that?"

"It came about in our conversation. I told her about the care you take of your friends, how you prevented Bingley from making a most imprudent match with a lady who was eminently unsuitable, though I told her I was not certain that it was Bingley. She deemed your interference officious."

In great agitation Darcy rose and crossed to the window, looking out into the night without seeing. "Edward, the woman Bingley admired is Miss Elizabeth's older sister, Jane Bennet."

"You counseled Bingley against offering marriage to the elder Miss Bennet on the basis of family objections, yet you offered for the younger Miss Bennet? Darcy, have you taken leave of your senses? What were you thinking?"

"I was thinking that I was being kinder to him than to myself!"

"I doubt that Miss Elizabeth will appreciate such generosity."

"I did not separate them out of my own desire," Darcy responded earnestly, turning to face his cousin. "I was convinced by my close observation of Miss Bennet that her heart had not been touched, that her affections were not engaged, and that Bingley was in serious danger of committing himself to a loveless marriage. I reminded him that the dutiful daughter of an ambitious mother like Mrs. Bennet would have to accept his attentions regardless of her own inclination. But for Miss Elizabeth to have taken such offense must mean that Miss Bennet truly did feel hurt when Bingley left her. It appears I misjudged her affections. That explains why tonight, for the second time in a week, Miss Elizabeth asked if I had seen her sister in town."

"And did you?"

"I did not. Miss Bennet called on Miss Bingley and Mrs. Hurst in January, and they eventually called on her in return. I understand that after that Bingley's sisters completely dropped the acquaintance. They were most anxious to avoid their brother meeting with Miss Bennet either by accident or design."

"So there you have it, Darcy. You have been discovered. Your plan to advance on Miss Elizabeth's defenses has been routed; and she not only has the upper hand, she has you in complete retreat. It is time to raise the white flag."

"My faults according to her estimation must be heavy indeed," said Darcy. "Yet there is a relief in knowing the worst. This is a mistake that can be easily remedied. I must undo the damage that has been done in separating Bingley from Miss Bennet, let Miss Elizabeth know that I have owned my error and made what correction I can, and then hope that we may continue."

The colonel eyed him with unrestrained curiosity. "Please tell me your strategy, for your ambition rivals that of Napoleon."

CHAPTER FOUR

The ladies of the parsonage were greatly surprised the next morning when Mr. Darcy and Colonel Fitzwilliam called upon them to make their adieus.

"We have just informed our aunt of our immediate departure," the colonel stated, "and have come to take our leave of you as well. My cousin finds that he has urgent business in town that cannot wait, and we shall be off before the afternoon."

"Is all well, Mr. Darcy?" Mrs. Collins inquired courteously. "I trust you have had no bad news? Your company will be much missed at Rosings."

"All is well, I thank you," Darcy replied. "I have merely become aware of an issue that needs my presence to remedy. I believe it best that it be resolved at once." He kept his eyes on Mrs. Collins as he spoke and Elizabeth could read nothing in his countenance.

"Lady Catherine must have been dismayed to hear of your sudden change in plans. I know how fond she is of you," said Mrs. Collins, which both gentlemen acknowledged with a nod.

"She is much disappointed, of course; but she knows that things like this come up from time to time and cannot be avoided. She will have consolation in your company, Mrs. Collins, and in that of your friends," the colonel responded graciously.

"Our own visit will be ending soon as well," Elizabeth said. "Our plans are to leave on Saturday."

"I am sorry to hear that," the colonel answered heartily. "I hope we may meet again soon, whether here or in another place. Will you go directly to Hertfordshire?"

"Not directly. We shall first stop at my aunt and uncle Gardiner's, in town."

Darcy addressed Elizabeth. "Miss Bennet, when next we meet I shall request the pleasure of your performance on the pianoforte once again. I look forward to hearing your mastery of the piece we discussed last night."

Elizabeth could not answer this in any way without embarrassment, so she merely nodded in acknowledgement. The gentlemen then took their leave and shortly afterwards they saw Darcy's carriage pass by on its way out of the park.

With her nephews gone, Lady Catherine felt the sudden and immediate need for the comfort offered by a visit from the group at the parsonage; and accordingly she sent her carriage for them at tea time. "The young gentlemen were excessively disappointed to have to leave," she said, "but so they always are. The dear colonel rallied his spirits tolerably till just at last; but Darcy seemed to feel it most acutely--more, I think, than last year. Their attachment to Rosings certainly increases every year."

"How could it be otherwise?" Mr. Collins answered her. "Who would not be sorry to leave Rosings when once they have seen it, and how could anyone ever bear to leave a place graced with such fine personages?"

Her ladyship ignored him. "Miss Bennet, I understand you will be leaving shortly as well, but I would have you extend your stay here in Kent. You must write to your mother and beg that you will stay a little longer. I had quite counted on your being here another fortnight, which would make a complete two months. Your presence here does not make up for my nephews' absence, but it is better than having no diversion at all."

"Your ladyship is all kindness, but as my father wrote last week to hurry my return, I believe we must abide by our original plan," Elizabeth replied.

"But if you stay another four weeks complete, it will be in my power to take you to London myself, in the barouche-box; for I am traveling there myself, and that is an honor you cannot decline."

"I regret to miss such a privilege, but believe that I must follow my parent's wishes in this regard."

Lady Catherine looked resigned. "Well, I suppose you must then; but it is all very inconvenient, and very vexing, the way young people must go traipsing about these days. In my day we stayed sensibly at home where we belonged and did not travel about as freely as is common nowadays. Have you decided what time of day you will leave? I always say that leaving at ten in the morning is the ideal time if one can arrange it; for it is late enough in the morning that the chill of the air is gone, but not so late that the heat of the sun has become oppressive. You may count on it; there is no better time of day to start a journey."

Elizabeth noticed that Mr. Collins had withdrawn a notebook in which he was now writing frantically, and she looked at Charlotte questioningly.

"It is a new habit," Charlotte leaned close and whispered. "He writes down important things that Lady Catherine says in order to study them later at his leisure."

Elizabeth focused just enough of her mind on the conversation around her as to be able to contribute a remark now and then, and to hear Maria conscripted to stay an additional four weeks with Mrs. Collins in order to mollify Lady Catherine. But her thoughts were more preoccupied with Mr. Darcy and his surprising declarations and actions of the past few days.

Darcy's sudden business in town felt like an excuse to her, an excuse to leave Rosings as quickly as possible, and she could not but wonder if it were connected with her in any way. Had he understood her question about Jane? If so, did it alter his sentiments towards her? His countenance when he visited to take his leave had given nothing away, but his parting words to her were an unmistakable message that all was not over between them. She would have no choice now but to wait to see when or if their paths crossed, and she was not certain if she anticipated or dreaded meeting with him again.

Elizabeth's attention was caught as Lady Catherine continued speaking. "When my niece Georgiana went to Ramsgate last summer I made a point of her having two men-servants go with her. Miss Darcy, the daughter of Mr. Darcy of Pemberley and Lady Anne, could not have appeared with propriety in a different manner."

"Certainly not," thought Elizabeth, "as the future sister of Miss Elizabeth Bennet of Longbourn." She was bemused to think that by now, had she so chosen, she might have been presented to Lady Catherine as her future niece; and she could just barely imagine what her ladyship's indignation would have been to such a perceived insult. She reflected that she had seen an unexpectedly humble side of Darcy several days ago when he apologized to her, and that the previous evening she had seen a new, humorous part of his personality. Surely he must also have much courage to even think of facing down his formidable relative, and she reluctantly added this trait to his list of attributes.

∞

Several days later, on a Saturday morning, Elizabeth made her farewells to Charlotte, promising to write soon and to visit again. A short, uneventful journey put Elizabeth on her uncle's doorstep in town, where she was met by Jane, her aunt and uncle Gardiner, and a crowd of little Gardiners, all gathered together and eager to welcome her.

It is a fine thing to be enveloped by one's family when that family gives nothing but joy; and Elizabeth gloried in the feeling and looked forward to its continuance for several days before she and Jane would continue on to Longbourn.

The house in Cheapside was a stark contrast to the parsonage in Kent. The presence of so many children added variation to the day; and although there was more commotion and less time for quiet reflection, Elizabeth found she could tolerate the change very well after the constant stillness of Charlotte's house. Her aunt and uncle were truly fond of each other. Her aunt employed no secret schemes to keep her uncle out of the house and out of mind as much as possible, nor did her uncle show anything but respect for his wife's behaviors and statements. While they made no overt displays of endearment, their contentment in each other's presence was reflected in their orderly house and joyful, yet well-behaved offspring. Elizabeth reflected once again that she had made the right decision in refusing Darcy's proposal of marriage. All the luxury in the world could not equal the happiness to be found in a marriage with true respect and affection.

The thought did cross her mind that perhaps if Darcy had understood her hint about Jane he would bring Bingley with him to call on them both at their uncle's house. But she could not imagine Darcy lowering himself to make a visit to Cheapside, even if he knew the direction; thus she was not disappointed when neither man made an appearance. Although he had seemed to desire to continue their acquaintance, it was possible that his affection would not stand the test of a rejected proposal. If so, she would not regret it.

Their handful of days at their uncle's home were taken up with shopping, outings to the park, calling on friends of Mrs. Gardiner, and a theater show in the evening. Elizabeth had little time to evaluate her sister's spirits, but she seemed tranquil enough. A quickly whispered conversation with Mrs. Gardiner told her that Jane was still sometimes given to fits of despondency, but that she exerted herself well in those moments and was demonstrating improved spirits over time. Elizabeth believed it was good for Jane to be a part of a bustling household with many varied activities to keep her occupied, and away from the prying eyes of Meryton. Jane had been away from Hertfordshire for three months. By the time she arrived home other gossip would have come to the fore, and Jane would no longer be so subject to the prying eyes and wagging tongues of their friends and neighbors.

The days of their visit passed swiftly, and then it was the night before they were to leave for Longbourn. Their bags were mostly packed, the carriage engaged, and all necessary preparations for their departure had already been made. All that remained was this final meal and to say their farewells in the morning. They would arrive at Longbourn in the early afternoon of the following day. It was therefore surprising as they left the supper table to receive a messenger directly from Longbourn with an urgent message from Mrs. Bennet addressed to Jane. Their mother was not a great writer and Elizabeth could not imagine what circumstance would make her put pen to paper when she would see Jane so quickly the very next day. Curious, she read over her sister's shoulder as Jane read the short note out loud.

My Dearest Jane,

Make haste and come back to Longbourn the moment you receive this letter, for he is come! He is come at last! Mr. Bingley is returning! The housekeeper at Netherfield has received orders to prepare for the arrival of her master, and she was going to the butcher's on purpose to order in some meat for his arrival in the next day or two! Mrs. Nicholls saw her there and came to tell me herself that it is certainly true! Oh! My dear Jane! You must return to Longbourn the very instant you receive this letter. Do not wait to pack your things for your uncle may send them after you, and you need not wait for Lizzy either unless she is ready to come with you. Only make haste to return as quickly as ever you can! I must stop this letter for my nerves are all a-flutter and I know not what to write. I must order in a fresh haunch of venison to have for his first dinner here!

Such was Mrs. Bennet's haste that she neglected to sign the note, but the handwriting and especially the style could not be easily mistaken for anyone else. Mr. Bennet had added his own note to the end of his wife's.

Jane,

You need not haste home in the exact moment that you receive this. I daresay a delay of ten seconds or so will make no difference to

Mr. Bingley. Return tomorrow as planned, and you may decide on the way how best to redecorate at Netherfield once it is yours. Please warn the carriage driver to avoid all the other carriages who will be transporting other young ladies to Hertfordshire post-haste.

Your affectionate father, etc., etc.

Elizabeth laughed freely at the absurdities in both notes and her aunt and uncle were also highly amused, but Jane's face was a study in embarrassment and anxiety. "Oh, my dear Mama! She means well, but his return may mean nothing to me. He lets Netherfield; why should he not come back to it when he wishes? Perhaps he is coming back in order to hunt. I doubt that he has thought about me at all. I do wish she would not draw such attention to it."

"My dear sister, I hope that he is indeed coming back to hunt! But perhaps he has a different quarry in mind than what you are thinking."

"Lizzy, you must not tease me so! I do not wish to return home and be subject to such speculation. I can see how it will be. Mr. Bingley will be kind and polite, I shall be kind and polite in return, and we shall remain as friends. I would rather not have an audience for every possible interaction between us."

"Yes, you shall be kind and polite, and he shall be kind and polite, and we shall all be kind and polite together and get along quite famously. But, sister, I do believe that matters will soon start up right where they left off last fall."

"You cannot be certain of that. My feelings are unchanged, but his may not be, if indeed he had any to start with. He may have met someone else who captured his interest or he may have decided that we should not suit. I shall not read anything into his return beyond the renewing of a very pleasant acquaintance."

"Oh, very pleasant indeed!" Despite her words of denial, Jane's face had lit up, a smile had appeared, and hope gave her face a new luster. Elizabeth was on the verge of commenting that only a very pleasant acquaintance could cause her to smile so brightly; but Mrs. Gardiner, sensing Elizabeth's mischief, cut her off with a shake of her head.

"Jane, your cheerful, patient attitude will be your strength when you see Mr. Bingley again. You are entirely correct in saying that he may have another purpose in returning to Netherfield besides seeing you. If he truly felt affection for you in the fall, it will have stood the test of a short time of separation, and he will make his feelings known when you see each other again. If he does not begin to demonstrate such interest you may still value him as a friendly acquaintance. Either way people will talk about you; but they will talk less, and will give up the topic sooner, when they see that you are just as free and easy with him as with any one else you know. Try not to be disturbed by their gossip, for it will be short-lived if they see nothing new about which to gossip."

"Thank you, Aunt--I shall remember." Jane smiled at her aunt and then hurried upstairs to see to the children before they went to bed. Elizabeth looked at her aunt.

"Seriously, Aunt Gardiner, I shall be very surprised if Bingley is not as much in love with her as ever as soon as he sees her. I hope he proposes to her before we take our trip to the Lakes, for I should hate to miss an opportunity to tell her 'I told you so.' "

"I hope you are correct, my dear."

CHAPTER FIVE

Elizabeth could hardly wait for the carriage to start off the next morning, for in the busy Gardiner household there had been no opportunity for the privacy she desired in order to tell her sister of Mr. Darcy's proposal. But now, inside the closed carriage, she divulged to Jane every detail of Mr. Darcy's speech to her that she could recall, as well as her own answer and subsequent exchange with him in the park, including his desire to court her. But she had resolved to suppress every particular in which her sister was concerned and so she gave only a brief recital of their conversation at Rosings, giving Jane to understand that she had given Darcy very little hope of ever changing her mind. For herself, she said, she did not care if she never heard from him again.

Jane's astonishment was considerable, but was soon overcome by the sisterly affection which made his attachment to Elizabeth seem only just and right. Soon she expressed regret that Mr. Darcy had made his proposal in a manner so unlikely to recommend his suit, and she was grieved for the unhappiness which her sister's refusal must have given him.

"He was wrong," said Jane, "to be so sure of himself, and to be so confident of your response. But I am glad that he was able to acknowledge what he said about you at the assembly and to make a suitable apology. Perhaps this will help him in the future to learn to guard his words more carefully; and to know how to show his admiration to a suitable lady before proposing instead of listing all his objections. Perhaps, in time, he might even try to renew his proposals to you. Would you accept him then, if he were to make you an offer in a manner more befitting a gentleman?"

"First I must be able to recognize such a proposal!" Elizabeth answered. "So far I have been the recipient of two offers of marriage, both of them offers made in such an exceedingly bad way as to forever blot out whatever I thought a proposal should actually sound like. I almost wish to have many more offers in order to have more stories with which to entertain others. But I suppose if Mr. Darcy can ever make an offer as charmingly as Mr. Collins, I might have to seriously entertain his for a minute or so."

Jane smiled, but Elizabeth readily saw that her sister's mind was too preoccupied with the sudden change in the neighborhood of Longbourn to dwell for long on the perplexing Mr. Darcy.

At noon they arrived at the inn in Meryton and pulling up outside, through the coach window they could see Lydia and Kitty's heads outside the window of the second floor, calling exuberant greetings and waving their handkerchiefs in the air. "I am so glad you came," Lydia called out to them from afar, "for I should have died of boredom if we had to wait another minute! We have so much news to tell you! But first let us eat! We have ordered and arranged a meal here for you, but you will have to give us the money for it for we have already spent all ours!"

After disembarking and making their way upstairs, Jane and Elizabeth watched as the two younger girls proudly displayed a salad they had dressed themselves, saying, "Is this not nice? Is this not perfect in every way?" The two girls had been busy, for besides arranging the refreshments they had spent no little time in the shops of Meryton. Lydia displayed the hat she had bought with her money, saying "Although it is very ugly, I did not buy it for its looks, for it has none. I have been using it to collect the names of the most handsome officers stationed in Meryton! Look, I have a piece of paper and a pen! Do write down who you think is the handsomest officer in the regiment and drop it in the hat, and then we will see who gets the most votes and invite him to our party!"

"Shush, Lydia, that is not proper," Jane began, but Lydia answered, "Oh! You need not write a name, Jane, for we know whom you find most handsome and he is no officer!"

Lydia apparently had not changed in the time that Jane and Elizabeth had been away. Throughout lunch her conversation dwelt on the officers she had seen, where she had seen them, with whom she had spoken, and what they were wearing. Although she professed great curiosity about her sisters' journeys she had yet to ask either one a single question about them.

"And of course you know that Mr. Bingley is coming back," Lydia stated loudly as they sat at the table. "Mama was in such a state when she heard, you cannot even imagine! I know she sent you an express last night to tell you about him."

Jane and Elizabeth exchanged glances, and the maid was told she need not stay. Lydia waited until she was gone and then said, "Well there is no need for secrecy! Everyone in Meryton is talking about him. I really grew quite tired to hear Mama exclaim over her poor nerves again and again."

"If I had such poor nerves I would never complain about them so; but all I get are headaches, and they are worse," said Kitty piteously, but nobody paid her any attention.

"Mrs. Forster says Bingley only came back because he could not get a wife anywhere else and he has decided that Jane will do very well after all," said Lydia in eager tones, "but Aunt Phillips says that his going away was meant all along, that he never meant to take up a settled state anywhere outside of town."

"Are Miss Bingley and the Hursts not with Mr. Bingley, then?" asked Elizabeth.

"The housekeeper was told she need only open one room, but others may join him later. He was to arrive today. Only think of it, Jane! If you and he both arrive back on the same day will it not appear as though you already have an understanding? What a great joke that will be! And Elizabeth, I have news of your favorite too!"

"My favorite? Who may that be?"

"Oh, do not act so missish with me, for we all know how you favored Wickham! You may rejoice! Wickham is safe from Mary King, for her father has sent her to Brighton to get her away from him, and now you may flirt with him again all you wish. I daresay he will call at Longbourn as soon as he hears that you have returned."

The carriage ride home was a great deal more crowded than when Jane and Elizabeth had arrived, for instead of two young ladies there were now four; and although the luggage of the elder Miss Bennets was stored in the boot, the recent purchases of the younger two were riding inside with them. Lydia had her head outside the window as much as inside, for the weather was fair, and she commented to her sisters on everyone she saw.

"Look! There is Emily Butler with Jane Parker, walking to Meryton. Emily!" she called out the window. "Come to Longbourn tomorrow and I will give you back the kerchief I borrowed, only I haven't had it washed yet so you mustn't mind doing it yourself!"

"I do not have her kerchief at all," Lydia said to her sisters as the carriage passed the two young ladies, "but I want to ask her all about her brother who is about to take a commission. He will be leaving for --shire in a fortnight. And there is Mr. Smithson and his daughter. Is she not monstrously ugly? They must be going into the butcher's shop. She was hoping for an offer from Mr. Terrance, but nobody would offer for a spindly thing like that; and besides, she is five and twenty years old. I should die of shame if I had not found a husband by five and twenty!"

"You are crushing the box I bought for my new ribbons!" Kitty complained. "Move your knee off my lap!"

"Nobody cares about your ribbons, Kitty; there's Mr. Denny!" was the sisterly reply. "Denny! Come call on us at Longbourn, for my sisters are home and there will be plenty of fun!"

The whole party disembarked at last at Longbourn, with many warm greetings from their remaining family members. Mrs. Bennet said repeatedly that Jane was more beautiful than ever, and that now that Mr. Bingley was returned, her beauty would certainly not be wasted; and Mr. Bennet told Elizabeth gravely, more than once, "I am glad you are come back, Elizabeth. Your mother's nerves have gone from being my long time friends to my most intimate acquaintances." Mary looked up from the Bible she was reading long enough to comment gravely, "In the book of Job we are told that the Evil One went to and fro on the earth, and walked up and down in it, and therefore I am content to stay at home. But I do not know that all travel is necessarily evil."

Mrs. Bennett now raised a topic which her husband wished had been forgotten long ago. "As soon as we hear that he is settled, Mr. Bennet, you must go and call on Mr. Bingley."

"Why? Why should I do such a thing?"

"Because it is the custom, Mr. Bennet!"

"'Tis a custom I despise," he answered, "and it will all come to naught. Last year you promised that if I called on him he would marry one of our girls, and yet nothing of the sort happened. So why should I bother to do it again? It seems a fool's errand to me. Call on him yourself if you are so inclined."

"Oh, Mr. Bennet! You know I could not do that! All I know is it would be abominably rude not to call on him, since you have already made his acquaintance; and I do not wish for anyone to accuse our family of poor manners."

"You may be certain that nobody will accuse our family of having poor manners within your hearing, my dear."

Lydia saw an opportunity to advance her latest favorite scheme. "And it would be very poor manners for me to turn down Mrs. Forster, would it not, Mama? She invited me to Brighton as her special friend, and I the youngest of us all!"

While Lydia continued to plead with her mother, who needed no convincing, and Mrs. Bennet implored Mr. Bennet, the elder Miss Bennets asked Kitty what Lydia was talking about.

"Lydia has become great friends with Mrs. Forster, whose husband is the commander of the regiment, and she has asked Lydia to come visit her in Brighton when they all remove there in a few weeks. It seems very hard that she should not ask me, for I am older by a whole year!" Kitty told them. Lydia had relayed the invitation to her parents, feeling that such a compliment to her would have to be answered in the positive. Mrs. Bennet then promoted the scheme to her husband. Lydia would be well supervised, and she would have all the company and activities so naturally desired by one of her age. Mr. Bennet had so far steadfastly refused to give an answer either positive or negative, which fact alone was enough to make Lydia redouble her efforts towards his approval. However, even Lydia and red coats could not long occupy Mrs. Bennet's mind now that she had Mr. Bingley to think about again.

Despite his careless speeches, Mr. Bennet had secretly planned to call upon Mr. Bingley as soon as he heard for sure that he had arrived. Sunday came and went with no such news, and Mr. Bennet decided that perhaps he might try to find out more information on Monday; but to their great surprise Mr. Bingley himself called upon the family at Longbourn on Monday morning.

Mr. Bennet was in his study and the ladies were in the drawing room when they heard his horse ride up to the house. They had not long to speculate on their visitor's identity, for a few moments later they heard his quick step in the entry way and then Hill was announcing him into the room. All the ladies stood and curtsied, and Mr. Bennet came out of his study in order to greet him properly. Both men then sat down, and the conversation was chiefly carried on between the two of them, with Mrs. Bennet making her own contributions.

Jane curtsied and smiled with the rest of them and then sat down to her mending with unusual attentiveness. Elizabeth was proud to note that her sister's manner was free of any resentment or ire and equally free from any special attentions or favor. From their manner of greeting, Jane may have simply renewed an old, casual acquaintance. Only her mending gave anything away, as Elizabeth noted several tangled threads were stitched over repeatedly rather than removed and repaired.

Bingley's conversation was with Mr. Bennet but his eyes were all for Jane as he politely discussed his travels, the state of the roads, the weather, and the condition of his estate. Although his tone was light and social, his hands twisted hard on his walking stick and his voice was occasionally tense. He inquired as to Mr. Bennet's health and the health of all his relatives, but in truth there was only one relative that really caught his attention.

When Bingley rose to leave Mr. Bennet extended him an invitation to hunt the next day, which Bingley gratefully accepted. "And perhaps," Mr. Bennet continued, "you will then feel free to join our little supper party here afterwards. We have a small group of officers gathering here before they are whisked off to other parts of the world." This invitation was agreed to with great eagerness and Bingley then left.

Elizabeth could not help but wonder about Bingley's sudden desire for the company of the Bennet family. Last fall he had been charmingly attentive to Jane, nearly inseparable from her whenever they met, yet had disappeared from all their lives most abruptly. Nobody in the neighborhood had heard a word of him all winter. Then Elizabeth had heard from Colonel Fitzwilliam of the role Darcy had played in separating Bingley from her sister, and she had hinted her disapproval to Darcy. Darcy had then suddenly traveled to London where Bingley probably still was, and now Bingley appeared on the Bennet front steps. Had Darcy spoken to Bingley? If so, what had he said? Or perhaps Bingley had simply returned of his own accord, and he might leave just as abruptly as he had returned. If Darcy had spoken to Bingley, she thought it more likely that Darcy would have accompanied his friend back to Hertfordshire. Only time would bring answers to her curiosity. Otherwise she might have to resort to tricks and stratagems to figure it out.

Of more immediate import was Mr. Wickham who would be included in the number of officers coming for dinner tomorrow. Elizabeth had kept the promise she made to her aunt before traveling to Kent; she did not believe that her heart had yet been touched by him. Though she had found him to be the most amiable gentleman of her acquaintance, she was aware that even amiable gentlemen must have a fortune to live off, and she did not possess that attraction. Undoubtedly he had formed an attachment to her, but his attachment to Miss King had been more pronounced, in keeping with her fortune. Still, she looked forward to an easy conversation with him, renewing a pleasant friendship and comparing their viewpoints of their common acquaintance, Mr. Darcy. Very few things bring such guilty pleasure as criticizing someone who is not present to defend himself.

CHAPTER SIX

Mr. Bingley arrived in good time the following morning but the ladies of the house did not see him then. He and Mr. Bennet left directly for a morning of shooting and did not return until shortly before supper. By then the officers had already arrived, and they all made a merry group as they sat at the table. Elizabeth watched eagerly as Bingley entered and looked for a seat. Mrs. Bennet had, of course, decided not to ask him to sit by herself so that he might have an opportunity to be seated by Miss Bennet. Bingley entered and by chance caught Jane's eye as she looked around and smiled at him just then, and all was decided. Bingley sat in the empty seat at her side to the general delight of at least half the people present.

By chance or design Elizabeth was seated next to Wickham and they made polite talk throughout the meal. She found that he had not changed in the six weeks she had been away. His manners were as pleasing as ever, and his appearance, at least in Elizabeth's eyes, was just as handsome. He remained the very picture of her image of an ideal gentleman. Despite her resolve to remain indifferent Elizabeth was gratified to find his attention fixed all on her.

"I am glad you are returned, Miss Bennet. The pleasure of your company was greatly missed. I can only hope that your time away from us was so well employed that you were able to put your friends in Hertfordshire completely out of your mind, and not miss us as much as we missed you."

"I had an enjoyable trip indeed, Mr. Wickham. It was a pleasure to see Mrs. Collins again and to see her new home. I believe her present situation is as agreeable to her as anyone can rightfully expect, under the circumstances."

"And her situation--is it a pleasant one? Does she see much of the inhabitants of Rosings?"

"Lady Catherine is a most attentive neighbor," said Elizabeth, smiling. "I believe the Collinses see as much of the inhabitants of Rosings as they could wish."

"I recall many of her visits to Pemberley when I was a boy. There was little that escaped her attention even then."

"Her attention could hardly be bestowed upon a more grateful object."

"In your journey did you happen to travel through the village of Kympton?"

"I do not believe that we did."

"I only mention it because it was the living that I was to have had, if circumstances had been different. It is a pretty parsonage, well situated, and a prosperous living. It should have suited me exceedingly well."

Elizabeth felt again the rise of indignation on Wickham's behalf that she had felt before her visit to Kent. "It is painful for me to believe that so much misfortune could be visited on you by one man. I had occasion to meet with Mr. Darcy several times at Rosings and I was surprised that his ungenerous nature was not more manifest there."

"Did you not state before that everyone in Meryton had found him to be proud and disagreeable?"

"I did," Elizabeth answered, "but as I came to know him a little more I found that he is not as disagreeable and proud as he seems at first, though his manners are still lacking."

"Truly!" Wickham exclaimed, with a flash of surprise on his face. "You need not worry that I will attack his character again in your presence, since he is become such a favorite." He turned his face away from her and looked steadily forward.

"You mistake me, Mr. Wickham. He is not a favorite of mine, and my overall impression of him is much the same as it was in the autumn," Elizabeth said with some confusion. "A spot or stain on a carpet may be smaller than first feared, but it is still a stain."

Elizabeth perceived that she had offended Mr. Wickham with her weak defense of Darcy and felt dismay at the misunderstanding. She had meant no affront to him. She opened her mouth to beg his pardon but stopped herself just in time. Why should she apologize to him for stating her honest opinion? She had given Wickham no just reason to resent her simply by saying that Darcy was perhaps not as bad as she had first thought. She could hold to her opinions without asking permission or forgiveness, from Wickham or anyone else.

"I am glad you see the stain is still there, Miss Bennet," Wickham answered after a moment. "It is painful for me to make new friends and then to have those friends turned against me by his hand. It has happened more times than I care to recall."

"My friendship is not so easily lost, Mr. Wickham," Elizabeth answered warmly. "My opinions are not swayed by entertaining false accusations, particularly when leveled by someone with whom I have such a passing acquaintance. Your reputation is safe with me."

"You are all goodness, Miss Bennet. I know not how he may attack my character, and I cannot defend myself against anything he says because of my respect for his father."

Elizabeth did not answer, for a new thought had struck her for the first time. She remembered that at almost the first meeting she had had with Wickham he had said much the same thing--that his respect for old Mr. Darcy would prevent his exposing the son. Yet within days of Darcy leaving Netherfield the whole neighborhood of Meryton had heard all of Wickham's complaints against him, turning the general opinion against Darcy even more than formerly.

Suddenly Wickham's manners seemed less appealing. Wickham had been sorely wronged by Darcy, of that she had no doubt; but she would not allow herself to completely overlook his sudden willingness to contradict himself. She resolved to be more guarded in her interactions with him, a resolve that was then tested by the renewal of Wickham's usual charm, for he seemed to regret his former outburst and to be bent on making up for it.

∞

Darcy pondered his cousin's final words at Hunsford as he rode in the carriage from London to Netherfield. The colonel had asked him about his strategy to win Elizabeth's consent but Darcy did not care for the term, as it hinted of trickery and deceit; and he abhorred disguises of every kind. His manner was as direct as circumstances allowed so that there would be no misunderstanding in his communications. It was his direct manner that had dictated his manner of proposal to Elizabeth, and in telling her afterwards that he wished to court her.

But, he admitted to himself, his straightforward way had not worked for his benefit in asking for her hand. It was possible to be too honest, to share too much of one's thoughts in the name of candor when courtesy should also be brought to the fore. Recalling his expressions during his proposal he began to regret how much he had dwelt on the inferiority of her connections and her family's lack of income. He was able to admit to himself that had he been in her shoes he would have been offended. In the days since last seeing Elizabeth, he realized that he owed her an apology for making a proposal that might have sounded more like an insult; and he vowed that he would beg her forgiveness at his earliest opportunity.

But first he must see her and gain a private audience. For that reason he was now returning to Meryton, to stay at Netherfield while he tried to win Elizabeth's consent.

He had done his best already to undo her ill opinion by hurrying back to London as soon as he could and speaking to Bingley about Jane. Bingley had been astonished, and then delighted, when Darcy told him that he believed he had been wrong about Miss Bennet.

"I have reason to believe," he told his friend, "that Jane Bennet was perhaps not as indifferent to you as I previously thought."

Bingley had stared at him, doubt written across his features. "You told me she was not attached to me, that I should be entering a loveless marriage if I were to take her as my wife!"

"Yes I did, and I acknowledge my error. I had no business trying to ascertain her feelings for you and I erred in discouraging you from pursuing her. Your happiness lies in your hands, not in mine."

"Darcy, with whom did you speak? How did you come to hear that she cares for me?"

"I did not hear any such thing. It is merely my own conclusion, after reflecting more on the events of this past winter, that I may have been mistaken in believing her indifferent to you. Her mother may be ambitious, but none of us should be judged by our relatives. Each person deserves to stand or fall on his own merits."

Bingley, ever trusting, did not press his friend for more details. "I should not have listened to you," he stated flatly. "I should have followed my own inclination and stayed in Meryton for the winter. What if she has another suitor by now?"

Darcy could not give his friend any guidance on that point. On his own Bingley decided to return to Hertfordshire at once so that he could see Jane again and determine her feelings for him once and for all. He also wisely decided to leave his meddling sisters at home with Mr. Hurst, for he had discovered the role they played in separating him from Jane. The long-suffering Bingley had had enough, for once, and had no patience for their protests. Darcy only hoped that Bingley's first meeting with Jane had gone well or he himself might be forced to seek lodgings elsewhere. Although Bingley was as generous a soul as ever lived, Darcy feared his reaction if he had lost all of hope of winning Miss Bennet.

The Darcy carriage pulled to a stop outside Netherfield. Darcy stepped out of the door as his footman held it open, looking about for

Bingley, but was disappointed to see only Bingley's butler, Hawkins, waiting on the top step. Hawkins welcomed him courteously and Darcy inquired as to Bingley's whereabouts.

"I daresay you will see him for dinner, sir. He is riding the estate with his steward at the moment but we are expecting a large party this evening."

Darcy pondered this for a moment. "A large party? For how many is Cook preparing?"

"The Bennets are the primary family invited, sir, but also the Phillipses and Lucases, Reverend Snow, and a few others from the neighborhood. It will be a farewell dinner for the officers as they are decamping from Meryton tomorrow."

"I can only hope that Bingley will not begrudge feeding one more person, then."

"I am certain he will not. He left Mrs. Dawson with instructions to prepare the rose suite for you, sir, in case you chose to join him here."

Darcy nodded with satisfaction, judging from this information that Bingley must have restored his relationship with Jane. "I thank you. Please have my trunks brought to my room; and if it is not too much trouble, I should like water to wash with as well." The ride from London was not a great distance but he still wanted to look his best when he saw Elizabeth that evening. He realized that Wickham might well be in attendance and although he had no desire to be anywhere in Wickham's company, he found that he would willingly endure far worse if such was the price for seeing Elizabeth again.

CHAPTER SEVEN

Bingley had been a regular caller at the Bennet household in the week since his first visit. The day after the dinner event he had taken the opportunity to call upon Mr. Bennet in the afternoon to ask his advice on plantings in his fields. It was, after all, his first spring season as the owner of a landed estate; and he said he found himself sorely in need of direction. The two men rode out briefly together and then returned to Longbourn, at which point Mr. Bennet conveniently disappeared into his study, leaving Bingley to attach himself to Jane.

From that day forward there was no pretense of his calling upon Mr. Bennet. Bingley would arrive at some point in the late morning or early afternoon and the rest of the day would be spent largely in Jane's company; probably, Elizabeth thought, to the great detriment of his fields. Jane said nothing more of her indifference to Elizabeth, and Elizabeth said little to Jane except to comment once that she must suddenly have become a great expert at farming. Unless outside events intervened Elizabeth thought their courtship would quickly reach its conclusion.

Elizabeth herself had little time to dwell on Jane and Bingley, for she also had a regular caller in the form of Wickham. Though he was not in as constant attendance as Bingley, he had gone out of his way several times to further their acquaintance. On one sunny afternoon he and Elizabeth had accompanied Bingley and Jane on a leisurely walk to Oakham Mount, and another evening found Wickham and Elizabeth singing a duet while Mary played on the pianoforte. She quickly found that his easy nature and amiability would have made it easy for Wickham to be as much a favorite of hers as ever had she not briefly glimpsed a different side to his personality. She wondered if that had been a brief, uncharacteristic moment of anger, or if he might be more ill tempered than she had previously considered.

She did find some little time to consider Darcy and his proposal to her. She was willing to give him credit for having restored Bingley to Jane, for she thought it most likely that he had spoken to his friend to inspire Bingley to return so quickly to Netherfield. But in the ten days since returning from Kent she had heard no more of

40

him. Surely, if he had spoken to Bingley out of concern for her feelings, he would have returned to Netherfield with his friend in order to pursue his suit. But perhaps he had had time to reconsider his choice, in which case she would see him no more. She was surprised to feel some disappointment that he might give her up so easily, but she would not let him touch her heart any more than she would allow Wickham to do so.

These thoughts and more occupied her mind as the Bennet carriages made their way to Netherfield for the supper party planned by Bingley. With Lydia in high spirits and Mrs. Bennet in raptures of joy over her plans for Jane, their arrival was immediately apparent to Bingley, who came out to meet them on the front steps. He smiled broadly as he offered his arm to Jane to escort her inside. Mrs. Bennet trailed behind exclaiming over the furnishings and decorations.

Elizabeth looked around inside the Netherfield hall, wanting to see if Wickham had arrived yet, but she did not see him. Instead she was confronted with the appearance of Darcy, who courteously extended his arm to walk with her inside. She could not do other than to take his arm in surprise.

"Miss Bennet, it is a pleasure to see you again," he said with warmth.

"And you as well." Elizabeth hardly knew how to answer. Apparently Mr. Darcy had not given up on her after all. "We had not heard that you accompanied Mr. Bingley back to Hertfordshire."

"I only arrived this afternoon. I trust you found your family well? They are all in good health?"

"As you can see for yourself, sir, the best of health."

They were silent for a moment as all the Bennets filed into the drawing room, from where they would go in to dinner. Darcy looked at her earnestly. "I trust that your oldest sister is especially well."

Elizabeth could not help glancing at her sister where she stood with Bingley, her face aglow with satisfaction. "I believe she has never been better, Mr. Darcy. A happy heart makes for splendid health."

"And you? Has your health been splendid as well, at seeing your sister's changed circumstances?"

"That remains to be seen, Mr. Darcy. Since returning from town I have felt quite hale and I can only hope to continue so." She turned away from him and moved across the room to greet her aunt Phillips.

Darcy observed her gravely but did not follow her.

Several minutes later Lydia's high voice was heard giggling over the noise of the general conversation. "Look! Here come the officers! There are Denny, and Forster, and even Wickham! Come Kitty, we must go outside to greet them! Lizzy, will you not come with us to meet your favorite?"

"I do not see why you need me to come with you. Colonel Forster is married, Denny looks only at you, and Wickham will only speak to Lizzy!" Kitty answered, but Lydia was already out the door.

Elizabeth flushed with embarrassment and looked at Darcy to see how he bore the new arrivals. His face was stern as he looked from her to the door and Elizabeth thought she saw his color rising. He looked at Bingley and opened his mouth as if to speak, but Bingley had eyes for no one but Jane, and it appeared that he was not aware of the arrival of the officers until they made their entrance.

Mrs. Bennet made up for her hosts' distracted state. "How good to see you, Colonel Forster, and Mr. Denny! Mr. Wickham, we are so happy to see you as well! I might have known Mr. Bingley would see to the happiness of my girls by inviting us for this occasion, for as you know they love nothing better than a man in regimentals!"

The colonel bowed. "The pleasure is all ours, madam. Bingley invited me and asked me to choose a half dozen or so of my officers with which to complete his number at the table, since there would not be room enough for all of them. I brought only the finest."

"I'm sure you did; and your choices do you credit, for they are already well known in our house. Denny is a great favorite with my two youngest, and Mr. Wickham has called on my Lizzy already three times this week! Such pleasant young men as they are. I do believe had he any money Wickham might even make an offer for her!"

"Mama!" Jane, jolted from her tete-a-tete with Bingley by this statement, attempted to stop the flow of words.

"I am jesting, of course; for Wickham cannot have serious intentions towards anyone with such reverses of fortune as he has had!" She said this with a pointed look in Darcy's direction.

Elizabeth resolved to draw no limits in the future to her family's capacity to expose themselves. "Mr. Bingley just had new wallpaper and carpets installed in the parlor, Mama. Shall you not like to see them?"

"Indeed I would! Come, Kitty and Lydia, we shall go see these improvements for ourselves. Mr. Bingley! I should dearly love to see how you are updating your rooms!"

Bingley happily led the way to the parlor with all but Elizabeth, Wickham, and Darcy following behind. Wickham, who had not yet noticed Darcy, advanced into the room and came directly to Elizabeth, taking her hand in his and kissing it lightheartedly. "Miss Bennet! It is a great pleasure to see you here again this evening! It seems far too long since we took our turn in the gardens yesterday afternoon!"

"Six and thirty hours, if one is to be precise; but of what use is such precision?"

"We have so few hours left here in Meryton that I am counting them all. I must be sure to make good use of what hours remain. After we leave tomorrow I do not know when or if we shall ever return to this county."

"And when friends are on the eve of a separation they like to spend the remaining time they have together. We have been good friends, have we not?" She stole a quick look at Darcy to see him standing stiffly at attention, his whole manner one of disapproval as he stared at Wickham.

"There are also those people whose friendship is a thing of the past," Darcy interjected in a stern voice, speaking for the first time in some minutes. "All good things must come to an end, after all."

Wickham absolutely started upon hearing Darcy's voice and wheeled around quickly to face him. After a moment he said, "I beg your pardon, Darcy--your presence surprises me. I had not anticipated seeing you here tonight." He inclined his head, adding, "It is good to see an old friend. When you did not return with Bingley I thought you had decided to stay in town."

"I had business matters to attend to which delayed my immediate return, some of it with gentlemen you know. I am happy to tell you that Brown and Lawdley were in the best of health when I saw them last."

Despite the courteous words Elizabeth sensed a powerful undercurrent of tension between the two men. Wickham hardly knew where to look, and his confident, easy manner had given way to an uneasy air. Darcy's face was immobile and his eyes were locked on Wickham as he spoke tersely. He then turned his back on Wickham and stood rigidly still, looking out a window into the evening sky, seeming to pay him no further attention.

Lydia and Kitty, already bored with the great rooms of Netherfield, returned to the drawing room in search of Wickham. "La! I don't give a fig about expensive furniture and rooms, do you, Wickham? I am happy with just a new gown every day or two and some pretty ribbons for my hair! When I am a married woman, you may be sure my husband will have enough to buy me silk every day! I would expect nothing less from my husband," Lydia declared.

"What if your husband is poor?" Kitty asked, being slightly more realistic. "You might not have any choice but to marry poorly."

"I was not born this pretty to be the wife of a poor man!" Lydia answered back in high spirits. "Don't you agree, Wickham? Shall I be the wife of a poor man or a rich man?"

"Miss Lydia, anyone fortunate enough to marry you shall be rich in good humor and love, and shall be a very fortunate man indeed."

Elizabeth found that where Wickham's charming remarks had previously held her attention, she could now pay them no mind. She was more desirous than ever to know exactly what lay between Darcy and Wickham. Although Wickham had protested his innocence in the face of Darcy's persecution, she realized that whenever the two men came face to face, it was Wickham who flinched first, Wickham who seemed to be in the weaker position. He spoke boldly of Darcy only when out of that man's hearing, and he had deliberately avoided Darcy's proximity on at least one occasion.

On the other hand, Darcy never spoke of Wickham at all. His dislike of Wickham was obvious, but he did not flaunt his feelings; instead he seemed to almost challenge Wickham whenever they met. Perhaps, Elizabeth thought, there was more than she had thought to the story of Darcy using Wickham so poorly.

When Bingley led them all into the dining room both men looked as if they would escort her in, and looked at each other in a manner none too friendly. Elizabeth smiled politely at both in their turn; but instead of picking one over the other she entered alone, moving to her designated seat opposite Jane who sat next to Bingley in the middle of the table. Darcy entered the room after her and, after a nod from Bingley, took the seat to Elizabeth's left. Of all the party Wickham entered last. Almost everyone else had already moved to a chair and the officers were rapidly filling the other seats on her side of the table, leaving only the seat on her immediate right empty.

Elizabeth looked to Bingley for guidance but he was speaking with Jane again and did not observe Elizabeth's distress.

There was no escape, no way of easily avoiding the awkward situation. Wickham took the only open place as gracefully as unbroken tension could allow him. Elizabeth realized that she would eat dinner exactly between two men who seemed to hold nothing but hostility for each other. She now wished earnestly that her limited education could have included military tactics and strategies, particularly the art of a hasty retreat. She anticipated no great pleasure from the evening.

CHAPTER EIGHT

For some few minutes conversation was hindered by the placing of bowls and cutlery and by the general good-natured laughing coming from Colonel Forster and Denny as they teased Lydia, who was seated towards one end of the table. Sir William, seated across from Darcy, was recounting his presentation before the king to anyone who would listen, and comparing the cutlery at Netherfield to what was used at court. Mrs. Bennet was speaking loudly to her sister of Lydia's upcoming trip to Brighton, although Mr. Bennet had yet to give his permission; while Mary spoke gravely with Reverend Snow about his sermon of the week past.

Very little attempt at conversation was made at first either by Elizabeth or the two gentlemen. Presumably they were waiting for her to make the first remark, and she was secretly wondering if there could possibly be a safe topic of discussion between two men so opposed to each other. At length she recalled that there were few subjects more universally acceptable than food, and she commented, "I believe Mr. Bingley has set a fine table tonight. My mother will certainly want to speak to our cook about imitating this ragout."

"I have never tasted finer," Wickham agreed. "What a pity, since we leave tomorrow, that I will never discover if your cook can match this."

"It is quite flavorful," Darcy concurred. "Bingley has been fortunate in his choice of staff for his home." Elizabeth inwardly allowed herself to relax slightly, glad that a pleasant conversation might yet be possible.

Darcy continued, "I believe he had some difficulties at first finding just the right mixture of maids, gardeners, cooks, housekeeper, and all the rest. Setting up a household can be quite daunting."

"I suppose it would be," Elizabeth answered, "if one had to start with an empty house, so to speak, and populate it all oneself. It would no doubt take a great deal of time. But I imagine Mr. Bingley hired a housekeeper first and then let her do the rest."

"Bingley had slightly more trouble than that, Miss Bennet. He asked me if I could advise him in a rather tricky matter that came up."

"How is that, Mr. Darcy?" She wondered why he was bothering to pursue the subject. Surely he could have no great interest in the intricacies of running a household.

"When Bingley first came to Netherfield there were a few members of the former household who wanted to stay on in his employ. One of the gardeners, for instance, had worked here all his life and could not imagine having to look for a new position, and one of the cooks was similarly attached to the house. Bingley was glad to have such loyal employees and kept them on."

"That seems straightforward unless they had other demands he could not meet." Elizabeth glanced at Wickham to see him watching Darcy guardedly.

"The head groom, however, was a special case. It seems the former owner had promised him that he would always have a home at Netherfield and the groom took that promise quite seriously. He even claimed that it had been the owner's dying wish for him to always be provided for at Netherfield. Apparently there was a great deal of affection between them."

"Mr. Bingley is a true gentleman and would no doubt want to fulfill any obligation even if the obligation was not properly his own. Was he unable to carry out that wish? Had he already engaged someone else for the position?"

"Bingley had not known about this request, and since the groom had already left Netherfield before Bingley took possession, he hired someone else. A week later the groom returned, having heard that there might now be employment available. Bingley was distressed as he takes his duties as master quite seriously. He had no wish leave anyone in a dire situation. It was then that he asked my advice."

Wickham spoke for the first time. "A true gentleman would honor the wishes of a loving master for his beloved servant, do you not agree?" Elizabeth noted, with surprise, his rising color and changed expression. She then looked back to Darcy who was taking a rather long sip of wine before answering. A lively suspicion entered her mind.

Darcy set his glass down carefully and then wiped his lips with his napkin, seeming to deliberate over his response. "Any gentleman would, of course, do his best to follow someone's dying wishes to the letter. In this case since the position was already gone, I advised Bingley to give the former groom a sum of money that would more than make up for his loss of income; enough so he could retire comfortably if he so desired."

"Did Mr. Bingley follow your advice, Mr. Darcy?" Elizabeth asked, looking between the two men.

"Yes." Darcy turned his head and looked directly at Wickham. "He received three thousand pounds, for which he gave up all claim to what had been promised him."

"Three thousand pounds is a considerable sum, sir, certainly more than enough to support anyone for some time, I think." Elizabeth spoke to Darcy but her eyes were fixed on Wickham. She willed Wickham to look back at her, to refute what Darcy was saying, but he would not meet her gaze and only looked down at his plate. She looked back at Darcy, raising one eyebrow. "I suppose he felt it was a fair settlement in light of the security that had been promised to him?"

"No indeed," Darcy answered, his look still dark. "I am sorry to say that the groom wasted all of his money in short order, all three thousand pounds and more, then returned to Bingley and demanded his position again. You can hardly blame Bingley for refusing. When that did not work he attempted to steal something very valuable from the house and was discovered at the last possible moment. He will never be welcome at Netherfield again, no matter how much affection the old master had for him."

Elizabeth turned her gaze back to Wickham, amazement and dismay playing across her face in equal measure as she caught his eye. He smiled back at her defiantly. She did not know what to say next. With such a tumult in her mind there seemed to be an embargo on any further conversation. Finally, feeling obligated to restore conversation, she said, "I am surprised by your interest in such mundane household matters, Mr. Darcy. Surely Miss Darcy handles such things at Pemberley?"

"At the moment we share such duties."

"You did not bring her with you on this trip," Elizabeth observed. "Does she not enjoy traveling?"

"She generally does." Darcy looked past her again to stare at Wickham. "But at present she has good reason to avoid Hertfordshire."

Abruptly Wickham pushed back his chair and stood. "Begging your pardon, Miss Bennet, I believe my attention is needed elsewhere. The colonel wants me." He made his way to Colonel Forster, spoke briefly in his ear, and then left the room without a backward glance, leaving Elizabeth with an indescribable torment of conflicting thoughts and feelings.

"I do not recall Mr. Bingley ever mentioning any problems with establishing his household, Mr. Darcy. Are you quite certain that you remember all of these events with his groom accurately?"

"My memory in this instance is impeccable, Miss Bennet. If Wickham ever returns you may ask him yourself."

"If he returns? You do not think he will return tonight?"

"At present he has good reason to avoid Netherfield."

"I see." Elizabeth looked away, her mind too full for any further conversation for the evening.

∞

Darcy felt a mingled sense of pride and anxiety as the last guests departed from Netherfield. He wondered what Elizabeth had thought of the conversation over the dinner table. He, Darcy, had for the first time publicly confronted Wickham point by point about his lies. He had answered item for item, held in his anger and temper, and come out the undoubted winner of the unspoken war. Wickham's defeat left him with the deepest feelings of satisfaction and vindication. Best of all, he felt certain from his close observation of Elizabeth that she had understood the true meaning of the story he had related about Bingley.

But he wondered greatly at Elizabeth's reaction to him after this. He did not know her exact feelings for Wickham, if she had any tender regard for him. If their interactions at Netherfield were any indication, he must believe that there was a chance Wickham had made inroads on her affections. How painful, then, to find herself the object of his deception. It was even possible, though he thought it unlikely, that she might still find ways to explain away or deny Wickham's misdeeds. But whether she excused or condemned Wickham, her feelings towards Darcy were likely to be in turmoil, and she might indeed hold anger towards him on Wickham's behalf. He had not been able to read anything from her expressions after Wickham had left so abruptly, and her conversation from that point on had been the barest that civility allowed.

∞

When the Bennet family returned to Longbourn that evening Elizabeth pleaded a very real headache and retired immediately, anxious for privacy to consider all that she had heard.

It was impossible not to conclude that she had been badly

deceived. Over and over again she weighed the words, the looks and manners, and especially the behaviors of Darcy and Wickham. Mentally she compared their two accounts. They coincided exactly, except that Wickham had never mentioned that he had voluntarily been paid in place of accepting the living in the church. Could Darcy have been speaking an untruth when he said it? Not likely, since Wickham had been right there, able to contest his account if he so desired. His sudden departure also appeared to be an admission of guilt. No, it must be true; and if so, what an unfavorable light it cast on her former favorite!

Wickham had not been treated shamefully as he had represented to Elizabeth and many others. Rather, he had been treated with great kindness by both his godfather and his godfather's son. He could have been secure as a gentleman for the rest of his life if not for his profligate ways. To insist on being restored to the living which he himself had discarded was shameful behavior. Worse still was to blame Darcy for his own choices, to impugn his character when out of his presence; when Darcy had apparently done nothing worse than to accede to Wickham's own wishes. "He may have been educated as a gentleman," Elizabeth thought, "but education does not always beget gratitude or decency. It may not change the basic character of a man. Mr. Wickham has behaved not as a gentleman but as a mercenary."

From disparaging Wickham it was a short step to disparaging herself. Now she saw, with unclouded view, the impropriety of sharing so much personal information with a person just met, as Wickham had done with her. "I was too trusting," she thought, "too unguarded, too willing to believe the worst of Mr. Darcy simply because he once insulted me! I found Mr. Darcy to be too proud but I let my own pride cloud the judgment I thought I owned. I should never have listened to Mr. Wickham so unguardedly; but his attention flattered my vanity so that I never even thought to question what he said. I have been my own worst enemy."

My opinions are not swayed by entertaining false accusations, particularly when leveled by someone with whom I have such a passing acquaintance, she had told Wickham, not comprehending that she was guilty of the very offense she named. Her humiliation was complete; and she did not know how she was ever to face Darcy again. He might not know how much trust she had placed in Wickham, how utterly she had despised Darcy; but she knew, and the shame burned through her.

Sometime later when Jane joined her, Elizabeth was induced to open her heart and share the substance of what had taken place at dinner.

Poor Jane! To think that so much evil was contained in one person she had not thought possible in the whole world. Again and again she tried to find some explanation that would exonerate Wickham but even she was unable to quite excuse his behavior.

"I wonder what object he attempted to remove from the house," she pondered aloud. "It might have been only a sentimental item, of no value to the family but with great meaning to him personally. Perhaps he thought the old Mr. Darcy wanted him to have it."

"This will never do. I defy even you, Jane, to find anything good in the character of such a man as he. You must admit he has all the appearance of goodness but none of the substance."

"I can find good in his apparent affection for you. Surely Mr. Wickham would not have been so drawn to speak to you so if he did not sense a sympathetic listener."

Elizabeth threw up her hands. "There! You have accomplished the impossible and made a virtue out of vice! But then perhaps you have made a vice of my virtue as well, since even a sympathetic listener should never be as uncritical as I was."

"Has all this changed your opinion of Mr. Darcy, Elizabeth?"

"I must admit that it has. Mr. Darcy appears to be an honorable man now instead of the proud, disagreeable person I thought he was. If he only knew the things I have said about him! At least I have the comfort that I have never said any of those things to his face. But please, quit trying to exonerate your very guilty sister and simply tell me how things are with Mr. Bingley. We have been so busy I have quite neglected you this week, knowing that my deficiencies were more than made up for by a certain gentleman caller."

Jane smiled contentedly. "I am satisfied, more than satisfied with matters as they stand now. I can no longer claim to be indifferent, for he has quite captured my heart. I only wish I could see you as happy as I am when I am with him."

"Until I have your goodness I cannot have your happiness. When am I to wish you joy, then?"

Jane turned color becomingly. "He has not spoken of marriage, but he has spoken of his affections for me, so you may wish me joy for that at least. And when he does speak you shall be the first to know of it, dearest Lizzy. I only wish you could find such a man."

"I believe, Jane, that I shall be more than happy as an old maid, to spoil my nieces and nephews when they arrive and to teach them to play their instruments very poorly indeed."

When they lay down to sleep Elizabeth could hear that Jane fell asleep immediately, for hers was the rest that comes to the deeply content. Elizabeth's mind, still reeling with astonishment, kept her awake for some time. But sleep did come at last, and on the morrow she awoke with the dread certainty that she must see Darcy again today if he accompanied Bingley on his usual call.

CHAPTER NINE

It was not Bingley, however, who arrived first the next morning. At eleven in the morning Hill announced that the Gardiner carriage was stopping in front of the house. As their carriage pulled up, the carriage door opened and the younger Gardiners poured out into the ecstatic arms of their older cousins. The Bennet family welcomed the Gardiners warmly, though surprised to see them arriving so soon. They were not due for several weeks yet when they would take Elizabeth with them on their trip to the Lakes.

"I am so glad you are come, Amelia!" Mrs. Bennet exclaimed to Mrs. Gardiner without bothering to ask why they had arrived before their time. "Such doings as we have had here! Jane is again the favorite of our dear Mr. Bingley, and we have become quite the envy of the whole neighborhood!"

"I am glad to hear it," Mrs. Gardiner replied graciously. "Jane, Elizabeth, and all my dear nieces--it is such a pleasure to be with you again. I want to hear all about everything going on here. But first let us get the little ones settled in with their nurse."

"Yes, yes!" cried Mrs. Bennet. "Lydia, Kitty, go find Hill and tell her that the Gardiners are here; and have her open the nursery and make tea for all of us. You older girls help us with the children and make sure the trunks are put in their right rooms." Mr. Bennet had already taken Mr. Gardiner into the house, allowing the women to handle the immediate commotion of arrival.

Jane and Elizabeth, delighted to be with their aunt again, escorted the youngest Gardiners to the nursery and saw them settled in with their nurse before returning to the sitting room, anxious to hear what had brought the Gardiners to them so quickly. It turned out to be news that mostly affected Elizabeth.

"We are hoping," Mrs. Gardiner began, "that Elizabeth would have no objection to starting out early on our trip to the Lakes. Mr. Gardiner had business which he had thought to conclude before our trip started but it has been delayed by some weeks, and it will now be necessary to make our travels beforehand rather than afterwards."

"It will also shorten our itinerary somewhat, I'm afraid," Mr. Gardiner added. "Due to time constraints we will not be able to travel to travel quite as far north as we had thought; but we will still have time to take in many fine homes and parks in Derbyshire. Lizzy, I hope this does not change your desire to travel with us."

"Of course not," Elizabeth acceded with a smile. "I will own that I am somewhat disappointed that we will not see everything we had planned, but I am sure we will still have much to see and do. I only wish we could talk Jane into coming with us; but I think that would be entirely out of the question at the moment, unless you can find room to pack her Mr. Bingley in a trunk and bring him along!"

"He is not MY Mr. Bingley, Lizzy!" Jane protested, her color changing.

"I think he might disagree with you."

"Of course he would!" Mrs. Bennet was eager to speak of Bingley again. "Would you believe, Amelia, that Mr. Bingley has called here every day this week? He has paid our Jane an excessive amount of attention and ignored all the other women in the neighborhood! And last night he had Jane sit next to him when we dined with the officers! I thought he was likely to make an offer right on the spot! But perhaps there were too many people in the room."

Jane looked away while Lydia began a loud description of the various officers, helped along by Kitty, and loudly complained of their immediate departure. Under the general noise of conversation Mrs. Gardiner addressed Elizabeth. "It is plain to see that Jane is restored her former state of happiness. I must confess part of the reason we were so eager to come to Longbourn this month was to see this Mr. Bingley for ourselves. Is he as smitten as your mother makes him out to be?"

"He is indeed. I have advised Jane to pick out her wedding clothes, and Mama is already deciding on which warehouses she will patronize when the time comes."

"And you, Lizzy? How do you feel about losing your sister if he does make an offer?"

"I shall not think of it as losing a sister, but as gaining a very rich brother. How can I possibly complain?"

"Shall you not wish to be settled in a home of your own?"

"I will never be as fortunate as Jane is in finding a true love match, so I shall do my best to be patient until another Mr. Collins comes along. Seriously though, Aunt, a great deal has occurred here in the last week; and when we are at liberty for a lengthy conversation I have surprising information to relate."

"I shall be pleased to have such a conversation with you."

Within a short time after the Gardiner's arrival Bingley and Darcy arrived for Bingley's usual appointment, and Bingley was introduced to the Gardiners. His manner was so open and free, so intelligent and willing to please, that they were instantly disposed to approve of him even without knowing his attachment to Jane.

They were also introduced to Darcy, about whom they could not but be curious. They had heard of his pride and arrogance; yet as a friend of Bingley, they were willing to make allowances on his behalf. But they found that no allowances were needed. Darcy might not speak as freely and easily as his friend, yet when he did speak it was marked with intelligence and good breeding. He was obviously surprised to see such fashionable relatives of the Bennets, but he did not keep his distance from them. Rather, he went out of his way to sit near Mr. Gardiner and to engage him and his wife in conversation about Derbyshire, where Mrs. Gardiner had been born. Mrs. Gardiner also noticed that Darcy looked at Elizabeth a great deal, and she did not think his look was one of criticism. These facts along with Elizabeth's desire to relate surprising information put a new idea into her mind; and she watched Elizabeth and Darcy closely.

Mrs. Bennet labored under the delusion that all Bingley lacked in order to make his proposal was privacy; and since the house was far too crowded for such an opportunity, she suggested that the young people might like to take a walk outside. Jane, Elizabeth, and Darcy all assented and the four made their way out of the house, through the garden, and along a small trail. Elizabeth and Darcy walked ahead and soon outpaced Bingley and Jane, who showed no sign of missing the other couple's presence. When they were out of sight of the house and of the other couple Elizabeth decided to take advantage of the privacy to speak to Darcy freely.

"Mr. Darcy, I am a selfish creature, and for the sake of relieving my own feelings care not how much I may be disturbing yours. Your story of the head groom last night shocked me, as much for what it revealed about my character as it did that of a particular officer. Mr. Wickham made slanderous attacks on your character in the past, and to my shame I gave credit where none was due. I offer my apology and ask your forgiveness."

Darcy's face, tense until now, noticeably relaxed. "You must not blame yourself, Miss Bennet. Wickham is a practiced deceiver. He has always been an amusing story teller, and as he grew older those stories more and more featured himself as first the principal character, and then as the tragic figure in a morality tale. You are not the first person he has deceived with his sorry tale, nor will you be the last."

"You are most generous, sir, but I cannot let myself off so easily. I have prided myself on being an impartial, fair observer of human nature, but I abandoned good judgment where he was concerned."

"The fault is entirely mine. I should have let the people of Meryton know what he was when I realized he was here last autumn; but when we first met I was too surprised to know what to do. Exposing him could possibly also expose others who have foolishly involved themselves with him, and I did not wish for any others to be hurt."

"Did you truly pay him three thousand pounds in lieu of the living?"

"I did. Three thousand pounds is a goodly amount, but still not enough to keep him in the style to which he aspired. When he wrote to ask me for more money he assured me his circumstances were quite dire, and I had no problem believing it. I had seen enough of his behavior in school to know that no sum of money would be enough to satisfy him indefinitely. Do you recall when I told him last night that his friends Mr. Brown and Mr. Lawdley were in good health?"

"Of course."

"Those are two creditors of his, both shopkeepers with whom he has run up a considerable debt. Since he had claimed an acquaintance with me, they came to me for satisfaction. Such has been the pattern with him for the past ten years. From time to time he has also tried to ingratiate himself with wealthy heiresses, but these plots were foiled."

Elizabeth could not help but smile. "If he was hoping for such a plan with me he chose poorly indeed! Our family has no fortune worth mentioning."

Darcy hesitated. "I fear you are correct. Wickham has kept company with many women, but he has never offered marriage to any of them that I am aware. With no fortune to tempt him you may have had a very narrow escape. He would think nothing of ruining your reputation."

Elizabeth colored as she realized his implication and looked away to keep him from seeing her mortification. "Rest assured he would not have succeeded with me."

"Of course not, but more than one woman has been ruined at his hands." Darcy looked as if he would say more but then apparently thought better of it.

"And he tried to steal something from your house? Something of great value, I assume?"

"Of tremendous value. Had he succeeded his revenge would have been complete indeed." Elizabeth longed to ask what the desired item was but felt the indelicacy of doing so.

"It is fortunate for us, then, that the regiment is now leaving Meryton," she answered instead. "If I never see a red coat again it will be too soon, though of course my sisters will be in deep mourning for at least a fortnight. Where do you suppose Jane and Mr. Bingley are? We have completely outpaced them. Perhaps we should go look for them; it would not do to leave them alone for too long."

"I think not." Something in Darcy's voice made Elizabeth look at him sharply. "Bingley was hoping for some time alone with your sister today as he had a very particular topic on his mind."

Elizabeth smiled at him mischievously. "Does Mr. Bingley always communicate his plans to you so thoroughly? He has been so reticent up until now, it is a wonder he does not ask you to make proposals on his behalf."

"My friend can speak for himself, but only if he has the time and space to do so."

"Then I suggest that we give them a great deal of space, but I do hope that he will not need much time. He will make my sister very happy." She quickened her pace, forcing Darcy to adjust his long strides to keep up with hers.

A little farther on Darcy saw a bench that had been set a little off the path and he guided Elizabeth to it. "Perhaps we might wait here for them to catch up with us," he suggested. "Surely they will not take too long, and we can then return to the house."

Once Elizabeth was seated the silence stretched awkwardly between them. Elizabeth saw Darcy looking at her earnestly. "Is there something else you wished to say, Mr. Darcy? We have any number of subjects open to us. We have not yet discussed the weather, so you might start there; or else we could speak of the state of the roads, or the current state of French fashions. I am honestly quite sick of discussing Mr. Wickham."

He smiled briefly, but then his look turned serious again. "I am trying to decide how to begin a much more awkward topic with you and I find that the easiest way is simply to say what I want to say to you and get it over with. Yet I fear to raise your anger."

She raised an eyebrow at him. "Could there possibly be another subject more awkward than what we have just discussed? Whatever it is, Mr. Darcy, I pray that you would just say it without hesitation. We do not have all day. My sister and Mr. Bingley will eventually join us."

"It is of your sister and Bingley that I must speak, and make my own confession. In the autumn when we were here previously Mr. Bingley was ready to make your sister an offer, but I interfered. I told him that your sister did not appear to return his regard and that if he persisted in his pursuit he would be disappointed in love. He believed me, taking my word over his own, and left your sister to return to London."

Elizabeth regarded him gravely. "You truly believed my sister to be indifferent, sir? By what authority did you feel you had the right to make that determination?"

"I had no such authority. My only defense is that I truly hoped to protect my friend from an imprudent marriage. Your sister's manners were such that I did not see that she held Bingley in any distinction. Later on when your sister was in town, I purposely concealed that information from him. I believed that if he knew, he would not fail to pursue your sister once again, and so I sought to keep him from what I thought would certainly be an unhappy relationship. Such deception was beneath me and I have come to heartily regret my actions."

"And why do you confess this to me now? What can you hope to gain from telling me this?"

"Since our conversation in Kent I have tried most earnestly to mend my faults in your eyes. From what you said I realized that your sister was not as indifferent as I had thought, and so I have done my best to repair the damage I caused. I spoke to Bingley, confessed my interference, and allowed him to continue pursuing the course he had already chosen."

"I see." Elizabeth's brow wrinkled, but gave him no indication how she felt about this revelation.

"Miss Bennet? May I ask what you are thinking? I hope I have not given you any cause to have anger against me."

"You may be at ease. I am thinking, Mr. Darcy, that one of the most noble characteristics any person can have is the capacity to see their own faults and to make amends when possible. You appear to have this trait in abundance."

"We have each confessed a fault today. If it were in my power I would make those things as though they had never happened."

Elizabeth smiled at him again. "I am also thinking that I hold quite an advantage over you. You are apparently trying to determine any possible fault that I might find in you so that you can make it up to me somehow. Perhaps I should be more critical!"

Darcy smiled, relieved at her lighter tone. "I stand ready to assist. What else should I make up to you?"

"That will never do. I would rather not tell you what I have in mind but make you guess it instead. If I am very fortunate, you may find more things for which to apologize than I had any idea of! And then my life will improve even more as I demand more and more tokens of your apology."

"What tokens would you require of me, Miss Bennet?"

"By and by I may admit to being unhappy that I have never seen the court of St. James; and after that I may confess a burning desire for a maharajah to appear in our parlor. But for now you will simply have to do the best you can."

Darcy bowed. "I am at your mercy. I will make a maharajah appear in your parlor at my earliest opportunity, and then make the court appear as well." His look turned serious. "But after that I would make one request of my own."

"You would make a demand of me, Mr. Darcy?"

"It is only fair, since we have both confessed faults."

"True. Ask what you will."

"I fondly recall a certain piece of music you played at Rosings on my last evening there. It would give me great pleasure to hear you perform it again, if you believe you have come to understand it better."

"I have had little time to practice since returning from Kent; yet I believe that I could indeed play that piece better now than then."

Unexpectedly, Darcy sat next to her and picked up her hand from where it lay on the bench, his eyes warmly intense. "If I have improved at all in your estimation, if you have come to at least tolerate my presence more easily than in the past, I ask if you would please do me the honor of allowing me to call upon you. When you have come to know me better I believe you will see how well we complement each other, how very well we might suit each other if we were to enter into a more long-term relationship. I ask for the chance to let you see this for yourself." He held his breath, waiting anxiously for her reply.

To her surprise Elizabeth did not immediately pull away from him, but instead kept her hand in his. She did not know how such a man had come to care for her, but it was plain that he did, and that he was a man she could respect. She smiled. "I would be pleased to receive you, sir, at any time."

CHAPTER TEN

The sound of steps on the path caused Darcy to stand and move hastily away from her, and a moment later Jane and Bingley joined them. Fortunately the joy of one couple prevented them from seeing any embarrassment in the other. The looks on their faces said it all, and Jane and Elizabeth embraced warmly as Jane confessed to being the happiest creature in the world. "I am so happy, Elizabeth; I do not deserve such happiness! It is so hard to believe that this is not all a beautiful dream!"

"I cannot think it a dream when so many of us thought for so long that it would happen," Elizabeth answered her. "Nobody in this world deserves to be any happier than you."

"I will make sure that she is as happy all her life as she has made me at this moment!" Bingley assured Elizabeth, and then embraced her, claiming all the rights of a future brother.

"I am sure you will be the most delightful couple in England, and no brother could please me more," Elizabeth responded. "Both of you with such cheerful dispositions, and so willing to accept the best in all you see! I wish you much joy."

"I can add nothing to what Miss Elizabeth has said already," Darcy said, shaking his friend's hand vigorously. "It is good to see two such deserving people find each other."

"I must go see your father," Bingley said to Jane. "I shall lose no time doing so. Darcy, would you please see the ladies safely back to the house? I want to speak to Mr. Bennet right now."

Darcy nodded, and with a quick smile for Jane Bingley left them. Jane and Elizabeth walked slowly back to the house, arm-in-arm, speaking of every joy that was to come and giving Bingley plenty of time to speak his piece, while Darcy trailed a little behind. His own heart was full to bursting, elated that Elizabeth had changed her mind about him and was now willing to entertain his interest in her. He hoped that someday soon he would stand in Bingley's position, asking Mr. Bennet for his daughter's hand.

They had not long to wait upon re-entering the house; for almost as soon as they had entered it, Bingley and Mr. Bennet came out of the study together, both looking highly satisfied as they shook hands expressively. Seeing Jane enter, Mr. Bennet smiled broadly and said, "Congratulations, Jane. You will be a very happy woman."

"I intend to see to it that she is," Bingley answered eagerly.

"Yes, well, very few prospective grooms admit that their goal will be to make their wives miserable."

Jane instantly kissed her father and thanked him for his goodness to her. "I should like to go to my mother now to acquaint her with the news. To know that what I have to share will cause such joy! I can scarcely contain it!"

"Certainly, go to her if you want, but do allow me time to plug my ears first. Too much happiness can deafen a man, or at least cause a raging headache. Elizabeth," he called as Jane left the room, "do not be eager to escape my company. I would speak with you in my study and with Mr. Darcy as well. Come in."

Greatly surprised, Elizabeth preceded Mr. Darcy into her father's study and took a seat, casting about in her mind for what might cause her father to call both of them in together when he knew nothing of what had transpired in their relationship. She suddenly wondered if he had somehow spied them as they sat together, and she anticipated with dismay all the explanations that would have to be made.

"I am certain, Elizabeth, that you know why I have called you here," her father began, looking at her severely. "You look conscious. Young ladies have great penetration in matters such as this."

"I am looking forward to your explanation," was all Elizabeth could offer.

"No, I believe I am the one looking forward to your explanation. I was upstairs minutes ago, retrieving a book from my bedroom for your uncle Gardiner, when I looked out the window that overlooks the garden and saw something I had never anticipated. Can you imagine what it might have been?"

"You are forcing me to guess. Perhaps you saw the cows from Mr. Tillsey's farm knocking down the fence again."

"Elizabeth, do be serious. This is a grave matter, and I am forced to give it my undivided attention for at least two minutes, which is taxing beyond words. I must be direct. Are you out of your mind to be accepting this man?"

"Papa, Mr. Darcy and I are not engaged."

Darcy spoke clearly and respectfully. "Mr. Bennet, I apologize for any misapprehension caused by my attentions to Miss Elizabeth. What you saw was completely innocent and honorable. I was asking for her permission to court her, nothing more; and I certainly have no desire to cause any discomfort on anyone's part."

"So you have not made an offer for my daughter?" Mr. Bennet asked.

Both Elizabeth and Darcy flushed and glanced away involuntarily, which did not go unnoticed. "Oh ho! My, what an amusing day this has turned out to be! You did offer for her, but you are not engaged! Elizabeth, did you refuse this man? I do not see, Lizzy, how you could possibly be your mother's daughter. No child of Mrs. Bennet would ever turn down a legitimate offer of marriage, and you have now done so twice!"

"Papa, this is a private matter between Mr. Darcy and me. I beg your leave to discontinue this conversation."

As she was speaking a loud shriek of joy escaped from the room directly overhead and they knew that the important communication had been made. A loud, "Lord bless me! I knew how it should be! I knew you could not be so beautiful for nothing!" followed. Elizabeth could not help herself. She shrank back as if trying to disappear into the chair where she sat, not daring to meet Darcy's gaze. At this moment no promise of future happiness seemed sufficient to overcome the present circumstances.

"Mr. Bennet, you are correct," said Mr. Darcy when the noise had subsided temporarily, politely pretending he had heard nothing. "When Miss Elizabeth and I were in Kent I confessed my sentiments of affection to her and asked for her hand. At that time she did not see fit to accept me. I have been striving since then to improve her impressions of me. I now ask for your permission to court her as well."

Darcy's speech was interrupted by continued explosions from Mrs. Bennet. "Hill! Call for the carriage at once! I must go tell my sister Phillips and Lady Lucas this morning! Jane, you will come with me that we may discuss your wedding clothes with Lady Lucas. She will know the best warehouses in London. Make haste, Hill, make haste!"

"When may we have a ball, Mr. Bingley?" Lydia added her voice to the general excitement. "Say that it will be as soon as you are married!"

"Why must we wait until they are married?" came Kitty's whine.

Mr. Bennet continued as though he had not heard. "I see. Yes, now I begin to comprehend very well indeed. You proposed, she turned you down, and you followed her here to Hertfordshire to continue your suit. In between those two events Mr. Bingley returned. I suppose we have you to thank for that? No, never mind; do not try to answer that question. You are right, Lizzy. Matters of the heart are a private matter and I do not wish to intrude, but please recall that in this house nothing involving eligible gentleman remains private for long. Only reassure me that this is your true desire, that you have no objection to being courted by Mr. Darcy, and I shall give both of you my permission." He paused, looking at her speculatively. "We know that he is a proud, unpleasant sort of man, but that would not matter if you really liked him."

"He is not proud or unpleasant!" Elizabeth cried, moved to anger by her father's poor manners. "What we heard about him from Wickham was a slanderous lie, and he has shown me the greatest humility! Indeed he has no improper pride, but a gentleman's true character. Pray do not pain me by speaking of him so!" She lifted her head as she said this and looked at Darcy. He gave her a smile such as she had never seen before on his face, and she flushed as she realized how her words would sound. How quickly she had moved from resenting Mr. Darcy to defending him! But she would not be intimidated.

"Forgive me, Mr. Darcy, for my harsh words," Mr. Bennet said. "I was curious to see the depth of my daughter's conviction and that seemed the most direct route. Lizzy, I can see that you are convinced in your own mind, and that is all I ask. Congratulations."

"Papa, I say again, we are not engaged!" Mr. Bennet continued as though he had not heard.

"But I would advise you to proceed with caution. Mr. Darcy is a gentleman and you are a gentleman's daughter. Thus far you are equal, but your styles of living are very different. Being mistress of a home like Pemberley is quite a different affair than being mistress of our own humble Longbourn. Your friends, your entertainments, your surroundings all would be quite changed. It would be well for you to understand your duties better ahead of time, should you choose to proceed to marriage with Mr. Darcy."

Without knocking Mrs. Bennet opened the door of the study and looked in with great eagerness. "Mr. Bennet! Have you not heard? Mr. Bingley has proposed to Jane and they are engaged to be married! I am in raptures of delight! I have such flutterings of my heart, so much shaking of my hands, that I know not how I will survive! Oh, I knew how it would be! I am excessively diverted!"

"You seem just as diverted as ever," her spouse answered drily. "Yes, Mr. Bingley did acquaint me with his hopes for marriage. Pray tell me when the wedding will be that I may make plans to attend."

"You silly man! Of course you will attend--you must give her away! We will be off to my sister Phillips directly to let her know what has happened!" In her agitation Mrs. Bennet failed to notice the presence of Elizabeth and Mr. Darcy which Elizabeth had momentarily dreaded. She withdrew in order to continue her preparations for her visits and Elizabeth sighed with relief.

"I hope you understand," said Mr. Bennet seriously, "that once word of your courtship reaches Mrs. Bennet's ears the present commotion will seem like nothing at all, once she overcomes her first shock. Indeed, the exclamations and noise that will then erupt will make me long for a quiet visit to Bedlam. I advise both of you to be discreet in your courtship, for my sake if not for yours. Continue to masquerade as chaperoning Jane and Bingley for as long as possible. I know it cannot be long. Where there is expectation of one wedding people will be eager to imagine another one in the offing, and Mrs. Bennet has an active imagination."

"Do you know if anyone else observed us outside?" Elizabeth asked, dreading the possible answer.

"I rather think that if they had we would know by now, although we cannot be certain," her father responded. "For your sakes, it would be much better if this courtship could take place somewhere other than Longbourn, somewhere where you will be able to have a moment's peace away from overly eager expectations." He paused for a moment; then looked significantly at Darcy. "For instance, I understand that Derbyshire is quite a pleasant county in the spring."

Elizabeth and Darcy looked at him in confusion for a moment, but did not have a chance to respond before a knock was heard on the study door. At Mr. Bennet's call Mrs. Gardiner entered the room and looked from Elizabeth's flushed face to Darcy's heightened expression, to Mr. Bennet's grave look, and instantly understood that a most important conversation had been interrupted. Fortunately Mrs. Gardiner possessed neither Mrs. Bennet's hysteria nor Mr. Bennet's sarcasm. "Forgive me, I do not wish to intrude. Lizzy, I came to find you when I realized you were not with Jane or your mother, but it seems that I must have broken in upon a rather significant event. I can only imagine one reason the three people here present would be engaged in a private conversation. Is this the news you wished to share with me earlier?"

"No, Aunt. We are not engaged," Elizabeth repeated somewhat wearily.

"They are not engaged," Mr. Bennet repeated, "but you see a minor miracle before you. It appears that Darcy insulted Elizabeth, Elizabeth rejected Darcy, and now, of course, they have decided that they wish to court. I do not understand it at all, but I have given my blessing since they are being so very entertaining. Mrs. Gardiner, do come in and join us. I believe you may be of some assistance in this situation, sister."

Mrs. Gardiner's expression was of utmost wonder. "I can see that this is a discussion that will take some time, and Lizzy's mother is looking for her to accompany them to Meryton." She disappeared for a moment while she spoke to Hill, giving her a message to relay to Mrs. Bennet. "Lizzy, when you see your mother again, you have a deep stain on the hem of your dress and I am helping you deal with the damage," she said when she rejoined them. "I also asked Hill to find Mr. Gardiner and send him to us, assuming nobody objects."

"Thank you, Aunt," said Elizabeth. "I doubt if my mother really sought my presence right now anyway, and she has enough on her mind that she will not miss my presence." She looked at Darcy to see what he thought of her family and all the happenings so far, but only saw an impassive look revealing nothing of his thoughts. He might have been amused, horrified, charmed, or any other emotion under the sun. Although she was coming to understand him better and trust him more, she realized that her father was correct in pointing out how very little she still knew about the man, his family, and the circumstances of his life--which would become her life if she continued her path with Darcy.

"Please do tell me about all this, for it is clear that I am behind the times," Mrs. Gardiner said as she sat next to her niece. "We had no idea the wind was blowing in this direction."

Elizabeth resigned herself to having to explain the situation once again but Mr. Darcy spoke instead. "It was never my intention to cause such disquiet to Miss Elizabeth, or to her family, by requesting the honor of courting her. I had not anticipated such an interested reaction to my request."

"Please allow me to introduce you to Mrs. Bennet sometime," Mr. Bennet responded pointedly, and Elizabeth smiled in spite of herself.

"If you wish to court my niece, Mr. Darcy, you will have to become accustomed to a lively family along with her," said Mrs. Gardiner. "I hope it will not frighten you."

He merely shook his head. "My intentions will not change, but I do wish there was a chance to conduct our courtship in a way that will not subject Miss Elizabeth and me to such unwanted attention."

"Any type of courtship will be somewhat difficult to carry out, at least in the immediate future," Mrs. Gardiner stated. "We leave for our tour of the Lakes district the day after tomorrow, as we were describing to the Bennets this morning, and Miss Elizabeth will be accompanying us. We will be gone for quite some time. Perhaps this courtship could begin upon her return."

"I was not aware of an impending journey," Darcy answered, glancing at Elizabeth, "but I am happy to wait upon your convenience. What will be the length of your tour?"

"I expect about four weeks. We were going to take a longer tour and go to the Lakes, but Mr. Gardiner's business has changed our plans; and we shall go no further north now than Derbyshire. I hope to spend time in the village where I grew up, in Lambton."

Darcy looked at her in surprise. "In Lambton?"

"Yes; are you familiar with it? I still have many friends there and am greatly looking forward to spending time with them again."

"I know Lambton quite well, madam." And now he also began to comprehend Mr. Bennet's intentions.

Mr. Bennet loudly cleared his throat. "Mr. Darcy, I believe you mentioned that your estate, Pemberley, is within Derbyshire, is it not?"

"Indeed it is, and not five miles from Lambton."

"And were we not just discussing how advantageous it would be to conduct your courtship as far from Longbourn as possible?"

"We were." Darcy looked at Mrs. Gardiner, hardly daring to hope that such an easy solution could present itself. Could it be so simple, and so perfectly suited to his desires? "Madam, it would be a great privilege if I could have the honor of hosting you and your family at my estate, Pemberley, when you are on your tour, if you have not made other plans. You would be my most honored guests, and I am certain you would find nothing lacking in your accommodations. You could come and go as you please, to Lambton or anywhere else, and you would have the entire estate of Pemberley at your disposal."

Mrs. Gardiner glanced at Elizabeth to see how she felt about the plan, but her niece had momentarily looked away. Mrs. Gardiner took her reaction for embarrassment rather than any real dislike for the scheme, however; and being confident of her husband's agreement she gratefully accepted the offer. No sooner had she spoken the words than her husband joined the group.

"You asked for me, my dear?" he addressed his wife, looking at the inhabitants of the room with utmost curiosity.

"Yes. It seems that Mr. Darcy has become aware of our impending journey to Derbyshire and my connections to Lambton, and he has graciously invited us to stay at Pemberley during our tour. What do you think?"

"I have no opposition," her husband said, looking even more intrigued, "but why would you, Mr. Darcy, be so desirous of our presence at Pemberley?"

"Mr. Darcy has announced his intentions toward Elizabeth," Mrs. Gardiner informed him.

"Toward Lizzy! Truly? A second engagement?" Mr. Gardiner asked in surprise.

"We are not engaged!" Elizabeth said emphatically to nobody in particular.

Mr. Bennet raised an eyebrow as he looked at her. "Methinks the lady doth protest too much."

CHAPTER ELEVEN

Elizabeth spent the remainder of the day trying to pretend to the outside world that nothing out of the ordinary had happened to her. The plans for Elizabeth and her aunt and uncle to travel to Derbyshire had been confirmed, but after speaking with Mrs. Bennet they were changed to include ending the trip in London in four week's time. Jane and her mother would be traveling to town at that time to purchase her wedding clothes, and so it was most natural that Elizabeth should rejoin their company at that point when her aunt and uncle returned to their home. Only Elizabeth, her aunt and uncle, and Mr. Bennet were aware that the entirety of the four weeks would be spent at Pemberley, and Elizabeth did her best to put it out of her mind lest her tongue slip and give up the information when least expected.

Her great joy in the day came from observing Jane and Bingley, the acknowledged lovers, in a state of such contentment that they made her a little envious. They anticipated a wedding date in a matter of weeks and spent the day in happy contemplation of their future state, whenever they were not recounting the story of Bingley's proposal again and again for Mrs. Bennet's benefit. Elizabeth rejoiced in her sister's happiness; but she did wish that it might come in quieter form, at least until she was able to leave with her aunt and uncle. She and Darcy spent the day in each other's company, along with Jane and Bingley, but they made every effort to avoid the notice of others and consequently spoke hardly a word to each other. Such continual avoidance led to a state of fatigue. Elizabeth escaped to her room as early as politely possible but her distracted mind could not even finish a chapter in her book, and she was happy to leave off reading when Jane finally retired and entered their bed chamber.

"Do tell me everything that happened between you and Mr. Darcy, Elizabeth, for I could see today that something came about. Are you engaged to him? It would make Charles and me so happy if you were!"

Jane's question was such a repetition of the earlier conversation that Elizabeth could not help rolling her eyes. "No, we are not engaged. We have left that honor to you and Mr. Bingley to carry out without us. What made you think that something has happened?"

"Lizzy, you are not as sly as you like to think you are. When Charles and I came upon you on the path this morning, it was clear from your expressions that something unusual had occurred; and then you were nowhere to be seen for the rest of the morning. Did he propose again?'

"Preposterous thought, Jane! Our own conversation today was, I believe, not nearly as interesting as yours, though interesting enough. I apologized to Mr. Darcy for misjudging him earlier, and he apologized for his pride and temper. He then asked permission to call on me, and I gave it."

Jane smiled. "That is more than remarkable. I am so pleased for both of you; but if he wishes to court you he must be disappointed that you will be traveling so soon."

"Not at all. I believe he is delighted beyond words."

More inquiries from Miss Bennet resulted in Elizabeth relating the entirety of the conversation in the study until finally Jane had all the information she wanted. "To be observed by our father in such an instant! How could you bear it when he asked you what had happened? I am happy that you have been able to look past your earlier dislike, and so pleased that Mr. Darcy is willing to change for your sake. I have the utmost faith that all shall work out as it should. I shall miss you on your trip, though. You must be sure to write every day and tell me everything that happens between you and Mr. Darcy."

"Perhaps nothing will happen."

"Whatever do you mean?"

"It will depend very much on exactly how large and beautiful Pemberley really is."

"Lizzy, do be serious, please. Do anything rather than marry without affection. You know you could never be another Mrs. Collins."

"I am relieved, then, that there is only one Mr. Collins. Seriously, Jane, this has all happened too quickly for my sensibilities. At this time just three days ago I was convinced that Mr. Darcy was the last man on earth whom I should ever be prevailed upon to marry; and now I am to travel to Pemberley to be courted by the very same man! And that visit came about with absolutely no input from me, though I own it worked out remarkably easily. I will happily spend four weeks at his home and become better acquainted with him, and perhaps then I can decide whether I wish to allow anything further. And of course Mr. Darcy may think better of our relationship when he sees me in his own home. The reality is never as attractive as the dream, and truly our stations in life are very different."

Jane shook her head. "Charles says that Mr. Darcy is as constant as the stars, and completely loyal in his affections. Whatever choice you make will be based on the state of your own feelings and not on his, for his feelings are already engaged."

Elizabeth gave her sister a teasing look. "Very well then, if Charles says it, it must be true! How can I compete with such a paragon of virtue as your dear Charles!"

"He is my dear Charles, Lizzy, and as he asked me today to call him by his Christian name, I think it is proper to do so. He is such a kind, generous man, and he asks for so little from me."

"Jane, please, I would ask just one favor of you, dear sister."

"Anything."

"Pray do not use that word "engaged" in front of me until I give you leave, for it has been completely overused today!"

Jane's answering smile was a study in radiance. "To me, Lizzy, it is the most beautiful word in the world."

∞

Darcy reflected on the events of the past several days with great contentment as his carriage bore him swiftly home to Pemberley. The possibility of a relationship with Elizabeth was, of course, first on his mind; but he also recalled his conversations with Mr. Bennet with satisfaction.

After the surprise of his daughter's courtship had worn off Mr. Bennet had made a point of conversing with him several times, careful not to let their conversation be overheard by others in the family. He was particularly interested in Darcy's history with Wickham, especially his habit of running up debt with various merchants. Darcy gave him an accurate recounting of Wickham's spending and gaming habits since the time of Wickham's entering Cambridge.

"I wish I had known about this earlier, Mr. Darcy," Mr. Bennet had said. "If this is true I should not be surprised to find that Wickham has left debts here in Meryton as well. A word in the right ear might have helped the shopkeepers protect themselves."

"I did speak to several of them discreetly in the autumn," Darcy responded. "I know not how my warning may have affected them, since they did not know either Wickham or me personally and did not know whom to believe. But I hope they were on their guard."

"It is well that Wickham has moved on, and the regiment with him. With any luck the merchants in Brighton will determine his true character on their own, and sooner rather than later."

"It is not just shopkeepers who are in danger when Wickham is near. He has also taken advantage of the company of women of some means, ruining their reputations when they were no longer of use to him."

"A regular Lothario, is he? Well, at least my family is safe from him. Still, you may have heard that my youngest daughter has been specifically invited to Brighton, there to continue her ceaseless chasing after anything in a red coat. If Wickham will be there perhaps it would be better to keep Lydia away from his vicinity. I say, Darcy," and here Mr. Bennet had paused to look carefully at him, "if Wickham is such a danger to female virtue you might have chosen to speak up against him earlier. He could have carried out his mischief with someone in this neighborhood."

"You are correct, sir. Perhaps I should have spoken, but to be honest I had no proof; and Wickham's easy manners and address win him friends wherever he goes, at least for a short time. Mine do not. And I could not expose him without naming specific women he has disgraced, which was of course impossible."

Mr. Bennet seemed satisfied. "I understand, Mr. Darcy. But I am glad that you have felt free to speak to me. Lydia shall be kept from his influence. I will keep her here at home where there are ample opportunities of exercising her foolish nature, and I thank you for your warning." Darcy wondered exactly how Mr. Bennet had informed the youngest Miss Bennet of the change to her plans. He could only guess at her disappointment.

His mind continued to rehearse its plans for the next several days, the first few which would be spent traveling to Pemberley. He had elected to leave the afternoon before the Gardiners and Elizabeth set out, wanting time to prepare his home for their arrival; and with luck and steady driving he would arrive two days before them. He wanted to make Mrs. Reynolds, his housekeeper, aware of the importance of this particular group of guests and ensure her discretion. He wanted to personally select the rooms his guests would use and verify that they were aired and cleaned in every respect. He would walk with the groundskeepers and ensure that the greenery and walks were in their usual immaculate state. He would visit the stables and select a horse for Elizabeth himself, so that he could show her every corner of the considerable estate. He would plan a dinner assembly at his home so that Elizabeth could meet other families of the neighborhood; and for this he would need time to compile a guest list, select a date, and write the necessary invitations.

Above all, he would take every possible step to advance a friendship between Elizabeth and his sister. Georgiana, a painfully shy sixteen-year-old, had grown up in a fairly solitary way, having lost both parents at a tender age and consequently having been left to the care of her older brother and cousin. Darcy and the colonel had done their best; and they had valuable assistance in the form of Mrs. Reynolds, who had been with the family for more than twenty years and who had become like a second mother to Georgiana.

But the elderly housekeeper could not gossip and confide secrets with the young mistress of the home, and Darcy and the colonel could not advise her as to the latest fashions, nor give her the sort of advice that she needed so badly to raise her confidence as she entered society. She had no female relatives who took a real interest in her besides Lady Catherine, and her ladyship was manifestly unacceptable. Georgiana needed someone with liveliness and good humor, poise and gentle sensitivity; someone who would be a bright, permanent presence in her life and give her everything that he and the colonel could not supply. She needed Elizabeth.

With Elizabeth's new acceptance of his suit Darcy allowed himself to hope as he had never hoped before. He would take every opportunity to court Elizabeth properly and give her as much opportunity as possible to get to know him. The Gardiners planned to stay at Pemberley for four weeks, and he would make the most of every day. With luck he would make a good start, if nothing intervened. After that, who could say what might happen?

CHAPTER TWELVE

Elizabeth and the Gardiners left Longbourn fairly late in the morning two days after the Gardiner's arrival there, with Mr. and Mrs. Gardiner giving their children a fond farewell as they set off. The children would remain under the special care of their cousin Jane, who had a winning way with them, while their parents took in the countryside of Derbyshire. Elizabeth gave her sister a warm embrace, followed by farewells with her mother and Kitty. Mary observed the occasion with a mere curtsey and Lydia was nowhere to be seen, as she was pouting in her bedroom after hearing the news that she would not go to Brighton after all.

"Come back to us soon, Lizzy, but not too soon," her father told her as they took their farewell. "Take as much time as you may reasonably need," he added significantly.

In front of Mrs. Bennet they dared not say too much but Elizabeth understood him clearly enough. She answered with a look at Jane, who was listening intently. "You shall hear my impressions of all of Derbyshire as soon as I can form an opinion."

"I am looking forward to your letters," her father answered. "They will be the only sensible communication made in this household for the next four weeks. Lovers are of all things most tiresome."

"Oh, yes! Pray write every day, Lizzy, and tell us all the fashions and current news!" her mother cried. "We shall see you in London in a month's time! Do not start shopping for anything without us there, for you will not know the best warehouses to use." Elizabeth solemnly promised that she would not shop for wedding clothes without the bride being present, the footman closed the door, and the carriage started off with Elizabeth and the Gardiners waving as long as they could.

Mrs. Gardiner, who had not been able to speak to her niece at length yet, eyed her from across the carriage before they even reached Meryton. "Now, Elizabeth, it is high time for you to tell us all about your Mr. Darcy." Such a conversation, Elizabeth knew, would encompass a great deal of time; and she was proven correct as the recital of all her interactions with Darcy, and her wrong impressions of Wickham, engaged their whole conversation until their first stop.

It is not the purpose of this narrative to recount all the scenes through which Elizabeth and her relatives passed, to describe the crowded streets or the quiet lanes of various small towns through which they traveled. On the third day of their travels Mrs. Gardiner began to point out familiar landmarks as they passed by, fondly recalling people and events from her childhood spent in that neighborhood. The day was fair enough to allow her to wave several times at old acquaintances outside the carriage as they passed by, and one or two returned the greeting. They were only five miles from the gates of Pemberley now and Elizabeth found her anticipation rising with every turn of the carriage wheels.

They passed steadily through the village of Lambton, crossing over a stone bridge where the countryside changed from homes to woods, and traveled alongside the woods until they reached the great, open gates of Pemberley itself. There they turned in and traveled for some time on the sylvan path, with the spring-greening branches of the trees forming a natural canopy overhead. Mr. and Mrs. Gardiner had been chatting merrily to each other as they first entered the park but their speech slowed and quieted as they traveled on, and all conversation ended as the carriage rounded an abrupt curve and the house itself came into view. Mr. Gardiner quickly banged on the carriage top and bade the driver pause while they took in the view.

Pemberley was situated against the backdrop of a rising hill; a great stone building, stately and with excellent proportions, with a green lawn spread in front of it like a smooth blanket of silk. Before this lawn spilled a large stream, springing up so naturally that Elizabeth could not tell from whence it came or where it went. Chestnut trees graced the lawn in various directions before giving way to the greater woods on both sides, and Elizabeth could only imagine the many paths to be explored in the days to come. Of the house there might be just as much exploring, for she found that to count the number of windows and other openings, and to guess at the number of rooms, was impossible. At that moment she began to feel that to be the mistress of Pemberley would really be something!

"And can it be," she thought, "that it is of this home that Mr. Darcy wishes me to be mistress? Could I ever find myself comfortable in such different surroundings, such grandeur and display?" She could not answer herself, but her aunt read the look on her face.

"One thing at a time, dear Lizzy. To visit the man is not to marry him; and I suppose once you are used to it, a house is just a house after all. But I do hope that Mr. Darcy will give us a bell to carry in case we are lost between the bed chamber and the dining room!"

It was just the sort of remark to make Elizabeth smile and to help her carry out her resolution of being at ease when she would see Mr. Darcy again.

That time was soon to come, for the carriage resumed its motion and in a few minutes they pulled to a stop outside the main entrance of Pemberley. While they waited for the carriage door to be opened and the stairs placed, Elizabeth observed Darcy proceeding out of the house to meet them with uncharacteristic haste. His eyes met hers even before the carriage door had opened and she felt herself relax a little at seeing the familiar face, though some anxiety still remained.

"Mr. and Mrs. Gardiner, Miss Bennet, it gives me the greatest of pleasure to welcome you to my home." The words were common and conventional as they exited the carriage, but there was a look in his eyes that was anything but normal. Under his controlled tone Elizabeth detected a tension reflected in his face, and she realized that he was at least as nervous as she was, though she could not imagine why. He was in a familiar place, with all the comfort of familiarity around him; and yet his sedate tone did not disguise the heightened expression in his eyes when he looked at her. Perhaps there had always been more uncertainty in him than she had previously believed possible.

"There are some visiting here who will claim the honor of an acquaintance with you, and one who wishes to be more particularly known to you as well, as soon as may be convenient. Mr. and Mrs. Hurst and Miss Bingley are visiting with us, and they are in the sitting room with my sister. When you have seen your rooms and been settled in may I introduce you to her?"

"Of course, I shall look forward to it." Elizabeth gave the standard answer to the respectful request and then allowed the housekeeper, Mrs. Reynolds, to take her to her room while a maid took the Gardiners in another direction. She was surprised and somewhat dismayed to find Miss Bingley at Pemberley ahead of her. No doubt she and the Hursts had come to visit Miss Darcy after

Bingley left them in town. Her memories of the days spent at Netherfield in their company were not pleasant, for she well remembered their cold civility and subtle snubs, and she also resented them for their attempts to influence Bingley away from Jane. But she resolved to be civil, though she hardly expected as much courtesy in return from the formidable Miss Bingley, who could not be pleased by Elizabeth's arrival.

Mrs. Reynolds led her directly up one stairway and then down a series of passageways before showing her into a suite of rooms decorated tastefully in pale gold with white. The bed chamber was adjoined by a wash room and a small sitting room furnished with a delicate desk and chair, with stationery already laid out; and the air of the entire suite was both cheerful and comforting. But though the entire room pleased her, Elizabeth's attention was fixed mostly on the oversized windows that afforded an excellent view of the lawn below and the start of the woods at some distance. The light permitted through the windows graced the bed chamber with as much light and air as could be wished in a much larger space, and Elizabeth anticipated happily the view that she would see upon waking each morning.

"Thank you, Mrs. Reynolds. The room is delightful."

Mrs. Reynolds smiled warmly. "Mr. Darcy said that you are fond of walks and would most appreciate a room with a good view of the outdoors."

"Did he direct you to choose the rooms for my aunt and uncle as well as myself?"

"No, ma'am, he chose all the rooms personally; and merely left it to me to make sure they were made ready. This is always his way, for he is a most particular man when it comes to his friends and family, and nothing can be too good for them."

"Are my aunt and uncle nearby?"

"Their rooms are but three doors down, but are more directly reached through a different corridor than we came through. Mr. Darcy and Miss Darcy are in the family wing, of course. The Hursts and Miss Bingley are in the back of the house overlooking the courtyard, close to the servant's entrance. If you have no objection I will send the maid in to assist you while you prepare for tea."

"I thank you."

When she had changed her clothing and briefly refreshed herself, Elizabeth followed the maid to collect her aunt and uncle, and then to the sitting room to join the party already grouped there. As they entered the room Darcy stood and greeted them with an easy manner and open smile she had not seen in him previously. She curtseyed to the Hursts and Miss Bingley, who looked at her with narrowed eyes, and then Mr. Darcy stood next to a young woman with fair hair, silently urging her to stand as he made the important introduction.

"Mr. and Mrs. Gardiner, Miss Bennet, may I have the honor of introducing my sister, Miss Georgiana Darcy."

Miss Darcy curtseyed and smiled hesitantly. "I am pleased to make your acquaintance, Miss Bennet. My brother has spoken of you a great deal."

"No doubt he told you of my poor manners when I have insisted on teasing him."

"Not at all. He spoke of your talents in playing and singing and could not praise you enough."

"Then you must ask him to speak more truthfully in the future."

"My brother always speaks the absolute truth," Miss Darcy assured her gravely, and Elizabeth could not help but smile.

They all sat. Mrs. Annesley, who served as Miss Darcy's companion, opened the conversation by asking about their travels; and from there one topic flowed naturally into another. The conversation was mainly carried on by Mrs. Gardiner, Elizabeth, and Mrs. Annesley, with occasional soft comments from Miss Darcy. The Hursts and Miss Bingley merely observed. Elizabeth recalled that Wickham had described Miss Darcy as proud, but a very little observation convinced her that she was nothing more than painfully shy. Little that she said was more than a monosyllable in length, and that said when it was least likely to be noticed. Upon these occasions Elizabeth was pleased to listen carefully and encourage further comments, wanting to help her be more at ease.

Darcy sat in a chair near Elizabeth, but not so near that it would be impossible for him to see her face; and she frequently glanced at him to find his gaze upon her with an open look of admiration. She quickly noticed that he forwarded every attempt of hers to interact with Georgiana and was most anxious for them to become acquainted. She also realized, from the looks and general attention she was receiving, that the suspicions of the whole party had been raised against her and Darcy; and that nothing she said or did, especially with Miss Darcy, would escape notice.

After sitting for some time she was roused by hearing Miss Bingley make a cold inquiry about the health of her family. She answered with equal brevity, and the other said no more.

At length, following a series of nods and hints from Mrs. Annesley, Miss Darcy called for tea to be served, and beautiful plates of fresh fruit and other delicacies made their way into the room. The atmosphere relaxed somewhat, for although not all could speak freely, all could certainly eat.

During a pause in the conversation Miss Bingley, who had been fairly quiet throughout the visit, addressed Elizabeth in a voice loud enough to carry throughout the room. "Pray tell, Miss Elizabeth, have the militia left Meryton yet? I believe they had planned to change encampments by now. That must have been quite a loss for your family."

Elizabeth perceived that Miss Bingley's jealousy had made her bring up the subject of the militia, hoping to injure her in Darcy's eyes by reminding him of her family's involvement with Wickham. She could not know that this particular venom had lost its sting.

"We tolerated their loss as well as we could, Miss Bingley," Elizabeth replied placidly. "Indeed, once we were aware of the good news of your brother and my sister we hardly thought of the regiment at all."

Miss Bingley's haughty expression changed suddenly, and the cup of tea that had been on its way to her mouth was replaced in its saucer rather quickly. "The good news, Miss Bennet? We have not heard from Mr. Bingley since he left London."

Elizabeth suddenly realized that their arrival at Pemberley had preceded the letter Bingley would surely have sent to announce his betrothal. She raised her chin slightly but kept her expression pleasant. "I refer to his engagement to my sister Jane, which happened the day before we left Hertfordshire. I assumed you would have received word directly. "

Miss Bingley's face was a study in shock, and Mrs. Hurst likewise froze as she took in the important communication. Mr. Hurst poured a glass of brandy.

"Perhaps your brother sent a letter to your house in town," Darcy commented, "as he did not know that you were coming here." His tone held just a faint tinge of rebuke. "I apologize that I did not mention it to you when I arrived. It slipped my mind in the excitement of the visitors I was anticipating."

Clearly Darcy had not been expecting to find Miss Bingley and the Hursts when he arrived at Pemberley. Had they imposed themselves on Miss Darcy? The shy girl would have been no match for them if they had chosen to arrive without an invitation. Miss Bingley tossed her head as Darcy's words sunk in. "I suppose congratulations are in order," she finally said without enthusiasm.

"What wonderful news!" Miss Darcy spoke with a hesitant, yet sincere smile.

"We are very pleased for them, indeed," Mrs. Gardiner said. "Mr. Bingley is an estimable young man, and we have no doubt of the happiness that he and our niece will find together."

"I can confirm Bingley's happiness," said Darcy. "He was as animated as I have ever seen him and his joy was palpable."

"It was certainly a most advantageous match for Miss Bennet," Miss Bingley sniffed.

"And just as advantageous for Bingley," Darcy replied firmly. "Miss Bennet has much to recommend her."

"Miss Bingley, you and Miss Elizabeth will soon be related!" Miss Darcy looked genuinely happy at the thought.

An awkward silence followed her words as Miss Bingley changed color and made no response, for being sister to the Bennets could not be her desire. Miss Darcy, sensing a misstep, looked around her uncertainly, but Elizabeth smiled at her.

"Miss Darcy, " she said warmly, "your brother speaks so highly of you, and I am so pleased to make your acquaintance. I hope we shall be able to spend a great deal of time together during our visit." Reassured, Miss Darcy's expression relaxed, and she recovered somewhat although not enough to make many more additions to the conversation. Darcy looked at Elizabeth gratefully while Miss Bingley was left to look more vexed than ever.

After tea had been cleared Darcy proposed giving Elizabeth and the Gardiners a tour of the house and surrounding grounds, to which they readily agreed. Miss Bingley, still smarting from her loss, declined to join them; and Mrs. Hurst declared that she had already seen it and preferred to stay with her sister. Mr. Hurst simply snored. Mrs. Annesley said that she had a letter to write, but Miss Darcy joined the group in response to her brother's request, and Elizabeth was touched to see how the girl was willing to exert herself in company in order to please her brother. Obviously they were devoted to each other.

Darcy guided them through the rooms on the first floor to start with, moving from the sitting room to the dining room, ball room and library. Elizabeth was pleased to see that great wealth had been married to an equal level of taste; and though the house was fully the equal of Rosings, she believed it to be superior in its furnishings, with no ostentatious display. From their exclamations of delight Elizabeth could hear that her aunt and uncle were similarly impressed. When they entered the library, her aunt and uncle walked with Miss Darcy to a small table where several rare volumes were displayed. Darcy led Elizabeth to a quiet corner of the spacious room, leaving the others to speak among themselves as they stood a little apart.

Elizabeth saw him looking at her with an open expression, reflecting an anxious pride mixed with a desire to please.

"I must apologize, Miss Bennet, for the presence of Miss Bingley and the Hursts. I would have preferred that their visit not overlap with yours, but I was not aware of their presence until I arrived. Apparently after Bingley left them in town they took advantage of a previous invitation Georgiana had extended."

"It is of no matter."

"It matters to me. Miss Bingley, I know, has long cherished her own designs upon me, which are of course bound to be disappointed. They are also perhaps not the most congenial company for your aunt and uncle. Truthfully, were it up to me, they would not be welcome at this time; but they are my sister's guests, and Bingley's family. Please do not let their presence intrude upon your enjoyment of your stay in any way."

"Are they not at all afraid of being polluted by being in such close proximity to Cheapside?" Elizabeth asked him solemnly.

"I will leave that to you to ask them."

At length they were led up the same stairway Elizabeth had previously used to enter the second floor, but turned in a different direction and made their way to the gallery. Here Elizabeth had leisure to look from portrait to portrait, some of them quite old, all of them of members of the extended Darcy and Fitzwilliam families. The portraits were of fine quality, painted by masters, in rich and ornate frames; and Elizabeth studied the faces of each subject at length, fancying in some that she could draw a resemblance to Darcy and his sister. She stopped for some time in front of the portrait of Lady Anne Darcy, painted a year or so before her death.

"You have discovered my mother. It is one of my favorite portraits in the whole house." Darcy materialized beside her, speaking quietly. "The artist does full justice to the kindness and sweet spirit she demonstrated every day."

"And this was your father?" She looked at the portrait immediately to its right.

"A most excellent man. He passed away just five years ago, leaving me with the administration of all his holdings and the guardianship of my sister."

"You were young to take on such responsibility."

"I was but three and twenty, and thrust into the role quite suddenly. I still feel acutely the lack of his guidance and advice."

"How did he and your mother meet?"

"It was an arranged marriage designed for the advantage of both houses, but it turned out to be a love match as well. They were a most devoted couple. The servants still talk about how my father dedicated himself to my mother in her final illness."

"That is a touching heritage to own, Mr. Darcy."

"It is a heritage I can only hope to imitate in my own marriage someday." He looked at her significantly.

From the gallery they were shown the billiards room and several other rooms of lesser significance. Assuring them that the third floor was not worth visiting, Darcy led them back downstairs and through the front entrance to the orangery located at one end of the house. "This orangery was begun several generations ago, to harbor a handful of citrus trees which would otherwise not survive the winter. Since then we have added a number of delicate plants to the collection. When my father saw how much my sister enjoyed the room, he had a fountain built and surrounded it with the benches you see."

"I enjoy reading here in the mornings," Miss Darcy volunteered. "William sometimes will have his breakfast brought here to eat with me."

"Are you very fond of books, Miss Darcy?" Mrs. Gardiner asked her.

"Yes. William always makes sure that I have a new collection to read every time he returns from town."

That explained some of the overflow of books in the library, Elizabeth thought. "It is well that you have the time to read so much, and a quiet area to devote to the pursuit."

"Do you not also enjoy reading?" Miss Darcy asked her. "I thought William said that you did."

"I dearly enjoy reading, but in a house with four sisters, the solitude needed is often in short supply."

"It must be wonderful to have so many sisters. I would be content with just one," she said wistfully.

Elizabeth looked at her sharply, but Miss Darcy's face held nothing but sincerity and an earnest desire. She was not scheming to speak on her brother's behalf but speaking from her own heart. "I am sure your desire will be answered one day, Miss Darcy." The two smiled at each other.

From the orangery they moved to the lawn and Mr. Gardiner asked how far it was around the park. Upon being told ten miles, they decided that it was too long a walk to attempt just then; but he asked leave to take a closer look at the stream, for he was fond of fishing. The party moved in that direction with the Gardiners and Miss Darcy walking together, and Elizabeth following on Darcy's arm. Elizabeth once again became aware of Darcy's intense gaze on her face.

"I hope, Miss Bennet, that everything you see is to your satisfaction. This has been my home all my life and I am certainly biased in its favor, but I hope that what you see pleases you in every respect."

"You hope that it pleases me? How could it not? I have heard of your Pemberley many times but the descriptions have not done it justice. No improvements could possibly be made to such an enchanting home."

"I disagree. There is one improvement that it still lacks, one that would make it perfect in every respect." His eyes were warm as they looked at her. Obviously he had no intention of being subtle. She decided to make a light-hearted reply.

"Mr. Darcy, it is traditional to conduct a courtship with a little suspense. One should not be too direct in their attentions but rather lead on their prospective partner with teasing and cajoling, all the while disguising the true intent of the heart." She looked at him with a raised eyebrow, waiting to see how he would respond.

"I am not experienced in courtship, Miss Bennet. You will have to show me the way."

"I hope that you know I do not speak from my own experience, but from the experience of others. I have read many wonderful novels on the subject. You may wish to improve your education with them."

He seemed amused. "And what advice do they generally give?""

"If their stories are to be believed, your efforts may be more successful if you pretend disinterest from time to time, or try to lead the lady to believe your attentions have shifted elsewhere. You might also consider deceiving the lady as to your true identity for a time, or confusing her with conflicting reports of your wealth. Such efforts almost always result in gaining the lady's affection in virtually a moment's time."

"I cannot pretend to be other than who I am. Disguise of every sort is my abhorrence."

She looked up at him. "Then I must ask, who are you, Mr. Darcy? You seem very different now than the man I met in Meryton. There you seemed proud and indifferent when we first met, and nothing could please you but yourself and your own company. But since your return to Hertfordshire you have been accommodating and amiable in every respect. Which Mr. Darcy is the true Mr. Darcy?"

"Mr. Darcy has never been indifferent. He is the man who has admired Miss Bennet since almost the beginning of their acquaintance. He is the man who listened to every conversation in which she was involved, covertly watched her at every opportunity, and found himself fascinated by her at every interaction. The true Mr. Darcy is the man who has longed to have Mrs. Elizabeth Darcy in his home for many months, and who desires most passionately that Miss Elizabeth Bennet will fall in love with Pemberley and everything in it. That is the only Mr. Darcy there is."

Elizabeth could scarcely believe the directness with which he spoke. Her attempt to relieve the tension had been ineffective, and had in fact resulted in another declaration of his affection before she had been three hours at Pemberley. This was too fast for her liking. She made no answer.

"Have I displeased you, Miss Bennet?" he asked at length with a furrowed brow, while they continued to stroll behind the others.

"Displeased is not quite the right word, sir. Indeed I do not know if there is a word for what I am feeling at the moment. You and I are going to be in each other's company constantly for the next month, and while you have made your own feelings for me clear, I am not ready to make any similar declaration. Such a circumstance could prove awkward."

"You fear that I will pressure you? I expect no such declarations from you, Miss Bennet, though I will welcome them gladly if they come."

"And are you willing to take the risk, to expose your heart and your affections again and again with no certainty that those feelings will ever be returned?"

He looked at her seriously. "I can take that risk so long as I have reason to hope. Can you give me that hope?"

Elizabeth looked away as she answered, "I would not be here otherwise, though I am far from being able to truthfully reciprocate your feelings as yet. A courtship is a matter of weeks but marriage is for life, and I must be certain of my feelings before taking such an irrevocable step."

"You have already taught me humility, Miss Bennet; and I shall be pleased to learn patience from such a teacher." They walked on in silence for a minute.

"Have you told your sister of your interest in me? Does anybody else know?"

"I have told no one besides the people you already know, not even my sister. Mrs. Reynolds probably guesses but I trust her discretion. "

"But they will know if you make no effort to disguise it. Already Miss Bingley eyes me with suspicion."

To her surprise, he chuckled. "Miss Bingley eyes any female within a hundred feet of me with suspicion. That is nothing new."

"I wish to carry out our visit here with a minimum of speculation and attention."

"Whereas I am anxious to shower you with every possible attention," he countered. "May I offer a compromise? When we are in company, when others can overhear, I will make every effort to treat you in every respect as an honored guest, nothing more. But when we are not observed or overheard, as we are now, I request the honor of expressing my feelings freely. I hope this will not intimidate you; but this is, after all, a courtship. I must have the freedom to speak my piece from time to time."

"My courage rises with every attempt to intimidate me, sir."

"Then may I say we have an understanding?" Elizabeth was about to protest the word when she saw that his eyes had lightened and he was teasing her.

"Not the understanding that you are seeking, but I am in agreement with your plan."

"Then I shall look forward to every attempt to intimidate you," he paused and added, "my dearest." He said the last two words with particular emphasis, and Elizabeth caught her breath; for although his words may have been few, she found his gaze eloquent. He smiled at her once more and moved away to speak to her uncle, leaving Elizabeth to conclude that despite his earlier words Darcy understood the art of courtship very well indeed.

CHAPTER THIRTEEN

Elizabeth did not write to her sister when she first arrived, knowing that her aunt would let Mr. Bennet and Jane know of their safe arrival. But several days later she penned the following letter.

Dearest Jane,

We arrived here at Pemberley five days ago. I am sorry not to have written to you sooner, but each day has been so full that I have scarcely had time to think, let alone to put my thoughts on paper. But why should I even bother apologizing to you, when you have undoubtedly been so involved with your dear Charles that you have not even noticed my absence? Pray forget that I even wrote these first few sentences.

Pemberley is everything that we heard described, and more. Upon our arrival, Mr. Darcy and Miss Darcy gave us a tour of the main parts of the house, and believe me when I say that Mama would faint dead away to see the many rooms, the curtains, the fine china, and the furniture. It must take a small army of servants to see to all of it. I cannot count the servants exactly for I have yet to see most of them twice! My aunt and I each have our own maid, as of course does Miss Darcy; and there are upstairs maids, downstairs maids, kitchen maids, and I believe even maids for the maids themselves!

Miss Bingley and the Hursts are visiting here as well. They came to Pemberley upon Mr. Bingley's leaving them in London. Imagine, if you can, the look on Caroline's face when she first saw us here! I thought her smile was likely to crack in half if it froze in place any more. She was, to put it mildly, quite surprised to hear of your engagement to her brother, about which I was only too happy to give her the good news. Mr. Darcy had somehow neglected to inform her of this momentous news, for reasons I can only describe as being mischievous. Since Miss Darcy is not out yet she really should not have had the burden of entertaining guests in his absence, and I suspect that letting me shock them with such news was his own way of punishing them for imposing on her. Clever man!

Miss Darcy is, as expected, completely the opposite of how Mr. Wickham described her to me. She is tall, as fair as her brother is dark, and absolutely not proud in any way. She is in fact quite painfully shy, which may be easily mistaken for pride in those who believe her to be superior; but after she overcomes her timidity she is perfectly amiable. She is guilty of nothing but a little reserve, probably from the lack of having siblings her age. Her gentleness and propensity to find the best in others remind me of a certain beloved sister, and I am certain that you would be friends immediately upon meeting each other. Meanwhile, her education has far outstripped ours, and I feel quite ashamed at my lack of diligence when I hear her play on the pianoforte.

But you do not wish to hear of Miss Darcy, but of her brother! Mr. Darcy has been most attentive since we arrived, devoting almost every waking moment to our entertainment. Two mornings after our arrival, he overheard my aunt express a desire to go around the whole park in a phaeton. No sooner had the words been spoken than a phaeton and two matched ponies appeared in the courtyard, together with a picnic basket, a great variety of food, a parasol, and a lawn blanket. The only item missing was a driver, for Mr. Darcy had already decided to drive us himself; and we spent the whole day out of doors, doing nothing but admiring the park and everything in it. I have rarely had such an enjoyable time, even on our picnics to Oakham Mount.

Such has been his way. Whatever we ask for, or express a desire for, is made to happen in the same moment; and it is difficult to imagine a request that he cannot fulfill, although I am sorely tempted to try. Two days ago I made the mistake of admiring a litter of kittens in the stable, and Mr. Darcy at once had it moved into the kitchen so that they may be visited more easily. He has given my uncle leave to use whatever tackle he has to fish, and shown him the best spots in the stream that runs through the park. Yesterday I repeated my request to see a maharajah appear out of nowhere--he merely smiled in that enigmatic way of his and bade me be patient, saying that good things come to those who wait. This makes me curious as to what he may have in mind, but I will not gratify his vanity by asking more.

His attentions sound overwhelming, do they not? But they are all carried out in such a gentleman-like way, with such propriety, that there can be no objection made. I asked him on our first day here not to make his attentions to me obvious, especially in front of others, nor to overwhelm me with them; and he has adhered to this request most diligently. But when we are a little apart from others, or when their attentions are directed elsewhere, he favors me with a secret smile, or with some small endearment, with such a look in his eyes that communicates clearly his true sentiments. Even these he limits out of respect for my own undecided feeling; but under such a determined onslaught, can I withstand for long?

Please do write soon; we all are anxious to hear about your wedding plans so that we may make plans of our own. Pray tell Mama that I said Chatsworth and Dovedale are quite fine houses, but I have not mentioned meeting any eligible gentlemen in either place. So long as you do not tell her that I have actually visited those locales there can be no deceit, and your conscience may be clear. The Gardiners and Mr. Darcy send their regards.
Your affectionate and thoroughly entertained sister,
Lizzy

Upon concluding the letter, Elizabeth addressed it and added it to the pile of outgoing mail which was kept in the study; then joined the others in the house who were all going to Lambton for the day. This number included Miss Bingley and Mrs. Hurst, who had tired of being left out of the entertainments the others enjoyed, even if it meant that they had to associate with a family in trade. The Gardiners would visit with an old friend of Mrs. Gardiner's whose friendship had been rekindled after a long discontinuance; and the others would visit the shops in town, so Miss Bingley did not feel the imposition would be too much. Elizabeth did not look forward to a day in the company of the two sisters, but with the company of Mr. Darcy and Miss Darcy she thought it might be tolerable.

The Darcy family did not often take their custom in Lambton, so it was a matter of some curiosity when the Darcy carriage with its livery pulled to a stop at a point near the center of the small town. Mr. and Mrs. Gardiner made arrangements to return to the same location late in the afternoon, and all the party went their separate ways for the day. Mr. Darcy looked at his sister. "Is there any particular shop that catches your interest?"

"I have little interest in most of the shops," Miss Bingley answered before Miss Darcy could. "Perhaps a milliner might be in the area?"

"That cannot be interesting to William," Miss Darcy protested, but her brother shook his head.

"I am perfectly at your disposal, Miss Bingley. Please lead the way."

Miss Bingley brightened at the inconsequential remark and took his arm as she stepped to the head of the little group, appearing to believe that Darcy was favoring her with attention. Elizabeth, following behind with Miss Darcy, was amused to see how neatly Mr. Darcy had trapped himself with company she knew he found disagreeable. Although Mr. Darcy had carefully guarded his behavior towards Elizabeth, some events, such as the picnic, could not go unnoticed; and Miss Bingley had redoubled her efforts to gain his attention. Jealousy had begun to make her desperate.

The little group made its way to a milliner's shop and waited patiently while Miss Bingley perused the various rows of ribbons, notions, and such like. The others scattered about the shop. Unable to devote himself to Elizabeth, Darcy trailed his sister; but Miss Bingley perceived that his eyes rested more often than not on the slim figure of Elizabeth as she perused the bonnets on display in the window. Elizabeth was likewise aware of Miss Bingley watching both of them, and was aware when she stopped in front of a display of fans.

Miss Bingley hesitated for a moment, then chose one and opened it up in front of her face. At the same time she maneuvered her way in front of the mirror that was placed there for the convenience of patrons, in such a way that her eyes could meet those of Mr. Darcy who stood off to the side and a little behind her. She fluttered the fan, closed it again, opened it and fluttered again. Mr. Darcy would not observe her, and she sighed heavily, but to no avail--his eyes were firmly fixed on a row of buttons. She repeated the ritual with the same effect and at length she threw the fan down again.

Moving to a rack of ribbons, she selected two rolls and began a more direct approach. "Do you think, Mr. Darcy, that this shade of blue would complement my eyes? Or should I choose the brown trim?"

Darcy barely looked up at her. "I could not venture to say. Either would, I am sure, be more than suitable. You must choose for yourself."

This did not suit Miss Bingley's goal. "But I asked which color you think should complement the color of my eyes. Surely there would be a difference between the two colors, if you consider the two shades. Only one color can show them to advantage and the other must conflict with them."

"I have never noticed the color of your eyes." Darcy looked again toward where Elizabeth had joined his sister, the two finding something to laugh about together.

"Oh! Men are so impossible; they never notice anything that is not right in front of them. Miss Elizabeth," she called, "do come to me and advise me on the color of ribbon for my best hat. Mr. Darcy is of no use at all."

Elizabeth was surprised at the application but she realized that Miss Bingley was trying to turn Darcy's attention from Elizabeth onto herself, just as she had when Jane was sick at Netherfield. She approached. "Show me the choices, please, and you shall hear my opinion."

"I have often been told that my eyes are large and uncommonly fine. Do you not think the blue would suit them better than the brown? Which color would you call my eyes?" She held up both ribbons to her face in turn while Elizabeth gravely considered.

"This, I believe, suits you most." Elizabeth reached past her and laid a length of green ribbon in her hand. "This is very like your eyes and sets them off beautifully. Do you agree, Miss Darcy?"

"I believe so," Miss Darcy answered hesitantly and looked to her brother, but Darcy still declined to give an opinion.

"Do not ask me to be the judge. Miss Bingley has already received a sound judgment from two who can discern these things better than I. She does not need my commentary."

"What do you think, Louisa?" Miss Bingley now addressed her sister, weary of fishing for compliments from the reticent Darcy. "I need to know which color would best set off my eyes before I can repair the trim on my hat."

"Which hat would that be?' Mrs. Hurst looked genuinely puzzled. "All of your hats are in fine repair. I saw to them myself when we were packing."

Elizabeth concealed a smile at Mrs. Hurst's unwitting exposure of her sister. Without meaning to, her eyes met Darcy's and she saw that he had the same thought, but she turned away quickly. Miss Bingley, looking between the two, intercepted the look and perceived that their shared amusement was at her expense. She flushed with anger but said nothing.

"While we are here should you not like to pick out some new bonnets or such like?" Mr. Darcy addressed his sister. "It has been some time since I was able to take you to town, and I do not believe you did much shopping then."

"I would love to pick out several new bonnets, William, if Miss Bennet can help me."

"I would be honored, Miss Darcy."

"Please, Miss Bennet, I would have you call me Georgiana if you like." She glanced at her brother, waiting for his approval.

"I would be honored. And you must of course call me Elizabeth." Though she did not look at him, Elizabeth could sense the satisfaction coming from Darcy.

They took some little time going through several bonnets and hats until Georgiana had found several that appealed to her, and Darcy directed these to be wrapped and delivered to Pemberley. Elizabeth and Mrs. Hurst made their own purchases and these were added to the delivery, but Elizabeth noticed that the green ribbon for Miss Bingley did not join them.

After several more shops and a few inconsequential purchases they made their way to the inn for a small meal. Entering the dining area with no private rooms apparent, the group made their way to a table by a window; and the proprietor hurried over to make them comfortable, spreading cutlery and napkins. He was a middle-aged man with that air of bustling friendliness typical of such establishments, eager to make conversation and an impression. "It's a fine day to be out with a notion of shopping," he said to Darcy, "fair weather, not a drop of rain, and with the company of such charming ladies, begging your pardon, misses," he added with a nod at the rest of the table. Obviously he had not recognized Mr. Darcy or Miss Darcy. "You'll find no better fare at any inn in this county, and we are most pleased to have you with us today."

"You look to have a fair business this afternoon," said Darcy, looking around at the well-filled tables, which were populated by a mixture of farmers and ladies and gentlemen.

"Ay, we have our hands full; but not to worry, you will be served most promptly. I'll send my girl out to you at once and the cook will have your food straightaway. We take pride in our service, sir, and we offer the best, if I do say so myself. Our cook worked at Pemberley itself if you can believe that!"

"An ideal recommendation," Elizabeth said smilingly.

When the maid came to the table she recognized Darcy at once, and curtsied. "Begging your pardon, Mr. Darcy, my master didn't tell me it was you."

"He has no reason to recognize me. How have you and your father been? I trust he is making a good recovery?"

"Yes, sir, he is. The apothecary says he'll be up and about in another fortnight, and we'll not be able to see that anything ever happened to him. It's most grateful to you we are."

"I was glad to be of assistance. Please do let Roberts know if your father experiences any further difficulties from his fall or if he needs the apothecary again. You have only to send word to the house and he will be attended to."

When she left the table again, Miss Darcy asked her brother, "Is that the family for whom I prepared the basket of food?"

"It is, and I would be most appreciative if you could prepare another. They are too proud to ask for charity, and what we sent previously will not be adequate to carry them through this crisis. Their neighbors are generous but we should do our part as well."

Miss Darcy murmured her assent, and Elizabeth commented, "You are a most attentive landlord, Mr. Darcy."

"I only do what is necessary, as my father before me."

"You are too modest, Mr. Darcy," Miss Bingley broke in. "I have heard of your generosity many times from my brother. Wherever any little matter arises you are sure to be found, distributing liberally and asking nothing in return. Everything that can be done for the poor will be done once you are made aware. Surely you set quite a high standard for others to follow, and all who know of it can do nothing but commend you for it."

"I do not do these things for the praise of others, and I would ask that you not advertise my supposed good deeds to the world."

"You are opposed to the praise of others for your acts of charity, sir?" Elizabeth asked.

"Charity that is performed for the praise of others is no longer charity, but mere pretense. The good that is done should be done for its own sake, not for want of recognition."

"Surely the objects of that charity would still benefit, no matter what the motive of the giver," Elizabeth countered.

"No doubt they would; but the act of charity will have a benefit for the giver as well as the receiver, if the motives of the giver are pure."

"You are entirely correct, Mr. Darcy," Miss Bingley joined in. "I have always felt an uplifted, pleased feeling when helping someone who is experiencing reverses of fortune. I am always glad to loan them a book, or a bonnet, or some other item within my possession, for one never knows when one may be in need of similar assistance someday. Louisa, do you not recall when I had one of my gowns refitted for you last month when your own was sadly torn?"

"But charity that is given with an object of being repaid is not charity at all," said Elizabeth. "To give with no expectation of being repaid, or as Mr. Darcy says, with no likelihood of being recognized or praised, is surely the only form of charity worthy of the name."

"Exactly so," Mr. Darcy answered. "And although I cannot look down upon the need for a new book or gown, I confess that the acts of charity that were in my mind were of a more substantial nature."

"There can be no harm in being recognized for your good character, although I should not advertise my acts of giving if I were you, Mr. Darcy," said Miss Bingley in a patronizing tone. "There are many people in this world who will take advantage of your generosity when they hear of it, and will hound you day and night in order to advance their own fortunes. When people are given too much assistance, they are likely to forget the sphere to which they were born and which they should not quit."

"And it is your opinion," Elizabeth asked Miss Bingley, "that a person should not advance from the circumstances in which they were born?"

"Certainly not," Miss Bingley answered with a false smile. "Even in marriage one should not wed too high above their station."

Elizabeth guessed that this snub was directed at her, and her guess was confirmed a minute later by expressive looks that passed between Miss Bingley and her sister.

"Insufferable, ill-bred woman," she thought to herself; and noted that, judging by the look on his face, Darcy agreed with her. But she would not give the two sisters the satisfaction of knowing that they had succeeded in needling her. Keeping her face composed, she instead directed her efforts to conversing more with Miss Darcy, which had the effect of drawing Mr. Darcy more into their conversation and away from that of the other two ladies. Thus Miss Bingley found that her cutting remark had hurt only herself in the end, in that Darcy's attention was now impossible to fix upon herself.

After finishing their meal, their last stop of the day was at a bookstore. Here Miss Darcy was in her element as she moved from one display to another, lost in the many titles competing for her attention. First a book of poetry, then a novel attracted her interest, and she set many others aside for further perusal as she moved through the store accompanied by her indulgent brother. Elizabeth, too, made her way through the various rows carefully, picking up one after another and then setting each down again. At length she found a book of poetry that especially appealed to her; and she found herself reading through its pages with delight, becoming oblivious to the rest of the party and to the passage of time. Miss Darcy's voice finally broke through her reverie and she wistfully laid the book down, aware that the purchase was too dear with her limited funds, and moved to join her friends.

Darcy stood still for several minutes watching Elizabeth as she read in her volume. The past four days with her at Pemberley had been some of the most pleasant days in his memory. Not since the time of his parents' presence had Pemberley been so full of laughter and good spirit. He delighted in every smile she directed his way, in every teasing comment from her lips, and rejoiced in the growing friendship between her and Georgiana. His only frustration was the boundary she had set on him, that of not expressing himself so freely as to overwhelm her. He already knew that when she left Pemberley in three weeks it would be a serious blow to his peace of mind.

But for now his mind was fixed on the present and he stood in happy enjoyment of the view before him. Without his knowing it his face softened and took on a tender expression; and if anyone cared to look at him just then, his whole heart was exposed. When Miss Darcy called Elizabeth's name, she looked up at both of them and smiled, and he smiled in return as she made her way towards them.

"Did you not find anything to your liking? You were looking at that volume for some time," Darcy said to her when she joined them, noting that her hands were empty.

Elizabeth shrugged, unwilling to admit her small purse. "Another time, perhaps. I do not wish to have too much to pack when I return home!"

Darcy frowned as he looked at her, suspecting where the real difficulty lay but knowing that he could not buy her a gift directly. He moved to where she had stood and retrieved the book, adding it to the pile his sister had selected. "I believe this will make an excellent addition to our library, will it not, Georgiana?"

"Indeed it will, if you say so," Miss Darcy replied loyally, and smiled at him meaningfully; for she had begun to realize where her brother's heart was hidden.

"We must give Miss Bennet every reason to want to return to Pemberley, after all," Darcy added, and Elizabeth gave him a bemused look.

Miss Bingley stood a little ways away from Darcy watching resentfully as the looks passed between him and Elizabeth. She had seen the reflective Darcy watching Elizabeth with an expression of deepest admiration, and she knew that she could no longer deceive herself. Darcy had no attention to spare for her and never would. His heart was given to another and there was no hope of retrieving it for herself. Not that Miss Bingley had any real interest in his heart. She was attracted to Darcy's purse, not his person, and her affections were not at all engaged in her pursuit of him any more than they would have been engaged with an attractive pair of shoes. But upon realizing that her efforts were in vain her vanity was sorely injured, and she began to plan ways to have some small measure of revenge.

CHAPTER FOURTEEN

When they arrived back at the house the ladies retired to their rooms to prepare for dinner, and there they found the various posts which had been delivered in their absence. Elizabeth sat at the desk in her sitting room to read a letter from Jane, which of course had been written before Jane could have received her own letter.

My dearest Lizzy,

By now you are safely arrived at Pemberley, no doubt enjoying the house, its family and its environs with my aunt and uncle. Please do describe all that you see and do, for I do wish I could have accompanied you on this momentous journey. We have always shared every new experience together, and it seems strange that you are there and I am here at such a time of change.

Charles has been a faithful caller every day and sits near me as I write this, penning the news of our engagement to his various relatives. Each moment we spend in each other's company here at Longbourn adds to the anticipation of starting our own establishment at Netherfield, or wherever Charles decides, as I do not think he is too attached to this neighborhood. I care not where we may be so long as I am with him, but I do hope that in the years to come you and I will find ourselves settled somewhere near each other.

Papa undertook a difficult endeavor the day after you left. Following his conversations with Mr. Darcy, he felt that his honor demanded that he acquaint Colonel Forster with Mr. Wickham's true character, and to that end he rode to Brighton two days ago. He returned just last night. He said that he spoke with the colonel at length and made known to him all the dealings which Mr. Wickham had with Mr. Darcy. To add to the story, he also took with him the list of the merchants in Meryton who extended credit to Mr. Wickham which had not been satisfied when he left. Colonel Forster became incensed and called Mr. Wickham into account. Our father says that Mr. Wickham did not attempt to deny the charges but made light of them, saying that on an officer's pay, the debts would be repaid sooner or later. Colonel Forster demanded that Mr. Wickham behave as a gentleman or else face removal from the militia, which reprimand Mr. Wickham took easily enough, seeming not outwardly disturbed; but our father seemed troubled at the interview. He says that Wickham will cause grief wherever he goes and that we may not have heard the last of him.

For my part, I am pleased that Papa exerted himself so much, and trust that under the colonel's watchful eye Mr. Wickham may yet live up to his best potential. He may want only a little direction and motivation in order to become a more useful sort of man.

Mama and I have been discussing wedding clothes at length, and I believe we shall be prepared when we meet you in town to empty half the warehouses that we see. I am afraid this will be terribly expensive for our father; but he tells me not to worry, that he will be pleased to see me off in such fine fashion and to such a deserving gentleman.

Mary and Kitty are much as they have ever been, but there has been such a change in Lydia as you would scarcely believe. When Papa first told Lydia that she could not follow the officers to Brighton she pouted and stayed in her room for three days, only permitting Kitty's company. As you know, this behavior in the past has induced Mama to lobby on her behalf and as often as not, Papa would give in for the sake of peace. But my father was not willing to weaken this time, and Lydia finally gave up and came downstairs to eat. I wish I could say that this episode has made her more mature and sensible, but I am afraid it has made another change in her altogether. Before she was loud and boisterous, but now she seems sly. I caught her and Kitty sitting on the couch yesterday, their heads close together, whispering together about a scheme to go to Meryton without our father's permission. Had I not overheard them they would have been to Meryton and back without our knowledge, exposing themselves to no end of folly. This new Lydia is in some ways worse than the previous version, and I confess to feeling that I need to keep a closer eye on her than ever.

I need to close this letter now if it is to be posted today. Charles sends you his affectionate greetings, and asks that you will pass them on to Mr. Darcy and his sister as well. Please do write soon and tell me how the romance goes, if you feel it is something you can share.

Your loving sister,
Jane

Elizabeth was well pleased to receive her sister's correspondence, if not by all the intelligence it contained. She wondered what Darcy would think of having his information conveyed to Colonel Forster; and she was also troubled by the change that Jane perceived in Lydia, aware that her parents were no match if Lydia were determined to pursue her headlong ways without restraint. She folded the letter to take to dinner and give to her aunt and resolved to tell Darcy of her father's actions at her earliest opportunity.

At the dinner table Miss Bingley and the Hursts announced their intentions of leaving on the morrow, to the surprise of all present. Such a plan had not been mentioned all day, and Mrs. Gardiner courteously asked if all was well.

"I thank you for your concern, though there is no need for it. Mr. Hurst finds that he has urgent business that just came to his attention," Mrs. Hurst replied and Mr. Hurst nodded his agreement obediently. Their tone did not invite further conversation, and Mrs. Gardiner looked questioningly at her niece, who could give no answers to her unasked questions. Though she had no proof, Elizabeth was certain that the urgent business was nothing more urgent than a response to Miss Bingley's frustration with Mr. Darcy.

Such an abrupt departure with no real explanation or apology could not be seen as anything but the most backward of manners, and Elizabeth realized that Miss Bingley's intention was to cause discomfort for the Darcy family. In this she was succeeding. Miss Darcy's expression was crestfallen, apparently wondering if she had somehow offended her guests, and Elizabeth wished that the two sisters might have exercised more common courtesy at least for her sake. Elizabeth herself could not let such an affront go unanswered.

Smiling brightly, she asked, "Were you able to locate suitable ribbons for your hat, Miss Bingley? If you need more, Mr. Gardiner has quite an extensive selection in his warehouses in Cheapside."

Miss Bingley could do nothing but thank her coldly and assure her that she had no need for more ribbons. Elizabeth felt that Miss Darcy had been somewhat avenged until Miss Bingley spoke again, in a tone of false sweetness. "Miss Elizabeth, when we were in Hertfordshire I recall that you had a great admirer in the person of George Wickham."

Elizabeth reassured her that Wickham had been no great favorite with her, endeavoring to make her tone light and careless. She saw that Darcy's hands had clenched tightly and his gaze was fixed firmly on Miss Bingley.

"That is well, for I understand that he has been the favorite of a great many ladies. I know that he is no longer in Meryton, but I thought to put you on your guard in case you meet with him again. I trust that you are not planning to meet with him once you return to town?"

"Our acquaintance is completely ended, I assure you." As she spoke these words, Elizabeth was surprised by Miss Darcy's expression as she sat across from her. Her face had paled and her breath came in short gasps while she stared straight down at the table. "Georgiana, are you well? Is there any way in which we can assist you? You do not look yourself."

Darcy instantly stood and moved to his sister's side, and for a moment all was confusion as he lifted her to her feet amid cries of dismay and concern coming from all around the table. Miss Darcy made no sound but hid her face against her brother's shoulder as he supported her; and then he led her from the room, calling for Mrs. Reynolds as he did so. He urged his guests to continue the meal without him, but they could not focus on eating at all; and after a hasty termination all congregated in the sitting room, waiting awkwardly for Darcy to return while they conjectured among themselves as to his sister's health. At length Darcy strode into the room, his face set sternly.

"I apologize that our dinner was so interrupted, but there is no cause for concern. Georgiana ate something earlier today that did not agree with her; and she is most embarrassed to be the cause of such disruption and the focus of so much attention. I expect that she will rest uneasily tonight, and she desires my presence; so please excuse me for retiring early."

"We quite understand, Mr. Darcy. Think nothing of it," Mrs. Gardiner answered, and the others echoed the same sentiments.

Darcy made to quit the room and the rest of the group turned away. Then he seemed to recall something and turning around spoke to Miss Bingley, who stood closest to him, in an undertone. The others could not hear, but Elizabeth stood nearer and could hear every word. "Miss Bingley, I have been considering your question from earlier today about ribbons. Upon reflection I find that I agree that green is the color that suits your eyes best."

"You believe my eyes to be green, Mr. Darcy?"

"No, it is because I believe that green has always been quite symbolic of jealousy." Miss Bingley gasped, but Darcy was not finished. "Tonight your jealousy has injured a sweet, trusting heart, and I pray that you do not forget it. Do not mention George Wickham in my presence, or in my sister's, ever again." With that he turned on one heel and quickly left her company.

Elizabeth pretended not to notice the exchange but her astonishment was great. She could not help seeing that Miss Bingley had no wish to remain in company for any length of time; and with the fatigue of the day setting in, the entire group retired much earlier than normal. As Elizabeth went to her room she pondered the significance of Miss Darcy's agitation and Darcy's words to Miss Bingley, but she could make no sense of them. She could only suppose that Georgiana's relationship with Wickham had been much closer than she had guessed. Perhaps he had been more like a brother to Miss Darcy and she felt his absence keenly, especially since he was closer to her age than to Darcy's. Elizabeth hoped that Darcy would see fit to enlighten her.

Once in her room, the maid had begun to draw up a bath for her when she heard a knock on her bedroom door. Mrs. Reynolds stood outside. "Begging your pardon, miss, but Mr. Darcy sent me to ask for you. Miss Georgiana is quite upset and told Mr. Darcy that she wanted to see you. I'm to take you to her room if you are willing."

"Of course, I will come at once."

Mrs. Reynolds led her through a wide corridor into a part of the house she had not yet seen; and at length, with a turn to the left, she led her into Miss Darcy's room, where brother and sister sat together on the couch in her sitting room. Georgiana's eyes were red and tearful as she looked at Elizabeth and Darcy kept a comforting hand on her shoulder. "Mrs. Reynolds said that you wanted me," Elizabeth said in her gentlest tones, sitting on her other side. "How can I help?"

"I need to talk to someone--to you--about what happened with me and George Wickham. It has been ever so many months and still I cannot hear his name without this reaction. I wish things had been so different."

"What is it you wish to tell me, Georgiana? Whatever it is, a burden shared is a burden halved, and you may depend on my discretion."

"Last summer," Georgiana began, fresh tears welling up, "last summer I was ready to elope with George, and I would have, if William had not come to visit me early. I cannot believe how easily I went along with his lies." She broke down into fresh weeping, covering her face with her hands.

Elizabeth's astonishment could scarcely be contained; but contained it must be for the sake of young girl next to her, if she were to be of any assistance. Elizabeth put her arms around Georgiana as her shoulders shook and looked appealingly at Darcy. "William, this is women's talk, and I think it would be most beneficial if your sister and I could speak privately. Would you please give us some time alone?" She did not immediately realize that she had used his Christian name.

Darcy stood and reluctantly nodded in agreement. "I appreciate your presence more than I can express. Please send for me if you need me." He left the room.

Elizabeth let the weeping continue for a few moments, and then urged Georgiana to calm herself. "I think it may be best, dearest, if you start at the beginning and tell me as much of the story as you can. Rest assured I will make no judgments and pass no censure upon you, no matter what has happened. You may speak freely."

Under this steady encouragement Georgiana began to tell her story, and bit by bit Elizabeth learned the terrible truth. George Wickham, so beloved of her own father, and who had spent so much time with her as a child, had come back into her life the previous summer when her brother had set up an establishment for her in Ramsgate. After a long absence from her life Wickham had reappeared and spoken to her so tenderly, with such evidences of his affection for her, that Georgiana had at length considered herself in love with him. Not only did she confess her love to him but she had also consented to an elopement! Their plans to run off to Gretna Green had been only one day from execution when Darcy had joined her unexpectedly.

Her brother's reappearance had made Georgiana think better of the plan and she confessed everything to him, at which point Darcy made her aware of Wickham's dissolute habits. When Darcy called Wickham to account, he steadfastly maintained his affection for her until Darcy stated that Georgiana's fortune of thirty thousand pounds would not be hers until certain other conditions had been fulfilled, and would likely not come about for a number of years. At that point Wickham gave her up entirely, stating that he had better make his fortune elsewhere, though of course he would miss Georgiana terribly and she was not to think too badly of him, etc., etc.

The veil of innocence had been ripped from Georgiana's eyes, her view of Wickham had been completely overturned, and her confidence in her own judgment badly damaged. At first, she said, she did not see how she was to survive the betrayal.

"It has been easier since then with some time gone by; but to hear his name hurts, and to think on what he almost brought about is agony. To know that Miss Bingley has heard of it and has decided to avoid my company! It pains me to no end. It is hard to know that I shall pay the price of my misjudgment for the rest of my life."

Of course, Elizabeth reflected--given Miss Bingley's remarks at the dinner table, and her announcement that she was leaving so suddenly the next day, Miss Darcy would naturally assume that Miss Bingley had somehow been made aware.

She suddenly remembered Darcy's statement at the Netherfield dinner about Wickham's attempted theft of something valuable from the home, and all the pieces of the story he had told then now fell into place. Darcy had been speaking of his sister's planned elopement, and he had been doing his utmost to warn Elizabeth as much as possible about Wickham without violating his sister's trust. How painful it must have been to Darcy to see Elizabeth herself possibly succumbing to Wickham's charms as well! How well he had managed speaking the needed truth without causing his sister any distress.

"Georgiana, Miss Bingley's remarks tonight at the table had nothing to do with you, and you must not mind what she said at all. Miss Bingley is not evil, just a petty sort of woman at times, and she thought to hurt me by making your brother think that Mr. Wickham and I have a relationship that does not exist. She certainly does not know anything that happened with you and him, and I am sure that she still holds you in high regard."

"I hope you are correct. It is so hard to believe, sometimes, what I almost did, what he almost talked me into. I owe my brother so much for protecting me."

"He is a good man and you are fortunate to have him for your brother. These feelings you have now of your own foolishness and inadequacy will diminish with time. You are still very young, and though it may be hard to understand now, one day you will come to realize how much Mr. Wickham preyed on you; how he took advantage of your past friendship, how you were led along in all your innocence. You are no more to blame for what happened than you would be for biting into an apple that some hurtful person poisoned on purpose. Please promise me that you will consider yourself innocent in this matter, and think of it as nothing more than a lesson learned."

"I will try, but it is a painful lesson."

Elizabeth continued to counsel Georgiana for some time, urging her to reflect on her own strengths of character and to focus on uplifting topics that would continue to draw her mind away from the memory of how George Wickham had used her. At length Georgiana's spirits had recovered enough to be able to smile and appreciate Elizabeth's good humor, especially when Elizabeth playfully re-enacted Miss Bingley's actions with the fan earlier that day. Elizabeth waited until Georgiana had gotten into bed and started to drift off before she quit the room. She was not surprised to see that Darcy had drawn up a chair and was sitting in it, opposite the door to his sister's room.

"She is well, Mr. Darcy," she assured him as Darcy stood with an anxious expression. "She is going to sleep now."

"I assume she told you all of her history with Wickham?"

"She did. I now understand the rest of the story you told me, when you said that Wickham had attempted to steal something very valuable from the house."

Darcy asked her to walk with him to the kitchens as there would still be servants awake in that part of the house. "We have much to discuss, and we cannot hold a conversation of any length here."

Elizabeth bowed to the need for propriety and followed him through the house, most of which was now dark, until they reached the kitchens on the first floor which were populated only by a maid noisily scrubbing a pot in an adjacent room. Elizabeth was somewhat amused at the thought of sitting with Darcy at the table where the kitchen staff normally ate. Surely this was not a common occurrence for Darcy; but she did not mind, especially with the presence of the kittens that Darcy had had moved there from the stable. She placed their basket on the table and sat stroking and caressing them as she told Darcy of her conversation with Georgiana. Darcy questioned her closely until he was satisfied that he knew the entirety of their discussion.

"I take it that Mr. Bingley and his sisters were not made aware of what happened with Mr. Wickham?" Elizabeth asked.

"No, certainly not. There was no reason to let them know

something that was so potentially harmful to her reputation."

"And you did not choose to tell me of it either."

"It was Georgiana's story to tell, not mine. I could not invade her privacy in such a way, though I feared for your safety and that of your sisters. Therefore I spoke of his womanizing in generalities only and trusted that, together with the other information conveyed, it would be enough to separate you from him." He paused. "Now you may perhaps understand better why I was such unpleasant company last autumn when I first came to Hertfordshire. My childhood friend who had once been as close as a brother had deceived me and tried to take advantage of my own sister, and had very nearly succeeded, only a few months previously. I blamed Wickham, but I also blamed myself for not seeing that such a possibility existed and warning my sister ahead of time. Her spirits took some time to recover; mine took a little longer, and when I attended that first ball upon arrival in Hertfordshire, my anger made me a most disagreeable guest. I have long been heartily ashamed of my behavior that night; nay, that entire month."

"It has long since been forgiven. You must endeavor to follow the advice I gave your sister and try to think of the past only as it brings you pleasure."

"I cannot begin to express my appreciation for your assistance with Georgiana. I have tried many times to explain that I hold her innocent, that her character is in no way called into question by what happened; but it appears to me that you explained it much better than I ever could have thought to do."

"I thought of my own sisters as I spoke to her and merely spoke the way I would have to them. Having four sisters close in age gives me somewhat of an advantage over a brother who is twelve years older than his only sister."

"I hope that one day soon you will be able to count Georgiana as a sister as well."

Elizabeth looked down at the kitten whose head she was now scratching. "It is rather late at night to have this discussion, is it not, Mr. Darcy?"

His hand came alongside hers as he caressed another of the kittens. "You called me William upstairs when you first came to Georgiana's room."

"Did I?" she asked, though she remembered it clearly now that he mentioned it. "It was a mistake, no doubt caused by hearing

Georgiana call you so much by your Christian name. I apologize."

"You need not apologize for that. I would have you call me nothing else, Elizabeth."

She looked up at him as he said her name, and felt his hand brush along hers as he moved it to the kitten she was stroking. She should have felt embarrassed, perhaps, but found that she could not feel anything but warmth. She stood. "It is time for me to say good night, Mr. Darcy."

She allowed his hand to envelop hers as he stood, and he responded quietly, "Yes, you should. Good night, my love." A strange warmth and energy were in his look, but Elizabeth forced herself to step away and make her way to her room. Sleep that night was a very long time in coming for her, and she realized that not all of her turmoil was caused by the newest revelations about Wickham.

CHAPTER FIFTEEN

The Hursts and Miss Bingley departed the next morning before Miss Darcy had risen, or perhaps before she cared to make an appearance; for Elizabeth had convinced her that such insupportable behavior as announcing that they would leave abruptly, just the night before, did not necessarily deserve the honor of a fond farewell. Elizabeth knew that the close friendship between Darcy and Bingley would not be materially harmed by the difficulties with Miss Bingley, but she did wonder how much more challenging it might be for them to spend time together if Miss Bingley persisted in her current behaviors.

Miss Darcy made a late appearance looking more cheerful than the night before, and was able to break her fast in seemingly even spirits. Darcy waited until she had finished before requesting that she and Elizabeth accompany him on a ride.

"I am not a great horsewoman, Mr. Darcy. Perhaps you and Miss Darcy would be more comfortable on your own."

"I think not. We would both be pleased to have you accompany us, and shall be pleased to moderate our pace to accommodate yours if needed. And, if I am not mistaken, there is something in the stable that may assist you in increasing your skills." Seeing that he would not be deterred and wishing to relieve her curiosity, Elizabeth sought and was granted her aunt's approval and prepared to accompany both the Darcys on their excursion.

In the stable Darcy led her to one of the far stalls where a small black mare stood eyeing them with gentle curiosity. "If she pleases you, this will be your mount. She is named Jewel for the white diamond on her forehead, and I have it on the best authority that she is even-tempered and easy to ride. She arrived two days ago, but I wanted her to settle in first and have the grooms put her through her paces. If a fear of horses drives your discomfort with riding, she should serve well to put that fear to rest."

"It is not fear, but a lack of familiarity." Elizabeth stroked the mare's head with delight. "The horses at Longbourn are often needed elsewhere; and as you know, I am fond of walking. Perhaps now I shall become just as fond of riding. Pretty Jewel, I am certain we shall be good friends. Thank you, Mr. Darcy, for your consideration of my comfort."

Darcy smiled with satisfaction. "Then if you approve, she is yours."

Elizabeth eyed him warily. "Mr. Darcy, you know I cannot accept such a gift from you."

"She is not a gift," he answered solemnly. "She is more of an inducement to keep you at Pemberley."

Elizabeth raised an eyebrow. "I am not certain that an inducement is any more proper than a gift, but I can hardly object to inducements that nicker and nudge my shoulder," for Jewel was doing just those things.

Together with Georgiana they rode upon a bridle path far into the woods that rose behind the house, ascending at varying degrees until they reached a sort of shelf just below the highest point. Elizabeth was glad to be mounted, for the distance and ascent together, on foot, would have been taxing even for her constitution. On the shelf they turned their horses and faced outwards, looking down through the opening that was now visible and seeing somewhat of the house and lawn below them with the stream just visible beyond it. The house, the woods, and the stream all combined to make a most pleasing view, and Elizabeth could only say, "It is beautiful." Darcy made no response but stood quietly absorbing the view with her.

"In olden days this is where hunting parties would stop and try to get a glimpse of deer in the area," Georgiana said. "If they were not successful at this point, they could dismount and walk up to the tower just behind us and gain an even better vantage point." Elizabeth looked at her with satisfaction. Her conversation with Georgiana the night before seemed to have brought a new intimacy into their relationship, and she had noted several times that morning already that Georgiana had been more talkative than previously. She spoke now with more certainty, in a stronger voice, and without looking to her brother to approve first.

"I would like to see the tower if it is permitted," Elizabeth said, and Georgiana was delighted to comply. Darcy volunteered to hold the horses to allow the two ladies to ascend, promising they could have all the time they wanted in order to investigate the tower fully; and after he assisted them in dismounting, Georgiana led the way.

A short climb led them into a small clearing where the tower, a stone structure of about forty feet in height, stood over them. The two ladies entered and climbed the stone steps, which were in good repair, until they reached the top and could look out freely through the window, seeing over where they had just been. The view here was superior even to the one from the shelf, as it enabled them to see not only the house and stream but a great deal more of the woods, looking down from windows on several sides of the tower. Georgiana freely described the history of the tower, when it had been built, when improvements had been made, and how much enjoyment the family now gained from it. The tower stood at the very top of the hill, and from one of the windows Elizabeth could also see a waterfall that coursed down the hill through the woods on the opposite side from the house. Leaning out of the window she did her best to see where the stream might originate and where it would end, and several minutes passed by in happy anticipation of other trips to investigate this area more.

At length she finally reluctantly admitted to herself that she was probably neglecting Georgiana and turned to speak to her, but was surprised to find Darcy standing next to her.

"Georgiana came back down to take her turn holding the horses," he explained. "I hope you do not mind my taking her place. She appears to be laboring under the idea that she is playing matchmaker between the two of us and is determined to do her duty fully."

Elizabeth smiled. "She is a delightful young lady. You have done well to guide her so well through such difficult days, for her age can be tricky even without men like George Wickham causing troubles. Someone with less support might have turned out far worse than she."

"I have not been alone in helping her. Colonel Fitzwilliam is also her guardian and he has done much to help her put the whole dreadful episode behind her. Still, neither of us could listen to her with a sister's heart and ease her distress last night the way you did. Please allow me to express my gratitude once again."

"It is the least I could do. You have been very generous to my aunt and uncle and me in our stay here, and it is the first thing that you have asked in return."

He looked at her seriously. "Nothing could be further from the truth. I have asked many things of you--your heart, your hand, and your companionship for life."

She decided to use his own words against him. "Good things come to those who wait, Mr. Darcy."

He smiled. "I can hardly argue the point, especially since I have used the same words with you."

She felt compelled to voice a thought that had run through her mind since the previous evening, though she was reluctant to raise the topic. "Mr. Darcy, have you given serious thought to the social consequences you would face if we married? Miss Bingley's attitude and comments last night might be a foretaste of things to come. I am well aware of the difference in standing between my family and yours, and there are many Miss Bingleys in the world. How would you face such censure? How would Georgiana react to it?"

"That there are differences between our two spheres I shall not try to deny. But among family and friends whose opinions I value, whom I hold in affection, there shall not be an impact on me if they do not deter you. Please do not think that all my family is like Lady Catherine. She, I am sure, will be dismayed at such an alliance, but she does not speak for my family. And even Lady Catherine, I believe, will eventually be reconciled to any marriage I make. As for Georgiana, the outside world means little to her. She is content to be at Pemberley or in town, or even at Rosings, so long as she does not have to mingle too much with society."

"And your friends and neighbors? How do you know you can trust their reactions?"

"You shall see for yourself when we have our dinner party here next week. I am not afraid of their reactions at all. Truly, Elizabeth, while some of society may gossip behind their hands at my choice, I believe the world in general will have too much sense to join in. And for those who do I care not."

She looked at him reproachfully. "You have called me by my name again, Mr. Darcy."

"Did I?" He smiled teasingly at her. "It was a mistake, no doubt caused by hearing Georgiana call you so much by your Christian name. I apologize."

She could not help laughing at his exact imitation of her words from the night before. "Now you are turning my own words against me!"

"Miss Bennet, I believe we have been so much in company and are on such good terms with each other as to make the constant use of 'Miss Bennet' and 'Mr. Darcy' unnecessary. When it is just the two of us, it would mean a great deal to me if you were to call me by my name, and if I could do the same in return."

Darcy's face had taken on the soft, expressive look she was coming to appreciate; and she felt unequal to the task of denying him such a small thing, if it brought him such pleasure. "I will permit it-- William," she answered with care, and was rewarded with a warm, approving smile.

"I would also ask one other favor. With the Hursts and Miss Bingley gone, the only people left in the house are those who already know of my interest in you--or at least Georgiana strongly suspects, and clearly approves. Our guests who will come for dinner next week have no connections to Hertfordshire or to any acquaintances of yours, so far as I know. If you truly wish to see how society will react to my marriage to someone outside our sphere, would it not be advisable for them to know of my interest in you as well? How they will react to the knowledge of a courtship is no different from how they will react to a marriage, and you may thus judge its effect for yourself."

"And how would you make your courtship of me known to all your guests? Shall you take out advertisements and hang them on the side of Pemberley for all to see? Or shall you have the footmen announce, as each new guest arrives, 'Here, Mr. So and So, Mr. Darcy would have you to know that he is engaged in a courtship with that lady over there'?"

"While either method would serve, I would prefer to simply devote my attentions to you without fear of wondering how to answer any questions they might make."

She considered this carefully. "So if I decline your request and they are not aware that you are courting me, then I shall lose the opportunity to benefit from their reaction, thus undermining part of the very reason for the courtship itself. But if I agree then it is one step closer to your stated goal of actually agreeing to an engagement."

"You can see how very well I have planned this out, but you have left out one important benefit to me. If it is freely known that I am pursuing you, very likely the other eligible gentlemen who shall arrive will leave you alone."

"Shall there be many other eligible gentlemen?"

"Three or four, all quite eligible; and none a day under five and fifty years of age."

She could not help laughing again. "Very well, Mr. Darcy; I grant your wish, on the condition that you acknowledge that I may still decline your proposal."

"We have an agreement," he reminded her. "Please call me William."

"Very well then, William," she answered, and his eyes glowed.

"That is all I can ask for, my dearest Elizabeth."

CHAPTER SIXTEEN

With the departure of the three least-desired guests the days took on a new and more delightful pattern, with more freedom of actions and expressions possible since there were no unfriendly eyes to appease, and no outings or entertainments to prepare for guests who would not appreciate them.

Each morning the household arose together, with all breakfasting together in the orangery on fair days and in the small dining room when the weather was not favorable. After that the ladies would be found together in the sitting room or the music room, taking turns at the pianoforte, writing letters, completing embroidery, or employing themselves in whatever pursuits might come their way. Darcy and Mr. Gardiner spent the mornings in their own way, fishing or hunting, or sometimes riding the estate and dealing with Darcy's steward; for Darcy had come to value Mr. Gardiner's business sense, education, and general company, and they frequently spoke of improvements which Darcy wished to make to the property. In the afternoons there might be a riding party somewhere about the park or even to the adjacent moor, or a day trip to one of the small villages nearby to see a church or some other fine building. After dinner the ladies and gentlemen stayed together and played cards, or played the pianoforte and sang together.

The ladies spent much time in discussion about the upcoming dinner party; for Darcy had given it to his sister to organize, knowing that she would have much able assistance from Elizabeth, Mrs. Gardiner, and Mrs. Annesley. The choice of menu, the seating of the guests, the decorations and flowers to be used, and the entertainments all took up considerable time; for none of them had organized something quite like this before on her own, and as often as not they asked for and obtained advice from the highly experienced Mrs. Reynolds. There was much good laughter and high spirits as Elizabeth proposed one completely impossible scheme after another, always with an air of pretended innocence.

"Why, Mrs. Reynolds, whatever do you mean by crossing rowboats off my list of needed supplies?" Elizabeth asked her one afternoon.

"I am sure the stream is too fast and the current too strong to launch rowboats in it at this time of year," Mrs. Reynolds answered her good-naturedly. "And it will be dark."

"Indeed, but the rowboats were not for the stream. I intended them to be used in the fountains on the lower terrace."

"Elizabeth, the fountain is but six inches at its greatest depth," Georgiana told her, thinking that Elizabeth did not understand. "Not even rowboats could float in such a shallow draught, nor have we ever put rowboats in the fountain."

"Now you are supposing that I meant for them to float. I meant rather for us all to eat in the boats as they sit in the fountains, two persons in each rowboat, each with their plates upon their laps. What could be more comfortable?"

"But shall the servants not wet their clothes as they wait upon each boat?" Georgiana answered, beginning to get into the spirit. "We must not allow their clothes to be ruined."

"Quite right. We shall have to drain the fountain, and we will all sit in the rowboats upon dry land while we eat."

Georgiana laughed at the absurd idea but Mrs. Gardiner smilingly shook her head. "May I remind you that the dinner is only two days away? There is a great deal to accomplish, and we must remain focused on our purpose lest we all embarrass Mr. Darcy with our lack of planning."

"Let us not embarrass the great Mr. Darcy," Elizabeth responded playfully, seeing the man himself walking past the sitting room just then. "Pray remove the magical phoenix birds from the menu, Mrs. Reynolds. They will not serve as food at all. We will instead have them walk freely about the grounds first and then Mr. Darcy may use his maharajahs, imported especially for the purpose, to catch them one by one and present them to each guest as a sort of thank you gift."

Georgiana looked astonished by Elizabeth's teasing of her brother, but she relaxed when Darcy bowed elaborately. "I have not forgotten about the maharajahs, Miss Bennet; but I trust that in return you will favor our guests with your performance on the pianoforte. There can be no doubt which piece I would ask you to play."

"I have not yet learnt it," Elizabeth retorted impudently. "You will have to wait your turn or else suffer disappointment with a very poor performance indeed." She spoke these words with such gaiety and charm and such cheerful humor that Darcy was delighted to laugh and move away.

With such pleasant company and pursuits each day passed swiftly away. The day before the dinner party Elizabeth rejoiced to receive another letter from Jane.

She opened it and read with pleasure as Jane described all the gossip of their various neighbors, the accounts of all the little parties and shopping trips they had had, and of course Jane's descriptions of her beloved Charles. She had little to say of Miss Bingley and the Hursts except to say that Charles had received word that they had returned to town, and that she herself had received a very short and unenthusiastic letter of congratulations from both sisters. Jane regretted their sentiments but could not be angry with them.

It is natural that they should wish for him to make a better marriage than with someone like me who lacks any kind of fortune or connections; but I hope that when they see how happy Charles is with me, they may reconcile themselves to the match.

To this Elizabeth shook her head, but she read on.

Colonel Forster made an unexpected appearance in Meryton yesterday and called on my father for above half an hour in his study. It seems that Mr. Wickham has run away from the militia and that they are now trying actively to find him and bring him back to face a severe justice. Naturally, since he had so recently passed time in this county, they came here first, asking if we had seen him or had any information of him; but we have not. The colonel asked Papa if he knew any of Mr. Wickham's past associations--his friends before he entered the militia, his family, and anywhere else that he might have connections. He already knew of his connection to Mr. Darcy, of course, so Mr. Darcy may well receive inquiries at Pemberley as well. I say this not to alarm you but so that Mr. Darcy may understand that Papa had no intention, and no part, in sending the militia to his doorstep.

Elizabeth paused to consider this and to be dismayed. She knew not what the punishment might be for desertion, if Wickham were found, but she could well imagine it to be something nobody would want to face. She had little doubt that he would be found sooner or later. By now there would be advertisements in the paper and notices posted in prominent places; Wickham's generally imprudent manner made it likely, in her estimation, that he would be discovered at some point. She did not relish informing Darcy that his family would of necessity be attached to the scandal. She would tell Darcy immediately upon concluding her letter.

Lydia continues much as before. Thrice now she has left the house without permission and without our knowledge, walking to Meryton or calling upon her friends. At least that is what she says has done and we have no information to contradict it. She is putting her reputation at such risk that even Mama has expressed concern. Papa has spoken of a plan to send her to our cousin Collins to remove her from temptation and attempt to curb her spirits, but I cannot imagine that such a plan would be conducive to anyone's happiness. How it shall end, I know not.

Elizabeth paused to consider the effect of Lydia on the parsonage at Rosings and on Rosings itself, and did not know whether to pity the Collinses, Lady Catherine, or Lydia the most under such an arrangement. In such a situation, nobody would be seen to advantage.

Dearest Lizzy, in your latest letter you spoke of Mr. Darcy's constant attentions to you, his unceasing devotion, his generosity, and of its possible effects on your feelings for him. May I say that it sounds as if you are rather in love with him already? I hope it is the case and that by now you have come to understand your feelings, and perhaps have been able to communicate those feelings to him. You are not a cowardly person, Elizabeth, not one to deny the truth about yourself when it is plain to even those around you.

Had Mrs. Gardiner written about her to Jane, Elizabeth wondered.

If you have come to love him already then you must find a way to tell him as soon as possible, within the bounds of decorum, and not lose any time that you have. Charles and I were separated for three months by the machinations of others and by misunderstandings; and I can say without a doubt that those months were some of the unhappiest ones of my life. Though three months is nothing compared to the years of the rest of our lives, yet they were still so miserable that I would not wish such a loss of time for you when one word could make you so happy. Life is uncertain, and every day a gift from Providence. Please promise me, dearest sister, that once you are sure of your feelings, that they are not the work of an instant but evidence of unswerving devotion, that you will waste no time in communicating them to Mr. Darcy.

Affectionately yours,
Jane

Elizabeth could not but be touched by such heartfelt advice from her sister, but she felt that it was misplaced. She had by now become well-acquainted with her own feelings towards Darcy, but she still felt something holding her back from declaring herself to him. She had a hard time putting a name to the reason for her hesitancy, for at times it seemed absurd even to herself that she had not already spoken to him. She knew his character and his personality enough by now to agree with Darcy's statement to her on that day back in Hertfordshire, that they were well suited to each other and would complement each other admirably. Her playfulness and good humor would relieve his tendency towards seriousness, while his education and exposure to the world would improve her mind. She knew without a doubt that they were ideally matched and had as great a chance of happiness as most couples upon entering the marriage state, and more likelihood than many.

No, her hesitation was not about her feelings. It was not even about her fear of society's reaction, though that was still a concern. Her hesitation stemmed from the lack of control she felt she had over the process. From the day of sitting with Darcy outside her father's garden until now she felt that events had pushed her along without her consent. Since the time they had been observed together, her father, her aunt and uncle, Darcy himself, and now even her sister were all pushing her towards what they considered a foregone conclusion--that she would marry Darcy sooner or later. She truly wanted to marry him, she knew that now; but in this most important decision of her life it felt that she had been more the observer than the participant, and that she had been thrust rapidly along with the current to some degree instead of making her own way in her own time. Darcy had been patient, it was true; but she still felt as though she might make a decision out of a desire to have the situation resolved quickly rather than out of a free choice of her own making.

She resolved to think no more of it at the moment, and instead took her letter with her to go find Darcy and make him acquainted with the news about Wickham.

CHAPTER SEVENTEEN

Elizabeth found Darcy in his study, having just finished dictating a letter to his secretary; and he looked up at her with a smile as she entered, happy that she had chosen to seek him out. She explained the nature of the information Jane had shared but found that he was already aware.

"I received word of this from my connections in the militia just this morning, and the letter I just finished with my secretary is being sent to Colonel Forster, though there is little I can add to what he already knows. I am aware of one or two friends that he had in town last year, and I have sent that information on; but Wickham has a tendency to alienate friends after some little time, and they will likely deny any knowledge of him."

"Do you believe there to be any chance that Wickham might return to this neighborhood?"

Darcy shook his head. "Wickham's habit has been to avoid confrontation, not to seek it out. He knows that he would find no refuge here. He must realize that I would happily hand him over myself, if I were to see him. No, I believe that Wickham shall never be seen in Derbyshire, or at least at Pemberley, ever again."

Elizabeth felt relief at his words, but she could not be completely at ease. Wickham was but one of her worries; the other was Lydia.

"You do not seem particularly relieved," Darcy observed. "Did Jane have other news that may concern you?"

"She shared information about my sister Lydia, who has become more unmanageable than before after my father refused to let her go to Brighton. I fear she may disgrace herself and our family along with her."

"I would like to hear more about this, Elizabeth. My work for the day is done and I was about to seek out your company. Shall we sit in the orangery for a little while? It is pleasant there at this time of day and your presence would make it even more so."

Elizabeth gave her consent and they made their way to the orangery, sitting together on one of the benches that surrounded the fountain. Darcy asked her to relate the details of Lydia's behavior, and she recounted for him the change in attitude that had started when her father had decided to protect Lydia from her own tendencies. "She has become sly, and openly opposes what is meant only for her own good. She cannot see the dangers in her behavior and I am not certain that she even wishes to do so. It is painful, exceedingly painful, to have a sister who seems so devoid of good morals and principles."

"She is young, and this change in her circumstances has been sudden. Her resistance is natural and to be expected. We none of us take well to having our lives ordered about."

"But it is also dangerous and may result in great harm to her and to those who love her."

"A steady guiding hand will, I think, eventually have the desired effect."

"We can only hope so. If she does decide to create a scandal, I do hope it will be something minor. Perhaps she will content herself by being seen in Meryton with a petticoat six inches deep in mud," she added, with an effort at humor.

Darcy smiled at the shared remembrance of Elizabeth's arrival at Netherfield. "Did Miss Bennet say anything else of significance?"

Elizabeth sat undecided for a moment, recalling Jane's advice. Truly she should not allow this baffling resistance to keep her from expressing her feelings; she should not be ruled by an emotion she could not even name, and which she certainly could not defend. Darcy deserved better than such suspense when she already knew her own heart. Making a sudden decision, she forced herself to meet his eyes.

"You asked me a most significant question once before, Mr. Darcy; and you have been most persistent in pursuing me, while making clear that your affections have not changed." She paused. "I can now say safely, sir, that my own affections have."

Darcy could scarcely believe his ears. "Are you accepting me, Miss Bennet?"

Suddenly emotional, Elizabeth let out the feelings she had been holding back, with tears welling in her eyes. "I am not ready to accept you, Mr. Darcy, but I am ready to tell you that my sentiments mirror yours."

Darcy was breathless with shock for a moment, joy, surprise, and dismay all meeting together in his expression in equal parts. "If I have won your affections, why will you not accept me?"

With sudden agitation, Elizabeth stood and walked away several paces before turning to face him again. "I do not know if I can make you understand this, for it is hard for even me to comprehend. Perhaps you will be angry, but I will make an attempt nonetheless. Everything about this relationship, this courtship, has occurred in my life in a manner not of my choosing. It is what I would have chosen, had I been given the opportunity; yet I want to make my choice in my own time, not to feel as though the end was known from the beginning."

"I have done my utmost to court you without overpowering you with my wishes."

"And you have succeeded. I could not tell you of these feelings if you had imposed on me in any way. The circumstances of our courtship are not your fault. The fact that everyone expects our engagement is not in your control, yet it still weighs on my mind. Perhaps, like Lydia, I do not take well to having my life ordered about."

He observed her silently for a few moments, his face revealing nothing, until Elizabeth was finally compelled to ask, "Have I angered you, sir?"

Darcy shook his head. "No, but I wish you would return to sit beside me so that we may discuss this further."

She weighed his reaction and her own emotions for a moment, then took her seat again and waited for him to speak. It was a relief to finally declare her own feelings for him, but revealing her affection without giving him the promise he desired brought its own distress as she looked at his sober face.

A silence fell between them, broken only by the constant flow of the nearby fountain. Darcy appeared to be deep in thought, in no hurry to speak, and Elizabeth could not make a sound for the tumult in her heart. At length, Darcy reached behind him to pluck a small flower off a nearby plant and spread it out on his outstretched palm.

"This is a rare specimen of a plant which my father had imported from the East Indies some years ago. Its normal home is in tropical climes; it is not a native of England at all."

Whatever Elizabeth may have been expecting Darcy to say, it was not this. She looked at him in wonder. "Do you know its name?"

"I do not. The gardener would know, of course, but I scarcely recall now. I remember when it was transplanted here and the attention my father paid to it week after week, watching it acclimate to its new surroundings. He, as much as the head gardener, learned all he could about tropical plants--the soil conditions they require, the amount of exposure to sunlight, and any other information he could glean in order to help it flourish. Eventually he succeeded, and it bloomed; and now, as you see, its flowers are the very embodiment of beauty and grace."

He laid the flower down gently on the bench. "I am sure that the tender young plant, while growing in its first home so far away, had no idea that it would one day have such changes forced upon it--that it would be transported to a new country, a new climate. Surely this was not its plan, if it could have made plans, to have events thrust upon it, and yet it thrives here. It does not refuse to take root or to flower simply because this plan was not one of its own making. Such a choice would only deny its own nature and deprive everyone who sees it of its beauty." He paused and looked at her. "Elizabeth, you know I am not speaking of flowers. I am a proud man, as you know better than anyone. I should not like to feel compelled to do anything, even something that would otherwise be my free choice. Yet I do not see how our courtship could have developed in any other way than it has."

Elizabeth was silent, because she suddenly understood the emotion that was still holding her back, keeping her from accepting him, for Darcy had named it for her. Her refusal to accept the inevitable conclusion to the courtship, her insistence that her life unfold on her own schedule, was born of pride. Her pride was what injured her feelings, what kept insisting, most stubbornly, on refusing that which would bring her the greatest happiness. At one time she had thought Darcy guilty of this fault; but she realized anew that pride has many forms, and with a flash of insight she acknowledged that she had her own full share.

Darcy looked down at the ground, afraid that he had said too much. "I know not what to say except to tell you that I understand your feelings well, and can only sympathize with them. In your position I might well do the same."

Still Elizabeth could not speak. She had observed before that in the moments of her life that were filled with the most emotion, her tongue was frequently the most silent. This was one of those times. She could not have said a word to save her life; her heart and mind struggled.

In the distance she heard Mrs. Gardiner call her name, probably summoning her to tea. Darcy sighed. "I believe your aunt wants you, my dearest. I should return you to her." Darcy stood and reached down to help her stand. "Will you take my hand?"

At last Elizabeth overcame the invisible barrier. Her heart and mind united in one purpose, and an overwhelming happiness overtook her. She looked up at him as she laid her hand in his. "I give you my hand, Mr. Darcy, for you already have my heart."

Surprised joy overcame his features. "Then I am accepted? You will marry me and live here with me as my wife?"

"It gives me the greatest of pleasure to accept you, William." She smiled radiantly as he took her other hand in his and lifted her to her feet, and then they stood barely apart from each other.

"My dearest, loveliest Elizabeth," he breathed as he looked in her eyes, and then he took her into his arms and kissed her for the first time. Elizabeth rested her head on his shoulder and felt joy suffuse every inch of her body. The battle was over; she was his, and she had never felt happier in her life. Jane's elation could be nothing to hers; surely, no one else in history had ever felt as she did at this moment.

Mrs. Gardiner's voice was heard again, coming closer.

"I am coming, aunt," Elizabeth called to her, but she and Darcy did not appear for many minutes; and when Mrs. Gardiner heard their announcement a little while later she made no inquiries about the missing time.

CHAPTER EIGHTEEN

All was now settled, Elizabeth thought, and she reveled in the knowledge all that evening as she and Darcy basked in the glow of their new understanding. Though they were in company, they freely communicated their feelings to each other through looks and expressions when they could not speak them aloud; and if they seemed somewhat distracted, the others did not see fit to mention it.

Nobody in the house seemed surprised to hear the news. The Gardiners, of course, had expected such a development and had thought it only a matter of time. Georgiana confessed that she had suspected her brother's partiality shortly after Elizabeth's arrival at Pemberley, and her suspicion had been confirmed by Miss Bingley's jealous actions towards Elizabeth. Even the staff smiled openly at them; and Mrs. Reynolds took the liberty of commenting that Miss Bennet was the most well-bred and genial of mistresses that Mr. Darcy could have selected, and that Miss Bingley would not have done at all.

"We would have had half the staff leave their positions, had Mr. Darcy chosen Miss Bingley," she told Georgiana confidentially. "And they'd have told all their families to stay away from service here, too," she added. Elizabeth smiled when Georgiana repeated this to her, but her mind was too busy to give much thought to poor Miss Bingley, who would now feel more put out than ever.

With the advent of this new agreement, all were agreed the next day that the dinner party that night would be a proper venue for the announcement of their engagement; and nothing could be more natural than having Mr. Gardiner stand in his brother Bennet's place to communicate the news.

"And then on the morrow I shall write to my parents, or at least to my father, to make him acquainted," Elizabeth said to her aunt and Georgiana as they sat together in the afternoon. "There is too much to do before the party tonight to write them just yet."

"Why would you not write to your mother?" Georgiana asked her. "Are you afraid she will withhold her consent?" Mrs. Gardiner smiled and Elizabeth laughed.

"Nothing so impossible! She will gladly give her consent to me, to Mr. Darcy, to my father, to my sisters, to all her nearest relations, and to the barnyard cats if she thinks they might stand in the way of the wedding. She will even give it to you if you care to ask. If word reaches her before we meet in London, perhaps the enthusiasm of her first response will have time to temper slightly; so perhaps I should inform her immediately."

"Now that you are engaged we might perhaps leave for town a few days earlier than planned. Some would not consider it proper for you to be under the same roof with Mr. Darcy," Mrs. Gardiner informed her niece.

"It is only six days until we would leave in any event. A difference of two or three days would not matter whether we go or stay, and I shall not be missish."

Georgiana looked as though she would like to ask a question but embarrassment held her back. At length she managed to ask, "How long have you been in love with my brother, Elizabeth? When did it start?"

Elizabeth considered this question carefully. "I could not say exactly when it started, for I was in the middle before I knew I had begun. But I believe I may date it from my first seeing the beautiful grounds here at Pemberley!"

"Lizzy, you should not tease your future sister so. Miss Darcy, I can assure you with all confidence that there was a strong attraction between Elizabeth and your brother before we came to Pemberley."

"Indeed, that is the reason we came to Pemberley, for how else was I to discover if I truly loved him? A woman should always look at a man's property first to see if love will be possible."

Another gentle rebuke from Mrs. Gardiner served its purpose, and Elizabeth explained how Darcy had changed her opinion of him, dwelling on the character traits she now found most desirable in him.

"William says that you used to hate him, but he must be mistaken; and yet he is never wrong."

"Perhaps there was a time when I did not love him as well as I do now, but I do not remember it now and shall never remember it again," Elizabeth responded cheerfully.

"And when will the wedding be? I should like it to happen as soon as possible."

Elizabeth smiled. "In this wish you are united with your brother, but there are preparations that must take place first. We were only engaged yesterday; pray do not rush me to the altar! I believe Jane and Mr. Bingley were considering dates five or six weeks from now;

perhaps our wedding might follow theirs."

"Or perhaps a double wedding?" Mrs. Gardiner suggested, and Georgiana smiled in delight.

"For now the only event we should be focusing on is the dinner party tonight; and after that we will have leisure to consider all else. I am counting on you, Georgiana, to remind me again this afternoon of everyone's names on the guest list, and of any salient facts that I should know. Your brother said this would be a small, intimate gathering of some of the oldest families in this neighborhood. I will confess that ten couples do not quite meet my definition of small and intimate."

"They are not all familiar to me as my brother has not entertained a great deal since our father died. He had so much to learn at first, and I do not think he cared to entertain or to be entertained for a long while."

"We shall have to make up for lost time then. Come, let us go over the seating again. Perhaps by learning where all will sit, I will be able to associate names with those seats, and avoid offending half the room by calling them the wrong person."

"I shall help you as much as I can." Elizabeth and Georgiana drew up around the table to look at the paper with the seating on it. Mrs. Gardiner drew a little back, but Elizabeth would not allow this.

"Oh no, Aunt Gardiner, you shall not shirk your duty. It is to you and my uncle that I am indebted for my present understanding with Mr. Darcy, for if you had not brought me into Derbyshire I cannot imagine what would have happened next. You must help me learn all this as well."

Mrs. Gardiner smiled and moved closer, but added her own comment. "Can you truly not imagine what would have happened had we not brought you here? Do you think Mr. Darcy would have been deterred by having to court you in Hertfordshire?"

"Perhaps, though he is a determined man. And yet my family can be fearsome indeed. I suppose he would have found a way."

"My dear, it has been my experience that when a man is violently in love he will suffer no interference until he has attained the object of his affection. Time, distance, and circumstances will not prove a barrier when once his mind is set. Rest upon it, Mr. Darcy would have courted you in front of your family in Hertfordshire, or followed you to the furthest reaches of the kingdom if need be."

"It is fortunate, then, that he needed only to go so far as Pemberley to pursue me. How very convenient for him!"

"It was not a convenience, but a blessing."

"The blessing is mine, aunt, for he is truly the best of men."

When they had reviewed the guest seating Mrs. Gardiner went to find her husband in the library and Georgiana went to her room in order to rest before the party. Elizabeth wandered rather aimlessly in the direction of the music room, looking out the various windows, wanting to see Darcy return from a visit to one of his tenants. She had not seen him since breakfast and found that she was eager to be in his presence again, as she relived in her mind the acceptance of his hand the day previous. In this happy recollection her thoughts naturally turned to the even happier moment to come, the day she would become his wife; and her mind was filled with dresses, wedding shoes, rice, and great quantities of punch. She wondered where the wedding would take place. As Elizabeth of Longbourn she would choose to be married from home, but as the future wife of Mr. Darcy of Pemberley perhaps a larger church would be necessary.

Her thoughts were interrupted by the sight of a carriage that came to a stop outside the front entrance. Elizabeth looked on curiously, wondering who it could be, as Darcy had not mentioned expecting any guests and the footmen attending the carriage blocked the sight of any arms on the door. She had not long to wait, however; the stairs were placed, the door was opened, the occupant made an appearance--it was Lady Catherine de Bourgh, and she did not look well-pleased.

Elizabeth wondered who was to receive the distinguished visitor. Darcy was out, and Georgiana would be in her room, resting, by now. She called a servant and asked him to find her aunt and uncle and make them acquainted with the arrival of Lady Catherine, and then to find Darcy and communicate the same. Until relief arrived she would have to entertain the great lady herself.

She made her way to the sitting room and awaited the visitor, not forgetting as she did so to feel that this was a role that would be hers in a matter of weeks. After their marriage she would be the one to accept calls and give them in return. Altogether she thought that she might have a kinder initiation to her duty than greeting the imposing Lady Catherine.

Lady Catherine appeared in the doorway as the servant announced her, her eyes fixing on Elizabeth in a most alarming fashion, but she said nothing beyond the usual ceremonious greeting. Elizabeth curtsied, Lady Catherine inclined her head in acknowledgement, and they both sat stiffly down, while the latter appeared to view the former as a kind of vermin that must be removed from the house at once.

"Your ladyship finds me at quite a disadvantage. Mr. Darcy is out, and Miss Darcy is indisposed. I regret that there is nobody else here to welcome you properly, but I have sent a servant to notify Mr. Darcy of your arrival."

"Very well, if that is the best you can do," was the lady's gracious response. "Are your mother and your sisters here as well?"

Elizabeth looked at her in surprise. "No, I am traveling with my aunt and uncle; and Mr. Darcy was kind enough to invite us to stay in his home while we explore Derbyshire. My family is all at Longbourn."

"That is a very pretty pair of slippers you are wearing," was the next unexpected observation. "They would appear to be of a quality your family could scarcely afford. Where did you get them?"

Elizabeth guessed that Lady Catherine probably would be incensed to know that Georgiana had given them to her several days before. "They were a gift, my lady. May I ask whether you left Mrs. Collins well?"

"She is as well as she can be under the circumstances." Elizabeth did not ask what circumstances Lady Catherine meant, and Lady Catherine did not volunteer them.

"And Miss de Bourgh? Is she also well?"

"She was when I saw her a day ago and a half, or at least as well as possible."

A strange phrase to hear spoken twice so closely together! But Elizabeth would not ask.

"We shall wait here until my nephew returns," Lady Catherine informed her with no attempt at courtesy. "I have something in particular I would discuss with him."

"As you wish." Elizabeth took up the embroidery she had set aside and began working on the design. She had no desire to carry on a conversation with Lady Catherine, who was being even more overbearing than usual.

Mrs. Gardiner arrived in the room and curtsied upon being recognized. Elizabeth made the formidable introduction.

"This is one of your Cheapside relations? This is a more

distinguished setting than she has perhaps seen in her life, yet she is more genteel than I expected," Lady Catherine observed. "I expect that she spends little time with your mother."

"They are very intimate, are you not, Aunt Gardiner?" said Elizabeth mischievously, willing to stretch the truth to see its effect on her ladyship. "My aunt and uncle were with us at Longbourn when my sister Jane accepted an offer of marriage from Mr. Bingley. Perhaps you may have heard of their engagement?"

"I did." Lady Catherine offered no comment or congratulations; and Elizabeth, after exchanging an expressive look with her aunt, returned to her stitching.

Several uncomfortable minutes passed. Elizabeth noticed that Lady Catherine was becoming increasingly restless, which was not surprising; for she had nothing to occupy her time, while Elizabeth and her aunt at least had their needlework to command their attention, and they made a little conversation between themselves about the design and the stitches. Her ladyship's agitation increased until she finally said, "Miss Bennet, I have decided to take a turn in the gardens, and you shall accompany me." She rose and left the room, and although Elizabeth would not have accommodated such behavior on her own, she felt compelled to follow.

Upon reaching the gardens Lady Catherine lost no time in addressing Elizabeth in a tone both cold and incensed.

"You can be at no loss to understand the purpose of my visit today, Miss Bennet."

"Indeed you are mistaken. I have not been able to account for the honor of your presence at all, except that perhaps you wished to visit with your nephew and niece."

"Do not be insolent with me, Miss Bennet. If this had been a customary social visit I would have announced my arrival several days in advance; but instead I rode here in haste after hearing alarming news just three days ago."

"Alarming news? I have not the pleasure of understanding you."

"Word came to me that your sister had made a very advantageous match with Mr. Charles Bingley and that you, soon after, would be united with my nephew, Mr. Darcy; that you and your family were already living in Pemberley and imposing upon my poor niece Georgiana; and that you had trapped my nephew with arts and allurements into a marriage that can be of no possible benefit to him. What have you to say to this?"

"Your presence here will prove a contradiction to such rumors, if rumors there are."

"Do you deny that there is any truth to the rumors? I see that you are indeed living at Pemberley, entertaining callers as though you are the lady of the house!"

"If your ladyship had notified Mr. Darcy of your impending visit Miss Darcy would have been the one to receive you, and Mr. Darcy too, no doubt."

"And your aunt and your uncle? How do you explain their presence?"

"We are visiting Pemberley at Mr. Darcy's kind invitation. Would your ladyship prefer that I visit him alone and unchaperoned?"

"Miss Bennet! This is not to be borne! This match to which you aspire, into which you wish to entrap my nephew, can never happen. Mr. Darcy is engaged to my daughter. Now what do you have to say?"

"Only this: if there is an engagement between Mr. Darcy and your daughter he has not seen fit to mention it."

Lady Catherine hesitated. "The engagement between them is of a peculiar kind. It was the favorite wish of his mother and of hers as well, planned while they were still in the cradle. And it was on the point of completion until you turned him aside and made him forget his duty!"

"This is a discussion you should have with your nephew, not with me," Elizabeth answered, with an effort at taming her rising anger. "You may ask him whatever questions you wish; but I am not compelled to listen to your arguments against a match, or to listen to such slanders upon my character. I beg you to allow me to return to the house."

"Not so fast! You will answer my question: are you engaged to my nephew?"

"Your ladyship has declared it to be impossible."

"It would be if you kept your distance; if you remained under separate roofs, if you had not inveigled your way into Pemberley, acting as a sister to Georgiana and a wife to Darcy in all but name!"

"You have now insulted me in every possible way," Elizabeth answered resentfully, "and I shall not stay to hear more." She turned and walked rapidly back to the house, followed by an infuriated Lady Catherine.

"Very well! I see now how matters stand, and I shall know how to act. Your reputation, already in tatters, shall be completely beyond redemption when I am done. Mrs. Collins, who is already distraught for you, shall have her worst fears confirmed, and so shall all your friends. Georgiana shall be removed from such an influence as you. You are unfeeling, immoral and unprincipled, a headstrong and insolent girl, and you shall never be Mrs. Darcy."

Elizabeth turned to face Lady Catherine one last time. "If I am all those things, do you truly think so little of your nephew's character as to believe that he would care for me? Could he be so lost to every good principle, to every notion of decency and the rules of society? I tell you truly, Lady Catherine, that he is the best of men, the most honorable, most decent, and most generous man of my acquaintance; and to insult my character in such a way as you have is to insult his as well. You should be ashamed of yourself."

Lady Catherine took a step back in shock, and Elizabeth could easily see that it had been many years since anyone had spoken to her in such a way; that perhaps this was the first such occasion in her life. She continued, "There has been no compromise, no failure in morals, no trickery nor deceit. The only fault that you may find is a fault that will be unforgivable in your eyes: Mr. Darcy loves me, and I love him. Given the nature of our characters and personalities, our temperaments and dispositions, there was no other possible outcome."

Elizabeth heard footsteps on the path behind her, and then Darcy appeared, stepping between her and his aunt as he faced Lady Catherine.

"Lady Catherine, I have not heard the entirety of this conversation; yet I have heard enough to convince me that someone is spreading slanderous lies about me and my intended wife, Miss Bennet."

"So you are engaged. They are not lies! Miss Bingley told me of the situation herself in an urgent letter which she sent to me at Rosings after you had her removed from Pemberley. Is it not true that Miss Bennet has forced an entanglement upon you? How else would you have come to be engaged to her?"

"The only entanglement is that of my heart. I have admired her for many months, and yesterday she did me the honor of accepting my hand. You have been deceived by an angry and vindictive woman."

Lady Catherine appeared to consider this briefly. "I would speak with you in your study, nephew. There are matters which we must discuss, and it would be best done in private."

"Miss Bennet shall come with me."

"She shall not! Until she is your wife I will speak with you alone."

She walked past him back to the house, and Darcy and Elizabeth followed. They had not time to speak to each other, for Lady Catherine kept a fast pace despite her age. Upon gaining the house, Lady Catherine marched into the study, Darcy followed her, the door of the study was shut quite firmly and loudly, and Elizabeth was left to face her aunt's startled face alone.

CHAPTER NINETEEN

Never had Darcy felt such a sudden change of emotions as when he faced his aunt in the study of Pemberley.

Each day with Elizabeth at Pemberley had seemed more appealing and memorable than the day before, to his thinking, and he foresaw many more such days after their marriage. From the moment of her arrival their relationship had grown more familiar, sharing more of their thoughts and feelings with each other, discovering points of commonality and similarities of taste and mind. His plan to court Elizabeth had succeeded beyond all expectations, and his only wish now was to use all his power to remove any delays in taking her as his wife. He had discovered that every moment not in her presence caused him only to wish to be with her even more than formerly; every moment of separation added to the sweetness of their interactions when they joined each other again. When his servant found him at a tenant's farm on the afternoon of Lady Catherine's arrival he was delighted to take advantage of the excuse to return to his fiancée's side.

But then he heard Lady Catherine's voice as he searched for her and Elizabeth in the garden; and though he could not make out each word, he understood her tone quite well. He felt a possessive pride in Elizabeth's poise and dignity as she refuted his aunt's charges, a pride that was nearly overthrown by the anger caused as he began to understand the nature of those charges. Miss Bingley's plan for revenge had been cunning in its execution; Elizabeth's reputation might never recover unless he could stem this tide with drastic action. His state of bliss had become earnest indignation within mere seconds. He closed the door of the study emphatically behind him.

"I will not be ordered about in my own house, Aunt Catherine, by you or anyone else. Say what you have come to say and let us be done with it."

Lady Catherine faced her nephew with all the dignity that injured pride can muster. "I will speak frankly, nephew. How is it that you have come to be engaged to a common trollop like Miss Bennet when you know you are intended for Anne?"

"You will speak of my betrothed with the respect due to the

future mistress of Pemberley, or you will not speak of her at all."

"Future mistress? Do you deny that she is already living here at Pemberley under your protection?"

"She has been given no more protection from me than what I give to all my guests. I will allow no aspersions upon her character or mine. Miss Bennet is a lady of decorum and utmost propriety and will be an exceptional mistress for Pemberley. Miss Bingley, who chose to leave this house of her own accord, has made a cravenly attack on her character by trying to work through you."

"Miss Bingley spoke no more than the truth! You forget your duty to your family. You forget your duty to Anne! Your mother and I planned this marriage while you were babes; while you were still in your cradles we spoke of it. You have been destined for each other by the respective voices of everyone in both your houses, and now these plans will come to naught for the sake of a girl of no standing, no wealth, with no social consequence at all. She is an inferior creature."

"With all due respect, Aunt Catherine, the only voices you have heard are those in your own head speaking what you wish to hear," Darcy answered angrily. "Most of our family is eager to approve whatever choice I make, and for that one who will insist on having her own way they will have no patience."

Lady Catherine changed her tone, trying a different tactic. "Anne wants this marriage, Darcy. She wants to marry you, to be the means of uniting our two houses, and to take her rightful place as the mistress of Pemberley. Have you no regard for her feelings?"

"I do regard her feelings, madam. I think too much of her to consign her to a lifetime spent with a man who has never loved her as a husband ought, whose affections are given entirely to another, who could never give her more than the embrace of a brother. Nor do I wish for her to suffer from the consequences of bearing children, for it is obvious to all that her health is precarious at best. I could never forgive myself for being the source of such misery for her."

Lady Catherine wrung her hands as she paced across the floor. "How can you say this? Being your wife is all she has ever wanted. You will crush her utterly with such rejection."

"I am certain that is all she wants, for you have allowed her to have no other thought since she was first able to speak! You have pushed, prodded, and prompted her along the path of your own choosing since time out of mind, with no consideration for her own comfort or wishes, and now you say that she wants this marriage! How could she desire anything else? And do you think I do not know what our life together would be like at Pemberley? I would gain two wives for the price of one; for you would be ever present, interfering, imposing your will upon us, and slowly grinding poor Anne under your heel. She would never be free of your smothering presence in her life."

Lady Catherine paused in her pacing and looked at Darcy closely. "You are determined on this course of action? Nothing will dissuade you?"

"Miss Elizabeth Bennet will be my wife, she and no other. It is time that you accustom yourself to the fact that I will not marry Anne, for even if I did not marry Elizabeth, I would not choose your daughter. There is no hope of it."

The great lady regarded him coldly. "If you will not listen to reason, I must think of Georgiana."

"What about her?"

"Being under the same roof with the likes of one like Miss Bennet is not in her best interest. She should not be exposed to such an influence."

Darcy's face hardened imperceptibly. "What do you propose to do about it?"

"This scandal will follow her as much as you, for when she is presented at court next year nobody of consequence will make an offer for the sister of Elizabeth Darcy. If you are not willing to take the necessary actions then I shall demand that Georgiana live with me at Rosings."

Darcy stared at her in disbelief. "You have no legal standing to make such a demand, madam."

"I do not need it! Miss Bennet is little known among society yet, but if you marry her with the current rumors beginning to circulate, our entire family will rise up in concern for Georgiana once they know who she is. All will be united; they will speak in one voice, demanding that she be separated as much as possible from your wife and the stain she brings with her. For her sake you will be forced to give your sister up, to live in isolation at Pemberley with your wife, while Georgiana enjoys the benefits of exposure to superior society under my sponsorship. Among our family it will be a punishment to speak your name; you will never be recognized by us again."

Darcy's anger rose to a cold fury. "Aunt Catherine, if you are convinced of the truth of your own statements, I tell you to do your worst. But I do not think that you will enjoy such unified family support as you now anticipate, and rest assured that once you start down this path, you will never see me or Pemberley again. All intercourse between us will then be at an end forever."

His aunt eyed him calculatingly for a moment. "This is your final answer? Obstinate, headstrong boy! Very well, then, I shall know how to act." She paused for a moment. "If you had married Miss Bennet before these rumors began to circulate the damage might have been contained. But it is all too late now." She turned to leave, but Darcy's voice held her back.

"One last thing, Lady Catherine, before you go. Behavior such as yours shall not stop me from wedding who I desire. But you do yourself no favors when you repeat baseless rumors such as the ones you have uttered today. They reflect on you as well as on me, and on the rest of our family. You would do well to suppress them, not to spread them further."

Lady Catherine appeared to consider this briefly. "I shall do my best, since you are so determined on this course of action; but my concern is for our family's sake, not for you. I take no leave of you and I refuse any compliments. With you I am most seriously displeased."

She marched out in high dudgeon, and Darcy could not bring himself to regret her leaving at all. His only concern was how this might have affected Elizabeth; and as soon as Lady Catherine left the house, he sought her out.

He found Elizabeth with her aunt in the dining room, overseeing the servants as fresh flowers were brought in and arranged in vases for the upcoming dinner. Their expressions, though serene, communicated that they had been watching for the end of his interview as well. Georgiana was nowhere to be seen and he found himself suddenly alertly searching for her, wondering if Lady Catherine had somehow already managed to take Georgiana away from him, though he knew such a thing could not have been carried out so quickly. Seeing his anxious look, Elizabeth reassured him as to his sister's whereabouts, although she could not account for his look of relief when she told him that she was resting.

"Lady Catherine has gone," he told them. "She is on her way back to Rosings or perhaps town first. I apologize, Elizabeth, for the unconscionable discourtesy she has shown to you, and for the malicious gossip she is only too happy to repeat to you. There is no possible excuse for her behavior and I made her aware of my feelings on the subject. She will never have the chance to insult you in such a way again. I hope you are not too upset by this unfortunate encounter."

"I am well," she assured him. "And I do not blame Lady Catherine for arriving at Pemberley and seeming to have those rumors confirmed, at least in some respects. She had been told that I was acting as the mistress of Pemberley, and when she arrived I was unfortunately the only one available to receive her. Also I believe she misinterpreted the significance of my slippers, as I told her that they were a gift but did not say from whom. It was an unfortunate happpenstance on her part, nothing more. My anger is reserved mostly for another object."

"I have enough anger for them both," Darcy responded heavily, "for there is another aspect to her visit which you do not yet know. Where is your uncle? I need his counsel straightaway."

"He is fishing in his usual spot, I believe," Mrs. Gardiner answered. "Shall I have a servant call him back to the house?"

"I thank you, but this is a discussion best held out of Georgiana's hearing. I will go to him."

CHAPTER TWENTY

Darcy found Mr. Gardiner up to his knees in the water, under a small willow tree at a bend in the stream where the depth and flow boded well for fresh trout for dinner. A small container next to him held several of his catches already, and Mr. Gardiner cast his line again as Darcy approached.

"What ho, Darcy! I heard a carriage depart a short while ago, after what seemed to be a short visit. Are there any messages for me?"

"No, there are no messages. I have come seeking your advice, if I do not ask too much."

"If you are having lady trouble, I am afraid I will be of no use at all. The fairer sex is as mysterious as they are lovely, which is why they catch us coming and going, no doubt."

"It is lady trouble, but not of the sort you are thinking. The visitor you heard was my aunt, Lady Catherine de Bourgh, and what she said involves your niece."

Mr. Gardiner retracted his line and returned to the bank where Darcy stood. "I am pleased to be of assistance, if possible."

The two men began to walk along the path that bordered the stream, wandering somewhat randomly as they spoke. Darcy repeated the particulars of his aunt's visit and her attacks on Elizabeth's character, ending with the threats she had made against Georgiana. He concluded, "I had hoped to have a peaceful visit with you and Miss Bennet, to see her return to Longbourn to plan our wedding, and to have her return here with me as my wife with no further difficulties. It seems that is not to be."

Mr. Gardiner pondered these things for a short time. "Is there any chance your aunt could succeed in removing your sister from your care? How would she overturn your father's will?"

"I was not made guardian by virtue of my father's will, for he had made no such provision. His death was sudden and unexpected, and I became guardian by the general acclamation of my family. My cousin was also made guardian by virtue of his relationship with Georgiana and to prevent against further difficulties in the event of my demise. We have both served in that capacity ever since."

"Do you believe your family will support you against your

aunt?"

Darcy nodded, his brow still furrowed in concern. "Lady Catherine is known for being obstinate and headstrong, traits of which she readily accuses those who oppose her. The family will support me, I have no doubt, so long as they trust my good sense. But if they become aware of these rumors, the situation will become difficult--perhaps even untenable--while they attempt to protect Georgiana's reputation."

"So then for the present Georgiana is safe. What about Elizabeth's reputation? Is it truly as damaged as your aunt has intimated?"

Darcy pondered briefly. "I do not believe so. Lady Catherine is given to exaggerations, particularly when she is not getting her own way. Elizabeth is not known to the Ton. Even if Miss Bingley speaks of her in London, society will take little notice of her until after we are married. So until then she is probably quite safe. And after that, accusing her of unseemly conduct now will not matter."

"Will your aunt not speak of her publicly?"

"She has no more desire for scandal than we do. I made it clear to her that my mind will not be swayed by threats, and if she believes that then she will know that repeating gossip against my fiancée will work against her own interests. But she is very angry with me. I cannot be certain what she will do. She may spread the rumors as quickly as possible to try to separate me from Elizabeth."

"It would appear, Darcy, that your goals are three-fold: to protect Elizabeth's reputation, to further your marriage to her, and to avoid any disturbance to your sister's future. Am I correct?"

"I believe so."

"Then your aunt has given you your solution, perhaps without meaning to do so."

Darcy regarded Mr. Gardiner cautiously. "I do not understand."

"Did she not say that she might have been able to stop the rumors if you and Elizabeth were already married? If you and Elizabeth were to marry immediately then Elizabeth's reputation would remain intact, for the rumors would be contradicted at once. Your aunt would not be able to separate you, and any concerns over Miss Georgiana's reputation would immediately disappear. Lady Catherine may have even been giving you a hint, once she saw your determination and realized her efforts were fruitless. She may have wished for a way to resolve the situation without lowering herself in any way."

"I cannot believe that is what she intended."

"Perhaps not. But it is an efficient solution all the same, whether she meant to put the idea in your head or not."

Darcy shook his head. "The idea is appealing, of course, for personal reasons--but it would not be fair to Elizabeth. I am sure she would like to make the transition to married life in a more leisurely manner; and she deserves the chance to be married alongside her sister, if that is her desire."

"I quite understand. Still, we might keep it in mind as a possibility, if any other circumstance arises."

"Then it is your counsel that at present we need do nothing? That seems too simple, and yet it is quite a sensible conclusion after considering all the possibilities."

"As you said yourself, Miss Bingley's comments about a person so unknown to the Ton will excite no interest; and Lady Catherine probably will want to distance herself from any scandal."

"You are a wise counselor, Mr. Gardiner."

"You did not need my counsel, Mr. Darcy. You simply needed a listening ear, and after speaking freely with a sympathetic hearer you were able to discern the situation for yourself. Wait and see what develops with your family, for they will be your only real concern. For the rest, you may put it out of your head and concentrate on matters more nearly at hand, such as the dinner party tonight."

"I thank you, sir." Although Darcy was most delighted to be taking Elizabeth as his wife, he reflected now that he would also be highly gratified at the prospect of gaining her aunt and uncle as a part of his family. Mr. Gardiner's manners and good sense particularly reminded him of his own father. His counsel was proving more valuable by the minute; and Darcy could easily imagine that in the future, the Gardiners would be frequent and welcomed guests in their home.

∞

With the dinner party hard upon them, the whole party made their final preparations and then gathered in the drawing room to meet the arriving guests. By common accord they put the troublesome visit from Lady Catherine behind them and resolved to simply enjoy the evening as planned. Darcy had made his sister aware of their aunt's visit and of her charges against Elizabeth, but for the moment he could see no benefit in frightening her regarding her future. So it was with a determined, cheerful air that Elizabeth began to meet the families who would soon become her own neighbors.

A Mrs. Mary Young and her son, Harold Young, were among the first to arrive. Mr. Young, a stately man of about threescore years, bowed low over her hand and kissed it; but Elizabeth felt no offense at the familiarity, for it was done with an air of kingly condescension, not of vulgarity, as if he were giving her a rare gift. Any offense would have disappeared in amusement the next moment when an unexpected canine head peeked out from Mrs. Young's reticule. Chelsea the pug, the elderly Mrs. Young informed Elizabeth, was her closest and most sympathetic confidante, accompanied her everywhere, and her company was often much more agreeable than that of any human she knew. She was, she said, completely unable to separate from Chelsea for the slightest period of time.

"Is she entirely in control of her faculties, do you think?" Elizabeth asked Darcy when they had moved away.

"She is in excellent health in both mind and body, and is more sharp-witted than many members of parliament. Her husband was a magistrate for many years before his final illness. You will find her conversation witty and full of acute observations."

Mr. and Mrs. Meadows claimed her attention next, along with their twin daughters Mary and Martha. The parents were courteous and anxious to please as they introduced their daughters to both Darcy and Elizabeth, for the two ladies had only recently entered society and this was their first visit to Pemberley. They both made painfully correct curtsies, seeming overawed by their surroundings. Darcy introduced his sister and the three moved off on their own, to Elizabeth's satisfaction, for she felt that Georgiana would benefit from the society of girls her own age.

She turned next to a finely dressed middle-aged couple, Mr. and Mrs. Roger and Harriet Worth. Mrs. Worth looked at Elizabeth with large, perfectly round eyes and said not a word, though she seemed perfectly amiable. Her husband made up for his wife's lack of speech.

"So you are from Hertfordshire?" he asked after introductions had been made. "Capital place, Hertfordshire, I lived there many years as a boy. And are you acquainted with a Mr. William Stafford of Shropley Hall? No," without waiting for or expecting a reply, "I suppose not, he is not much in company, yet he keeps a fine table, a very fine table indeed. Did you travel here on the S-Road? Of course you did, it is the usual way; and it is a good road, kept in excellent repair. I am certain you enjoyed your travels upon it. I imagine you probably stayed at the Blue Hen Inn as it is quite the most logical stopping place. Have you ever eaten their white soup? It is superb, perhaps the best in the country, and it is simply not worth taking that road if you do not stop and eat that soup. When you return you shall stay at that inn. Do have the white soup, and tell Mary in the kitchens that I sent you so that you may be certain of having the best."

Elizabeth had not had a chance to say a word, which was fortunate since she would have had difficulty deciding which of these topics to attack first. She was saved from the effort when Mr. Worth received a small nip in his elbow from Chelsea, whose owner had maneuvered to a place behind him. Mr. Worth and his silent wife moved away with an indignant, "Begging your pardon, madam!"

"And that is the most sensible thing he has said or is likely to say all night," Mrs. Young said with an air of satisfaction, replacing Chelsea's head firmly within the reticule. Elizabeth decided she would like both Mrs. Young and Chelsea, with their obvious mission of ending tedious and pointless monologues, and instantly resolved to spend more time with both.

She was enjoying the evening immensely, she decided as they sat at dinner; and much of the enjoyment came from having Darcy beside her constantly, his eyes warmly upon her, and his obvious pride as he introduced her and her relatives to all. She thought with amusement of the bargain she had made with Darcy just a few days previously, when she had given him permission to make his attentions obvious in this crowd so that she could see the effects of their relationship on his neighbors. It was quite an unnecessary bargain now and she could not imagine having it any other way. She gloried in his every affectionate gesture toward herself, in his careful attentions to her comfort, and especially in the joy apparent as he stood to make the important announcement with her uncle.

Darcy called for the attention of the table as he and Mr. Gardiner stood; and surely half the people present, at least, must have already guessed his intent as he asked for the honor of their attention to a toast being offered by the other man.

"I have the pleasure of announcing the engagement of my niece, Miss Elizabeth Bennet, to Mr. Fitzwilliam Darcy, our most gracious host tonight. Pray join with me in wishing them a long life and a happy future together! May their joys be many, their troubles be few, and their home filled always with laughter!"

The general acclaim around the table was genuine and heartfelt, and Elizabeth could detect no resentment or unspoken condescension in any face. The Misses Meadows looked identically and politely joyful, Mr. Worth applauded loudly, and even little Chelsea poked her head out and seemed to wink at Elizabeth before she stole a dinner roll off the table. Through the remainder of the evening, which included an impromptu performance from Georgiana and the Meadows sisters, Elizabeth felt warm approval and welcome from all the families. Some of their congratulations were given in a more stately form than others, but all seemed determined to show her their good intent. She realized anew the esteem and affection held for Darcy; for such warmth towards her, she knew, was very much a reflection of their opinion of him. She was able to go to bed that night with a heart much lighter than she would have believed possible just a few short hours previously.

CHAPTER TWENTY-ONE

Dearest Jane,

I must thank you again and again for your last letter to me, for I took your advice very much to heart and threw myself shamelessly at Mr. Darcy in the very same hour that I read it. We are now engaged. William begs me to send you his gratitude as well; and wishes that in your next letter you may encourage me to be even more effusive in my declarations of affection for him, for the results are quite to his liking. I have not reminded him that there will be no letter, for we will see you in London shortly, and then you may encourage me in shameless declarations to your heart's content. When I see you in London there is a great deal more that I shall have to tell you, for I must describe the visit of Lady Catherine, who came to separate us, and the departure of Miss Bingley, whose departure led to said visit. I also simply must tell you everything about our dinner party last night; but in the interest of time I shall now close this letter, for I must still write to Papa.

Your most affectionate and thoroughly engaged sister,
Elizabeth Bennet
~Elizabeth Darcy~
~Elizabeth Marie Darcy~
~Mrs. Elizabeth Darcy~
~Mrs. Fitzwilliam Darcy~
N.B. No, we are not yet married, but I simply had to write my new name out once, to try it out ahead of time; and then I could not make myself stop. Does it not look well? Yours, etc., etc.

With such high spirits she addressed the next letter.

Dearest Papa,

I was slightly cross with you when we parted company in Hertfordshire, for then you supposed that more existed between me and Mr. Darcy than there actually was. But now, suppose as much as you wish, let your imagination take flight, and unless you suppose me actually married you cannot go much wrong. When next I see you I shall defend him much more than I did in your study. You may tell Mama as much as you wish, but if I were you, I would tell her sooner rather than later. Perhaps you will be able to plug your ears in the carriage on the way to town. I look forward to introducing you to my fiancé in just a few days.

Affectionately,
Your engaged daughter,
Elizabeth
N.B. The next time I tell you that I am not engaged it will be because we are married already!
Yours, etc., etc.

After penning these letters Elizabeth joined her aunt, Mrs. Reynolds, Georgiana and Darcy in the family wing of the great house; for Darcy was eager for Elizabeth to see the quarters that would become hers upon their marriage and to allow her to begin to choose furnishings of her own. He was determined that all decorating should be completed before Elizabeth returned to Pemberley in her married state. Darcy stayed with them long enough to show them the spacious bedroom with its four poster bed and canopy; the sitting room with a settee, desk, and its own fireplace; and the small balcony with its French doors. He then left them to consider patterns and colors while he met with Mr. Gardiner in the study, beginning to negotiate a marriage contract; for he was determined to be far more generous than Mr. Bennet would want to agree to, and thought it would be best to begin the work of the settlement with Mr. Gardiner instead.

The ladies gravely considered bedding, wall coverings and curtains, furniture and paint, and all manner of accessories; while Elizabeth secretly wondered where she was, for she felt she might as well have been handed the moon for a play thing. Never had she been given such license and responsibility for a suite of rooms. Besides this, the rooms were so stamped with Lady Anne's presence that she felt like an intruder. She would not hear of removing any of the things that the former mistress of the house had used every day. But Mrs. Reynolds prevailed upon her to make a clean sweep, for Darcy had left particular instructions that anything personal belonging to his late mother was to be removed so that Elizabeth would feel free to make whatever changes she wished. He would not have her live with a ghost, as Mrs. Reynolds repeated to Elizabeth, and Elizabeth again had reason to be grateful for the sensitivity of the man she was to marry.

Bemusedly she authorized several small changes in the curtains and bedding, but she would not approve of replacing the costly furniture, although it was somewhat dated. "I am quite comfortable with the rooms as they are, and the settee and desk are entirely serviceable just so," she told her aunt, but Mrs. Gardiner shook her head at her.

"My dear, you must allow him to do this for you. He is driven to provide for you, do you not see? To be able to give you so many things you do not expect from him--to him, this is as much a declaration of his affection as any words he might speak to you. Allow him this freedom and show your appreciation to him as best you can, for he will not be happy otherwise. Consider how you would feel if you were to plan a surprise for him and he protested that he did not want such gifts from you."

Elizabeth recognized that her aunt's words were true. Darcy had courted her with many gifts throughout the preceding month and she realized it was part of his pattern with Georgiana as well, that he would not rest until he had expressed himself in this way as much as possible. Philosophically she decided that she must accustom herself better to such tiresome duties, and gave way fully to Mrs. Reynolds's suggestions. The ladies then spent several hours making decisions that were carefully written down to be completed as soon as possible.

Following a late lunch her aunt and uncle left to take a turn about the park while she and Georgiana joined Darcy again in his study. He and her uncle had worked out most of the marriage contract in the morning; and he was now prepared to tend to some estate matters while she and Georgiana sat nearby, intending to take up their needlework. Elizabeth set this aside as the footman came in with the day's posts, anticipating correctly that there would be a letter from Jane. She sat back and opened the letter in a leisurely way, noting that Jane had written the address in an uncharacteristically rapid scrawl. Darcy also began to work his way through a small pile of correspondence.

Jane's letter opened with the usual affectionate greeting and then moved on into a description of their little parties and engagements of the past few days. They had been to the Lucas' home once for dinner; several girls from the village had called on Kitty and Lydia; Mary had a new piece of music she was learning; and Bingley was planning some small improvements for Netherfield. After several rambling, unimportant paragraphs, the handwriting changed markedly from Jane's usual careful hand to something that appeared to have been written in more agitation.

Since writing the above, Elizabeth, something has occurred of a much more serious nature. I am afraid to cause you any fright but I know that this news can do nothing less, for the tidings are dreadful--Lydia has run away! She retired a little earlier than usual last night saying she had a headache, which we did not think to question; for since her anger at our father started she has been unpleasant company in the evenings when the family all sit together, and we were just as happy not to be afflicted with her mood. But this morning when she did not come to breakfast, Hill searched her room and found a note saying that she was gone and that we are not to worry about her nor try to find her. As if such a thing was possible! Upon investigation we found that she removed ten pounds from the house with her, and a good selection of her clothes are gone; so we suppose that she has every intention of making good on her threat in the note--that of never returning to Longbourn! She must have left the house immediately upon seeming to retire last night, and gone down the stairs while we all sat together in the drawing room. All that is known after this is that she might have been seen early in the morning in a hackney coach on the London road, and that there may have been a gentleman in the coach with her, but of this we are not certain. Papa has gone to Brighton to look for her, for he believes it more likely that she would try to follow the officers than go to town by herself, completely unprotected.

I fear Papa blames himself for her behavior, but who could have foreseen such an event? He did his best to curb her high spirits, and rebellion was the result--and now rebellion may bring about all our ruin.

Shall I own, Elizabeth, that your presence is sorely needed here, and that of my uncle as well? It is hard to ask you to leave the comforts of Pemberley at such a time, and yet your visit is almost over in any case. Pray return with my uncle and aunt as soon as possible so that we may help support my mother, and consider what to do next to recover my sister. Charles is a great support to me, but he is of little assistance in calming Mama's hysterical nerves, and much more might be accomplished if I had not the responsibility of tending to her. Kitty and Mary are of little use. Please come right away to Longbourn. Until this situation is resolved there can be no visit for us in London."

Elizabeth darted out of her seat and blurted out to both her companions, "Oh! Where is my uncle? I must find him at once! I have not a moment to lose."

"Good God, what is the matter?" Darcy cried, rising from his own seat, and Georgiana likewise rose. "Are you well, Elizabeth?"

"I am quite well, William, but I have just received distressing news from Longbourn," Elizabeth answered, and burst into tears as she alluded to it. She stood wretched and unsure, the letter in her hands, as Georgiana left the room in search of the Gardiners. Elizabeth felt Darcy's strong arm around her as he guided her to sit again, then pulled a chair to sit opposite her with both of her hands held in his.

"Tell me, my darling, what has happened? Are you sure you are quite all right? Allow me to get you some wine--it may help to settle your nerves."

"I need no wine, William, just you," she answered passionately if not fluently, and Darcy moved to sit next to her with one arm around her.

"Can you not tell me what has happened?" he asked, and in response Elizabeth gave him Jane's letter, for she could not trust herself to speak. He skimmed the first paragraphs rapidly, and then his face changed expression as he reached the section which detailed Lydia's disappearance. Elizabeth saw his lips tighten and narrow and his brows furrow together; and for a moment he looked not unlike how he had appeared on his first evening in Hertfordshire, rather stern and unapproachable. Was he already regretting his decision to ally himself with such a family? Certainly he had reason to do so with this proof of family failing now on display. She made as if to move away from him, but his arm tightened and kept her in place.

"We shall have to locate and retrieve her," was Darcy's only comment.

"But how? How is such a thing to even be attempted? She might be anywhere by now!"

"Your uncle and I shall handle this; you need have no worries. We will retrace her steps from the hackney coach and determine a likely direction for her; with only ten pounds she must surface sooner or later, for she cannot survive on her own. If she is in

Brighton, a few coins in the right quarters will quickly yield her location."

As he spoke he seemed to suddenly recall something to mind and gave a great start and an oath. He moved back to his desk and began to sort rapidly through the letters he had just received, muttering another oath as he took one from the stack and opened it, while Elizabeth could only watch in bewilderment. Darcy silently read for a minute and then looked gravely at her. "This concerns your sister. I thought in passing that the writing of the address looked familiar, and now my suspicions are confirmed. My sweetest, loveliest Elizabeth, you must be brave."

Elizabeth nearly tore the letter from his hands. It started without the customary salutations:

Darcy,

When we met so unexpectedly at Netherfield last month your attentions to Miss Bennet gave me pause. I have never seen your preference for one lady made so markedly, or at least it seemed marked to me, for I am familiar with your disposition. Am I correct in thinking that you have developed a tendre for the lovely Miss Elizabeth? It hardly matters now, for if I am not to have a living, then you shall not have her.

You took Georgiana away from me and destroyed my reputation with Miss Elizabeth. Your words to Mr. Bennet, repeated to Colonel Forster, have likewise ruined any prospects for me in the militia, and you have already damaged my future in the church. I now take my revenge upon you in the only way I can. Lydia is ruined. When I am done with her no other man shall have her; and the disgrace will make it impossible for you to join yourself with the Bennet family, if that was indeed your hope. But if you truly had no designs upon Miss Bennet, then my revenge falls only upon Mr. Bennet; and that motive, combined with Lydia's willing charms, is more than enough for me. You will still have enough guilt over the situation to satisfy my desires.

If you care to retrieve her, you may find Lydia in the care of our old friend Mrs. Younge at her boardinghouse in town. You shall not find me.

George Wickham

Elizabeth covered her face with her hands and gave herself up to despair.

CHAPTER TWENTY-TWO

In short order Georgiana returned with the Gardiners, and Darcy gave all of them to understand the dreadful occurrence, aided by the two letters he handed to them. Exclamations of shock and dismay followed, amid many cries of, "No! This cannot be! Surely not!" Georgiana also gave in to her tears, and Darcy was forced to go to her aid and allow Mrs. Gardiner to comfort her niece. At length the party began to recover, to talk of what had happened, and to make plans for what to do.

"How did they even meet?" Elizabeth cried. "He was in Brighton and she was in Hertfordshire. Where did they meet, and how did their association start?"

"He was not in Brighton, as it is now apparent," Darcy answered her, still sitting with his sister. "He must have retained some connections in Meryton, unknown to us, which induced him to return there after he left the militia."

"And those walks Lydia was taking which caused my sister so much concern," Elizabeth answered him, thinking aloud, "they must have brought her to his attention."

"I doubt that," Darcy said, looking grim. "This letter of Wickham's shows a viciousness I had only guessed at before and never seen on full display. The tone of it reveals all. He returned to Meryton with the express intent of hurting your family in some way, and me too if he could. He may have encountered your sister by chance; but it is more likely that he deliberately threw himself in her way, making communication with her by some secret means. When your sister made her trips to Meryton she was then undoubtedly meeting with him and he was able to carry out his plans without resistance."

"If only I had warned her against him!" Elizabeth cried passionately. "If I had only told what I knew of him before leaving Hertfordshire, at least told my own sisters!"

"The fault is mine," Darcy responded, "for if I had made his character known to all last autumn, none of this should have occurred."

Mr. Gardiner held up a hand to stop them both. "May I remind all concerned that the fault lies with the two people involved, Wickham and Lydia? Wickham is using Lydia to lash out against those who would hold him accountable for his behavior, and Lydia is doing much the same. But she will be left to pay the full price of both their folly."

"Foolish, foolish girl," said Elizabeth. "Papa tried to correct her willful ways but it was too little and too late."

"Perhaps not too late," said her uncle. "Our first object must be to try to recover her. Though Jane begs for our immediate presence, I believe we can all agree that we are more needed in town. Jane is not aware of the information Wickham sent here. While we know of Lydia's location we must go to her and retrieve her from her present situation."

"Yes, and it must be done as soon as possible," Darcy added. "I am familiar with the boarding house Wickham mentions. It is no place for a gentlewoman even with Wickham protecting her. If Wickham has already abandoned her, I fear for her physical safety. We must secure her at once."

"But what then?" asked Mrs. Gardiner, also in tears. "If we recover her we may return her to her home; but as Wickham said, she is ruined. She will never be able to marry, nor will any of her sisters. Who would ally themselves with such a family? More things have been destroyed today than just Lydia's reputation." As she spoke she looked doubtfully at Darcy, and he comprehended her meaning at once.

Momentarily leaving his sister, he crossed the room to sit next to Elizabeth and gathered both her hands in his, disregarding the impropriety of the action. "I can assure you, madam, that my intentions have not changed; nor will this situation cause them to change in any way. Elizabeth shall be my wife regardless of the actions of any of her family, so long as she is willing to have me. And though I cannot speak for Bingley, I feel sure in saying that his engagement with Miss Bennet is safe." Mrs. Gardiner thanked him with a weak smile.

"We do not have leisure at the moment to consider what will happen when we find Lydia," said Mr. Gardiner. "Darcy and I must make preparations to leave immediately and find her, if I may depend on his assistance." Darcy nodded in agreement and made to stand, but Mrs. Gardiner stopped him.

"I believe we must all go. Elizabeth will be needed for dealing with her sister, especially if Lydia is reluctant to return home. And of course I must accompany my husband."

"I shall not be left behind," Georgiana stated suddenly, surprising everyone with her vehemence. "I wish to be of assistance in whatever way I can in this crisis." Darcy considered this briefly, weighing her determination with the increasing self-assurance he had seen in her lately, and nodded again.

"If we can all be off in an hour's time, we may make a good start towards town, and be at Lydia's side two days from now." With those words, they all scattered and made rapid preparations to leave at once.

∞

Their departure took a little longer than they hoped and they were only able to make thirty miles the first day; but it was still thirty miles closer to Lydia, and Elizabeth took heart. She was apprehensive about Lydia's stay in a boarding house such as the one Darcy described, knowing that Lydia was ill-equipped to protect herself from those who might take advantage of her undefended person. All her life she had been petted, protected, and pampered by her indulgent mother, never made to bear any responsibility for herself, never learning to consider the interests or concerns of other people. She could have little idea of the designs that others might have on her now. Elizabeth dreaded what they might find at the end of their journey.

At the end of their second day on the road they were able to reach town, for they had driven hard each day and had several changes of horses along the way; and without pausing at the Gardiner's or at Darcy House they drove directly to the address Darcy supplied. Elizabeth's heart sank as the carriages made their way through streets that grew darker and narrower by the moment, with decrepit houses on all sides and disheveled men and women lounging carelessly about. At length they turned abruptly to the left and stopped in front of a long, low building with tired lights shining out of the few windows. The building's wooden exterior was covered with innumerable stains and had boards hanging loosely from its façade; the short walkway leading up to the door was littered with refuse.

Darcy went inside briefly, accompanied by one of the footmen, and returned in a very few minutes. "I will need your assistance now, Elizabeth," he told her and handed her out of the carriage. "Mrs.

Younge easily yielded the location of the room where your sister is, but she was unable or unwilling to give me any more details on her condition. I cannot properly enter her room without any idea of what I may encounter. I must ask you to allow me to escort you inside, and then we shall see what her state may be. Please stay as close to me as possible."

"Is Wickham there?"

He shook his head. "From what Mrs. Younge said, I think not."

He left Mr. Gardiner and a footman to guard Mrs. Gardiner and Georgiana and took another footman inside along with him and Elizabeth. Inside the building Elizabeth wrinkled her nose at the foul odors in the unkempt dining room as she closely followed Darcy to the stairs on the far side of the room, followed by the footman. They climbed the stairs and turned down a dark hallway where Darcy firmly knocked on the third door on the right. A muffled sound came from inside, as if something had been dropped, but no greeting or other sound of welcome was heard. Pushing heavily on the door Darcy forced it open and allowed Elizabeth to enter ahead of him, and then followed directly behind her.

Elizabeth's eyes adjusted slowly to the dim light, for there was only one small lamp on a rustic table by the unkempt bed. She called her sister's name hesitantly, and was rewarded by a loud, "Good lord, Lizzy! What are you doing here?" Lydia stepped forward into the light.

"Lydia! You are here! And are you safe? Are you well?"

"I shall be, now you are here. I would have been off in another hour or as soon as I could climb out of this window. Can you believe Wickham brought me all the way here and then ran off without a word to me? La! Mr. Darcy, whatever are you doing here? What a joke that you and Elizabeth should be the ones to find me! Wickham quite hates you both, you know."

"Why would you need to climb out the window? Why could you not use the door?"

"Wickham took the last of my money, and Mrs. Younge would not let me leave without the room being paid for. I tried to go past her door very early this morning, but she heard me and sent me back directly. I do not like her at all; she is not very nice. How did you find me?"

"We shall speak of this later," Darcy said firmly. "Your room is paid; you are to come with us."

"Nothing should please me more, for I have not seen a single show at the theater since I have been here. Wickham would not take me, although we have been here six days; and I should think my ten pounds ought to count for something!"

"Oh, Lydia, you thoughtless, headstrong girl," Elizabeth began, but Darcy stopped her with a small gesture.

"May we assist you in gathering your things, Miss Lydia?"

"My things are all together, for I should have made my escape shortly. There, pick up that hat box and put it on top of the valise, and here is my other bag. That is all. Where are we going? You are not taking me back to Longbourn, are you? For I hate it above all other places and if you take me back, I shall not be long in leaving again. Lizzy, you are grown so brown and coarse! Have you been walking outdoors a great deal?"

"We are taking you to the Gardiner's house and then we will see what to do next," Elizabeth told her, sick at heart at the folly being continuously displayed by her youngest sister. "You have had a narrow escape, Lydia, and I do not think you yet understand it at all."

"I have not had such a narrow escape as all that; for as I told you before, I should have been gone from here very shortly, and there is no end of amiable gentlemen in this neighborhood. I should like to see a play tomorrow; do you think my aunt will let me go?"

With such thoughtless talk they ushered her quickly out of the building and into the waiting carriage, where the palpable relief at her safe return was rapidly replaced by disgust at the attitude that had made rescue necessary in the first place. Both carriages speedily traveled the short distance to the Gardiner's house in Cheapside, where all got out; and the Gardiner's luggage, along with Elizabeth's, was removed. Lydia was taken upstairs immediately for a hot bath, for the stink of her temporary lodging was all too apparent; and while a maid tended to Lydia, the others gathered in the parlor on the first floor to discuss their next actions.

"What was she thinking? Where was she to go next?" Mrs. Gardiner asked. "It is a relief to know that she is safe, but I cannot account for her frame of mind at all. Has she no comprehension of her situation, of the difficulties this has caused for everyone?"

"I do not think she had any fixed idea in mind. She was merely going to climb out the window, find any reasonably handsome gentleman in the area, and attach herself to him," Elizabeth answered. "She has no idea of the danger into which she would have placed herself."

"Did she say where Wickham went?"

"No, for she does not know. He left sometime yesterday or the day before and she has not seen him since. He was gone long enough, apparently, for her to realize that he was not coming back."

"I sent messengers ahead of us yesterday to try to discover Wickham's whereabouts," said Darcy. "They should report back to me tomorrow."

"If we were to find Wickham," said Mr. Gardiner heavily, "what would we do? We cannot force him to marry Lydia, and yet married she must be if her reputation is to have any prayer of survival."

"We cannot force him, but we should be able to bribe him," Darcy answered. "He has always had a price. After hearing Miss Lydia speak about him tonight, however, I do not know if she would accept him as a husband."

"So, even if my father had the resources to convince him to marry her, there is no certainty that she would go along with it. She might stand at the altar and refuse him to his face, for I have never seen her so determinedly against whatever my father might suggest. And Wickham would certainly demand far more than my father has to give. It seems a hopeless business."

"Do not give up, my love. We shall find a solution," Darcy assured her. "We must find a way to restore your sister's reputation enough so that she may be seen in Hertfordshire again, and we must find it quickly."

"Does Lydia realize that she cannot return home even if she wanted to?" Mr. Gardiner asked. "Would she be motivated to marry Wickham if she were made to want to be at home again?"

"Not at the present," Elizabeth answered. "Just now she has no desire to return to Hertfordshire at all."

"But she might feel differently about returning to Hertfordshire if she were on the arm of a handsome husband and could show him to advantage," Mrs. Gardiner pointed out.

"I am not at all certain that she even ought to marry Wickham," Elizabeth said with conviction. "Both his letter and his behavior have shown a tendency towards cruelty which frightens me. He need not have singled out my sister in such a way merely to avenge himself on my father; he had other means at his disposal. If he were to marry Lydia, she could not look forward to anything but a life of misery with him, though she is too stupid to see that right now. I cannot consign my own sister, foolish though she is, to such a fate. But nobody better than Wickham will offer for her now once it is known that she was living with him."

"I believe the solution to this may be found in your own words, Elizabeth: find a better gentleman, one who needs a wife, someone who is willing to disregard her past for a price and who has the character to treat her well," Darcy stated. "It will not be a love match, but it is her best chance to rejoin respectable society."

"It cannot be that simple. Is there a decent man anywhere to be found who will be so willing to be paid in order to take on a wife of doubtful character, and to assume responsibility for any possible consequences of her liaison with another man? Are such things even done?"

"They are done every day, though you may not be aware," Mr. Gardiner answered. "Sometimes they turn out to be happy matches. I might even have a suitable gentleman in mind," he continued, beginning to brighten a bit. "There is a clerk in my office, two and twenty years of age; well-spoken and intelligent, from a plain family, and ambitious. He wishes to advance in the company, and I have no opposition, for he has worked for me from the age of fifteen and has always shown a scrupulous character. He might do very well for Lydia, though he is a bit young."

"Forgive me, uncle, but I believe Lydia will require a steadier hand than that. Your young man may be very capable in your office, but she needs someone who will not be afraid to stand up to her, someone who will be very much in charge of his own household and of her. She is so much more willful than we have previously been led to believe; and this must be nipped in the bud if she is ever to lead a productive, useful sort of life."

"Edward!" Georgiana exclaimed, and all the rest stared at her, for until now she had been entirely silent. "I do not mean that Edward should marry Lydia," she said, seeing the surprise on their faces. "I mean that she would benefit from a husband in the military, and Edward could find the right person. Would not a soldier, accustomed to giving orders and having them followed, be best?"

"My sister speaks of our cousin, Colonel Edward Fitzwilliam," Darcy explained to the Gardiners. "I believe she is correct. A husband who is a soldier, preferably an officer, would be an ideal match for Miss Lydia."

"Lydia might take well to the idea of marrying a man in regimentals, especially an officer," Mrs. Gardiner added, the look on her face showing her approval of the idea.

"But it will not be enough." Mr. Gardiner frowned. "Finding such a man will take time, for a careful search must be made. We do not wish to exchange one mercenary for another. His background and character must be thoroughly examined, and then we will have to negotiate his price. But every day that Lydia is gone from Hertfordshire, when she is known to have left in such a public way, is a day that will damage her reputation more." Mr. Gardiner paced the room as he spoke. "We need to buy time, to distract any gossip about Lydia onto something more worthy of attention; and it must be something rather surprising, something sure to gain everyone's attention, but which will not cause further harm to the Bennet family." He paused and looked at Darcy.

Darcy was silent as he returned Mr. Gardiner's look, for he felt fairly certain of the other man's intent but was not sure if he dared pursue the subject.

"This is the possible additional circumstance we were looking for, is it not, Mr. Darcy? Surely you can see now what must be done. It shall end any possibility of gossip against Elizabeth before your aunt has a fair chance to begin; and if it is made known as publicly as possible, as quickly as possible, even in Hertfordshire it will outweigh the news of Lydia running away. Nobody will even think about Lydia's situation, let alone talk about it anymore, if you take the step we discussed."

The three ladies looked at each other in confusion for a moment until Elizabeth asked, "Of what step are you speaking?"

Mr. Gardiner would only observe Darcy in careful silence, while Darcy gathered his courage and asked, "Elizabeth, if it is not too much of an imposition on you, do you think there is any way that you might be able to marry me," he hesitated, "tomorrow?"

"Tomorrow, sir?" she cried in the deepest shock while Mrs. Gardiner and Georgiana gasped.

"It is not as difficult as you might think," Darcy answered. "I can speak with the bishop early tomorrow morning to obtain a license and we could be married by noon."

"Tomorrow," she repeated helplessly, her breath leaving her.

The rest of the room remained silent as they looked between her and Darcy.

"Tomorrow," she said again, beginning to feel the room around her again. "Tomorrow is quite impossible; I had not thought to have our wedding for some weeks yet. There are preparations that must be made. I am not ready, just yet, to leave my family."

"I wish you would consider it," Darcy responded softly. "It would offer a means to solve a number of problems in one stroke." He stopped, looking at their silent crowd of observers, and made an eloquent plea with his eyes; in response they all rose and quietly left the room, while Elizabeth remained seated, her eyes on the floor. When they were alone, Darcy knelt before her and took her hands, forcing her gaze upon him.

"My dearest, I beg of you to take my hand in church tomorrow and become my wife. You are my love, my all, and you have been my wife in my heart for many weeks now. If you were to join your life to mine tomorrow you would have no cause for regrets."

"I shall not have a chance to say farewell to my family," she began, "and Jane shall not be here."

"Regrettable, but necessary, if we are to save Lydia and protect your family," he answered. "If we marry tomorrow, I shall make certain that it is advertised as widely as possible both here in town and in Meryton. Coming so swiftly when so few people know of our attachment, our marriage will be a development of such interest that none who know you will speak of anything else for days. And among my family it will make any gossip spread by Lady Catherine or Miss Bingley of no effect. Your reputation will be safe. Afterwards, we will make our way to Longbourn so that you may make a proper farewell."

"I have not the proper clothes," she said weakly, faltering in her resolve as she saw the familiar warm, soft look on his face. He smiled.

"Of all the reasons to put off being married, I have always thought that one the worst. When two people discover that they wish to share their lives, it seems folly to me to wait weeks and weeks while they wait for the proper wedding clothes, when so many more important things call for their union. After we are married you shall have all the clothing you could want, and more. It shall be my privilege to provide anything you wish."

"You wish me to marry you tomorrow," she said, still in shock, locking her eyes with his.

"That is the general idea," he admitted, gently teasing. "I wish you to become my wife, to stay with me and never be separated again, to share my life in every way. It shall be as you wish, of course; but I think you see that even if it is not quite as we might have planned it, our wedding could never be anything less than perfect no matter what the circumstances. We will send a messenger to Longbourn tomorrow to let them know what is happening."

"And Lydia? How will this help to explain her absence from Longbourn?"

"We shall say that her excitement at the upcoming nuptials of her eldest sister and her resentment at not being the center of attention led her to impulsively travel to town on her own in order to meet her aunt and look at wedding clothes. While she was in town, she caught the eye of an eligible young man who made a sudden offer for her, which her family was delighted to accept after your rather abrupt wedding."

She allowed herself a small smile. "You have planned for every contingency, sir."

"You must allow that I am persistent in pursuit of my goal."

She considered this carefully, eyeing him shrewdly. "You are indeed. You spoke of this with my uncle while we were still at Pemberley?" she asked, recalling her uncle's words to him.

"Your uncle suggested it on the day of my aunt's visit as a means of protecting your reputation, but I did not think it was fair to ask of you then. But now, with this need to protect Lydia, it seems the only sensible plan."

"I must remind you--good things come to those who wait."

"I have waited long enough, and marrying you is a very good thing. What do you say? Will you marry me tomorrow? Shall we begin our married life immediately or do you still want to wait?"

She took a deep breath and looked at him archly. "Very well then. I have no set plans for tomorrow; so if I can convince my aunt not to expect me for tea, then I shall marry you, William."

An excited squeal from beyond the doorway led Elizabeth to believe that their exchanges might not have been as private as she could have wished, and her guess was confirmed a moment later as Georgiana fairly leapt into the room, embracing first Elizabeth and then her brother. She bore her excitement as well as possible, her mind beginning to race through all the preparations that now must be made before tomorrow. Mr. and Mrs. Gardiner likewise re-entered the room, smiling but less noisy than Georgiana in their approval.

"It would seem we have matters to settle then, Darcy," began Mr. Gardiner in his business-like way, "yet perhaps not as many as one would expect in the circumstances. My brother Bennet will have no objections to the settlement you and I already discussed, and if you brought the paperwork with you from Pemberley there can be no difficulties in that quarter. I am authorized to speak on his behalf."

"On our side there is also not as much work needed as might be expected," said Mrs. Gardiner. "Elizabeth's trunks are already packed, though we will have to find a suitable dress for tomorrow. Elizabeth and I are of a size, or close to it; I will find something for her."

"Then Georgiana and I will return to Darcy House," Darcy decided. "You may expect me at ten tomorrow morning with the license if all goes well. I will not be able to have the settlement finalized with my solicitors by then, but if Mr. Gardiner can trust me to be honorable, it will be in his hands and ready for signature by the end of the day tomorrow. I will direct that my solicitors sign on my behalf."

"And after the wedding," Mr. Gardiner added, "I shall send the necessary announcements to Longbourn and to the paper in Meryton, and begin to look for a husband for Lydia. With your cousin's assistance we may make a speedy process of it."

"There must be something in the air in London," Elizabeth observed, "that makes husbands appear out of nowhere, where only pleasing fiancés and worthless young men were previously seen. Perhaps we should tell Mama to bring Mary and Kitty to town right away."

"No indeed!" said Mrs. Gardiner emphatically. "No more hasty weddings! Two will be quite enough!"

Lydia's clear voice was heard from the adjoining room. "Two weddings? Who is getting married? Am I to be invited?"

CHAPTER TWENTY-THREE

Elizabeth was waiting before ten o'clock the next morning, wearing a blue silk that her aunt had previously purchased for an occasion that did not materialize. She sat in the parlor nervously, watching as the hands of the clock proceeded on to a quarter past ten; but she need not have worried, for Darcy appeared shortly thereafter. He was accompanied by Colonel Fitzwilliam, who bowed gallantly over her hand.

"Miss Bennet, it is a pleasure to see you again; and even more of a pleasure for it to be on such a momentous occasion. I could hardly believe it when I received Darcy's message last night that you were to be married today. The last I knew you were playing the pianoforte and using the music to tell him that his attentions were not wanted!"

"Your cousin can be quite persuasive, sir; and it turns out that he has a fine appreciation of music."

"I assure you, Edward, it took all my powers of persuasion, and I was not at all certain of my success."

"Once you told me of Wickham's failings in such a clever way, my heart was half yours."

"And when did I gain the other half?"

"I believe it was upon your promise of making a maharajah appear in our parlor at Longbourn, or perhaps upon seeing you unable to discern between brown ribbon and blue."

The colonel laughed. "A maharajah, Miss Bennet?"

"A story for another time, cousin," Darcy told him. "Right now we have an appointment to keep."

So saying, the small group made their way to the church, with Georgiana and Darcy in the Darcy carriage, the Gardiners and Elizabeth following separately, and the colonel following on horseback. They had to wait for a few minutes as another couple was marrying just ahead of them; and a glimpse at the bride's tortured face and the grim face of the groom convinced Elizabeth that all was not well in this union right at the start. When they turned and faced away from the altar her condition was apparent. Elizabeth's heart went out to the girl, who reminded her of Lydia; and she was convinced again that their sudden marriage was the best and most beneficial step that she and Darcy could take at this time to protect her family.

It was their turn. Darcy and the colonel stood at the front while Mrs. Gardiner and Georgiana took their seats as witnesses, and Mr. Gardiner prepared to walk down the aisle with his niece. With all her heart Elizabeth wished at least one of her sisters might be present at this occasion, but Lydia's reactions could not be trusted, and the others were out of reach.

They repeated their vows to each other in the usual style but with hearts overflowing, their eyes communicating more than their words ever could; and before either had time to really think about it they were declared man and wife. Darcy took her hand in his as they walked back from the altar and held it so tightly that Elizabeth was convinced he might never surrender it; but she had no complaint to make, for she had no wish to be separated from him. They signed the register, Elizabeth signing for the first time as Elizabeth Darcy with a proud flourish, and then left the church, walking out into the bright London day.

"What do we do now, Darcy?" Mr. Gardiner asked his new nephew, seeming at a loss for the first time. "I know you would like to devote your attention to your new wife, but there are a few things to which we still need to attend."

"Let us return to Darcy House," Darcy responded decisively. "My housekeeper, Mrs. Allen, has prepared a small meal for us as a kind of celebration though I gave her precious little time to prepare. After the meal we will have a little time to discuss the possible terms to settle upon a husband for Miss Lydia."

Accordingly they all traveled to Darcy House on Grosvenor Square, the only difference being that Elizabeth and Georgiana traded places in their carriages so that the newlyweds had a few minutes of privacy. It was not nearly enough time to please them, however, as they arrived at Elizabeth's new home quite swiftly. "In other circumstances, Mrs. Darcy, I would like to have the staff assembled to meet you, but it was not to be," Darcy told her. "Due to my unexpected arrival last night not all the staff is on hand at this time, as their services are not all needed when we are not in town. They will arrive tomorrow. But I can introduce you to Mrs. Allen at least."

Elizabeth, with her head and heart so full, barely took in her luxurious surroundings as she entered the townhouse with her new husband and made her first approach into her new life. She had a quick impression of a stout, middle-aged woman with an air of sonsy, keen-eyed capability, and knew that the wedding meal was in good hands. Whether the meal was served expertly or with many errors she did not care. Her only thought was for Darcy; and she could scarcely believe that the anxiety, the separation, the difficulties were behind her and she was Mrs. Darcy at last. She stayed as close to her new husband as possible, enjoying occasional whispered endearments in her ear, trusting him to keep her from making any accidental errors in her new role.

When the meal was finished Georgiana volunteered to show her and Mrs. Gardiner around the house, starting at the kitchens and working their way up the three flights to the servant's quarters on the top floor. The furnishings here were not as extensive as at Pemberley, for the house was of course much smaller, but their quality was just as fine. When they came to the mistress's chambers Elizabeth saw that Mrs. Allen was busily unpacking her dresses, shaking them out briefly and arranging them neatly in a wardrobe. "I trust your room is acceptable, Mrs. Darcy? We did as much as we could to make it ready in such a short time; it has been airing since last night. It shall be more thoroughly cleaned as soon as possible, of course; and Mr. Darcy said that you are to redecorate as you wish."

"I cannot imagine wanting to change a thing," Elizabeth said, meaning it sincerely; for the room was in a rose blush pattern with oak paneling, and large windows overlooked the small yard at the back of the house. There was no sitting room here although a writing desk graced one corner. A door in the left hand corner of the room connected, she knew, to her husband's room. After a short inspection they returned to the first floor, where the men were just leaving the study with the air of having accomplished a great deal.

"We shall meet again tomorrow at noon, then?" the colonel was asking. "By then I should have several possible candidates in mind and we can take our time discussing each one."

"My agents have so far not found any sign of Wickham," Darcy said, seeming not too troubled by it. "I am sending them out again and perhaps they may have news for us when next we meet."

"I will now leave my niece in your capable hands," Mrs. Gardiner told him, with a smile directed towards Elizabeth. "I look forward to seeing you both again tomorrow." Georgiana embraced Elizabeth once more, welcoming her as a sister; and then went to the waiting carriage, for it had already been determined that she would spend this night with the Gardiners. Mrs. Gardiner whispered a few words of motherly advice and encouragement in Elizabeth's ear, Mr. Gardiner congratulated her once again, and then they were gone.

Darcy pulled Elizabeth close to him, taking her hands in his and kissing each one in turn. "My dearest Elizabeth, my wife," he said, "Do you think you can live without the assistance of the servants for one day? I wish to have you all to myself for a little while now."

Elizabeth smiled at him. "I believe you said your mission now was to advertise our marriage to as many people as possible."

He kissed her more directly this time. "And so it is. I will accomplish both goals at the same time, if you would care to observe."

Releasing her, he rang the bell for Mrs. Allen, smiling at Elizabeth as he did so. When Mrs. Allen appeared he handed her a small purse of coins. "Mrs. Allen, has the food from breakfast been laid out on the sideboard as I requested?"

"It has indeed, sir; and all other preparations have been carried out just as you requested."

"Very well then, I have one final duty for you. I wish for you to take the coins in that purse and disburse them among the servants now present for them to use to celebrate our wedding in whatever way they desire. They may take a meal somewhere, buy a new suit of clothes, or do exactly what pleases them the most with it. I only request that they drink to the health of Mr. and Mrs. Fitzwilliam Darcy at some point this evening to as many people as possible. I am the most fortunate man in the world, and I wish that all may know it."

Mrs. Allen glanced inside the bag briefly. "You are very generous, sir. It shall be done as you desire."

"Then you may stop whatever you are doing now and distribute the coins at once. All of you are to consider yourselves at liberty immediately for the rest of the day; we will not require your services at all before ten o'clock tomorrow morning."

"Ten o'clock, sir?"

"And not a moment before."

Darcy's intent was so clear, and his means of carrying it out was so pleasing to all, that in a very few minutes the servants were all making a speedy exit. Mrs. Allen waited until all others had quit the house and then notified him that she was leaving. Darcy and Elizabeth stood together in his study, listening as her footsteps made their way to the front door. The footsteps paused on the threshold; the door opened and closed; the footsteps echoed briefly on the stone steps. She was gone, and Mr. and Mrs. Darcy found themselves alone for the first time.

CHAPTER TWENTY-FOUR

There is no point in saying how thoroughly happy Elizabeth and Darcy were when they awoke to their first day as a married couple, for there are no words adequate to convey their feelings upon that event. To say that they were deliriously happy is to understate their joy; to say that they were content leaves too much unsaid; and if they were to say they were elated they might just as well state that rain in its normal state is generally wet. In short, the readers must use their imaginations and perhaps their own past experiences in a similar situation, to have any idea of the state of mind enjoyed by the Darcys on the morning after their wedding.

But reality must intrude even into the sort of bliss as the type the Darcys now enjoyed, and it intruded first in the form of Mr. Bennet.

Mr. Bennet was desperate for news of Lydia, and he had no idea that she had been found and secured as of yet. Indeed, no letter from Jane had found him for over a week. He had been in Brighton trying to determine if she were hidden there; and now he made his way to London, knowing that Mr. Gardiner was due back any day, and hoping to enlist his help since his own search had been so fruitless. Rising with the early summer sun, he rode hard and fast and stood upon the Gardiner's doorstep at fifteen minutes before eight. In answer to his rapping a servant opened the door and informed him indignantly that the family was still in bed.

"I am Mr. Bennet, and I need to see Mr. Gardiner immediately, or else Miss Bennet."

The servant was confused. "You wish to see Miss Bennet? Which Miss Bennet, sir?"

"I mean Miss Elizabeth, of course. She was traveling with the Gardiners," he answered impatiently. "If I cannot see the Gardiners, I will see her."

"She is at Darcy House, of course," the servant answered with some surprise.

"Darcy House! Where may that be?"

The servant gave him the address and Mr. Bennet left without another word.

The clock showed eight when Mr. Bennet first rapped loudly upon the door of Darcy House; an hour entirely too early for polite social calls, but more than adequate for the arrival of an irate father demanding answers as to the whereabouts of his daughter.

The Darcys were sitting comfortably together in the dining room, breakfasting upon foods left by Mrs. Allen on the sideboard and feeling very domestic. It was their first meal since their late wedding breakfast the day before and they were eating freely, with no fear of being interrupted by any servants, for the servants were not expected to return for another two hours. Both were dressed, but with no valet or maid present to help them, neither could be considered entirely ready to receive their first visitor. Darcy wore a shirtwaist and trousers, but his feet wore only stockings since he could not put on his boots without his valet's assistance. His jacket and cravat were, of course, entirely absent. Elizabeth was slightly more presentable in a simple morning dress, but her hair hung untidily over her shoulders instead of being carefully arranged.

When the loud rap on the door came, Elizabeth looked at her husband. "I believe somebody wants us, my love."

"At this hour? It is too early for social calls. It is probably just a delivery for the kitchens."

"Do you not think we should answer it?"

"I am of the opinion that we should totally ignore it," Darcy answered firmly, giving his wife one or two convincing reasons why he would rather disregard any external demands on his attention.

"But they are rapping again and it sounds quite insistent. I do not think it sounds like a delivery."

Darcy muttered something indistinct and continued reasoning with his wife. The rapping came again, even more loudly now. Elizabeth tried again.

"My dearest, that rapping is from the front door, not the kitchen. It is not a delivery."

Darcy sighed and stood. "Very well, I shall answer it." He moved towards the entry.

"You have my permission to slam the door in their face if it is anything less than a French invasion," Elizabeth called after him playfully.

Mr. Bennet, listening hard upon the doorway, thought he heard a feminine voice inside just before the door opened and showed Darcy's surprised face.

"Mr. Bennet!" exclaimed Darcy.

"Mr. Darcy!" Mr. Bennet responded, almost as surprised,

especially on seeing his unkempt state. "Why have you answered the door and not your servants?"

"They are not here," Darcy answered automatically without considering the effect of his words.

"Papa?" Elizabeth asked in disbelief as she showed her head behind Darcy.

"Elizabeth! What the devil are you doing here?"

"Father!" Elizabeth answered, aghast. "That was most inappropriate!"

"You are most inappropriate, Lizzy, to be in this state! You are engaged!"

"Papa, we are not engaged!" Elizabeth began, but Darcy cut her off hastily.

"We are married, sir. We married yesterday. Elizabeth is my wife."

Mr. Bennet stared at them with an open mouth for a second. "Married? How is it you are married?"

"In the usual way, Papa," Elizabeth began, starting to see the humor of the situation, but Darcy answered again.

"We married in church yesterday morning, with the Gardiners and my sister present. All is well, sir; you need have no fear."

Mr. Bennet glared at him for a moment. "Had it been otherwise I would have skewered you to the wall, young man. As it is I am clearly behind the times. Let me in and tell me what has happened since we last met."

With alacrity they bade him enter and offered him a share of the food from the sideboard, but he refused. "I have no appetite, and have had none since Lydia disappeared. And now you tell me that my Lizzy is mine no longer. I congratulate you; but I shall never forgive you, Darcy, for giving me the scare of my life. Elizabeth," he turned to address her, "how could you have consented to be married so quickly, without any of your family present?"

She felt all the disappointment conveyed in his tone and replied apologetically. "It was absolutely necessary, Papa, once we discovered Lydia here."

"Lydia is here?" he asked in surprise.

"She is at the Gardiner's, at least as far as we know," Elizabeth answered, and with Darcy's assistance she told her father of Wickham's treachery, their departure from Pemberley, Lydia's discovery, and of their marriage in its immediate aftermath. Mr.

Bennet absorbed the succession of astonishing news with his usual practicality.

"And so you have arranged for it all, Darcy. You have engineered the marriage of my least deserving daughter, taken my most deserving daughter away from me, protected both their reputations and gained yourself a wife all in the same day. You are something of a miracle worker, I think. It is a most effective solution."

"Papa, in your study at Longbourn, did you not tell Aunt Gardiner that she was observing something of a miracle in front of her?"

"Had you told me on that day that you would be married just a month later I would not have believed you. Had you told me last autumn after your first meeting that you might develop any interest in each other I would have called you a fool. It seems the joke is on me."

"I hope you have no objection, sir?"

"None at all! It has saved me a world of trouble and economy. I am sure he will insist on bearing the entire cost of purchasing Lydia's husband. If it were your uncle's doing I must and would pay him; but I shall offer to make the match, Darcy here will rant and rave about his love for you, and there will be an end to the matter."

"I will hear of nothing less, sir," said Darcy emphatically. "Elizabeth's family is now my family and it is only appropriate that I provide for them."

"See, Elizabeth? These violent young lovers carry everything their own way, and all I can do is absorb their generosity. But you must have missed having your family with you at such a time. I am sure you and Jane would not have chosen to be separated on your wedding day."

"I did miss Jane, and you, very much. But it was done for the best. I only wonder what people will say when they realize that none of my family was present for the event. It may occasion some talk."

"Oh, I doubt that most sincerely. Nobody who knows your mother will wonder at Darcy choosing to marry you out of her hearing; and I am the fortunate beneficiary, for I do find weddings quite tedious."

"No, Papa, I am the beneficiary, as I have said before. I could not imagine finding another such splendid man anywhere, one who is so generous and kind, so perfectly suited to me in every way."

"No," Darcy answered, "I am the one who benefits the most from our relationship, for you are liveliness, generosity, and kindliness personified, and your personality merely brings out those traits in me."

"Enough!" said Mr. Bennet, moving away from them both. "Do you have any port, Darcy? I believe that I shall need a full portion of it today. Lovers are of all things most tiresome."

CHAPTER TWENTY-FIVE

With the return of the servants a short while later Darcy and Elizabeth were able to restore their appearances to something more appropriate, and Mrs. Allen assembled the staff to be introduced to their new mistress. The household began to fall back into its normal daily routine, while Colonel Fitzwilliam and Mr. Gardiner arrived and met with the other gentlemen in the study. With the greatest of curiosity Elizabeth made her excuses to Mrs. Allen and joined them.

"I have found a gentleman who is eminently suitable to be Miss Lydia's husband," the colonel started off by saying. "He is Jonathon Fret. He is thirty years old, an officer I served with several years ago, and recently came into an inheritance of landed property due to the death of his older brother. He will resign his commission soon in order to take up this new responsibility. After him there are no heirs for his estate and so he must marry, but the property brought with it several encumbrances and little else."

"So he needs a wife but he is too poor to attract a suitable bride at this point?" Mr. Bennet asked. "He seems ideal for our Lydia, though I am sure she would prefer the life of an officer's wife. Where is this estate of his?"

"In Newcastle."

"She will be quite out of the way there," Mr. Bennet began reflectively, but a messenger entered just then and gave Darcy a note. Darcy paid for it, sent the messenger on his way, and then read the message briefly.

"Wickham has been located," he announced. "He has been arrested for his debts and placed in prison. He is in the Clink."

Exclamations of dismay rose all around. "I care nothing for Wickham," the colonel said, "but I would not send a dog to that place. What are his debts?"

"They are thought to be several hundred pounds, perhaps a little more," Darcy answered. "I could easily pay them off and have him released to me if he agrees to marry Lydia. What is the price for this Mr. Fret?"

"About five thousand pounds, I think, a mere trifle. Though he would like more he is too wise to ask for it."

Elizabeth blanched at the sums involved but Darcy's expression did not change. "Besides discharging Wickham's debts there is the little matter of his desertion of the militia. How could that be settled, Edward? Would we have to pay an additional fine?"

"I think not. There is a great deal of discretion used in punishments for desertion. A word from me in the right ear would probably result in his being flogged in the square, and then he would be all yours, or rather, Miss Lydia's."

"If she would have him!" Mr. Gardiner scoffed, and the others laughed.

"My dear," Elizabeth spoke to her husband, "I would not have Lydia shackled to such a man for the rest of her life. She is young and stupid, but she does not deserve such a fate as Wickham, who has shown a shocking ability for cruelty. Married to a decent man her character may yet improve, but with Wickham she will have little chance of change."

"Elizabeth, you do not know what you ask," her father answered. "Darcy is more generous than I could have imagined to even be considering five thousand pounds for your sister's happiness. It is a sum I could not hope to repay without ending up in prison next to Wickham myself. It is too much. A good flogging will do wonders for Wickham's character, I am sure, and Lydia for once will have to live with the consequences of her own actions."

"What do you say, cousin?" the colonel addressed Darcy. "I begin to agree with Mr. Bennet. Wickham deserves a good flogging and more, and we could settle him in some out of the way place with a steady income. It would be nothing to keep a regular eye on him and make him aware of the consequences he would face for mistreating his wife."

Darcy looked around at all of them, his gaze ending on his wife and softening as he saw the imploring expression there.

"Five thousand pounds is not too much to ask for my wife's happiness, and I know she could never be happy while worrying for her sister," he said finally. "Edward, please make the deal with Fret. But I cannot leave Wickham in prison either. It is no place for the son of my father's steward, and I believe my father would be most pleased if he were to have a chance at a new life. You say a word in the right ear would get him flogged. Would it also get him transported?"

"If that is your desire, I can have him on the next boat to the Americas."

Darcy looked at Mr. Bennet, then at his wife, and nodded to his cousin. "Please see to it."

"I shall see to the flogging myself first, personally." He left eagerly.

"And I shall be on my way now as well, for somebody has to tell Lydia the fate that is about to befall her," Mr. Bennet told the rest of the group. "It might as well be me; it is likely to be the only significant role I will play in this wedding. Brother, I would return with you to Gracechurch Street if I could. I want to get this over with quickly, as I believe Lydia is not likely to take this news well. As much as she has run after men for the past year, though, I should hope she would express a little gratitude at having a husband practically thrown at her head."

"You will be disappointed if you hope too much for that," Mr. Gardiner assured him, as they made their farewells and then departed.

When they had gone Elizabeth moved to her husband's side. "I can never thank you enough for your kindness to my poor sister. Were it known to the rest of my family I would not have just my own thanks to convey."

"I did not do it for them. As much as I respect them, I believe I thought only of you."

"Mr. Darcy, I believe that I have at last discovered a fault in you!"

"You discovered my faults many months ago, Mrs. Darcy. I would like to think that I have made some small start at correcting them, and that I have not added any to the list."

"I found this one some time ago but I have been waiting to mention it. You do not accept thanks gracefully! All you have to do is say 'I thank you for the favor of your compliment,' as most fashionable men do."

"Oh, but if you remember, Mrs. Darcy, when we were in your father's garden you said that you would find as many faults as you could with me so that I could find ways to atone for them with you."

"And I told you that although I might invent some rather outrageous requests by and by, for now you would simply have to do the best you could."

"I believe that I have now determined an excellent way for me to make up this latest fault to you," said Darcy, giving her one or two convincing tokens of his affection.

174

"Mr. Darcy! You are quite incorrigible!"

"Excellent," he said, "another fault. I must atone for that one as well."

With that Darcy closed the door of his study, and the servants did not see fit to disturb them for some time.

CHAPTER TWENTY-SIX

The next day brought two surprising visitors to Darcy House, one welcome and the other perhaps less so. Mr. Jonathon Fret arrived at precisely ten o'clock accompanied by Colonel Fitzwilliam. Fret was a distinguished looking man, not overly tall but with piercing eyes that took in every detail of the world around him and weighed it all in the balance. His manners seemed to indicate that if anything was found lacking in his inspection, it would be speedily corrected after merely one request to the person responsible, and with no delays expected. But his smile was kind and open, and Elizabeth found that she could only regard him with respect, not fear.

"I am told you are the man I must thank for my immediate good fortune, if Miss Lydia accepts my suit," he said, addressing Darcy, "and thus, making your acquaintance before meeting Miss Lydia is the least I could do."

"Your consideration is appreciated. Treat Lydia well and we will have no complaints."

"You may rest assured on that point. I take my responsibilities seriously." He now addressed Elizabeth. "Mrs. Darcy, if you could be so kind as to give me advice on how to approach Miss Lydia in order to make her more amenable to my suit, I would be appreciative."

"You see he is a military man," the colonel said. "No nonsense, right to the point; determine your objective and what you must do to take it."

"Really, advice in this matter escapes me," Elizabeth answered. "Were you any other man I would simply say to flatter her with what she wants to hear, but I sense that you are not the kind of man to offer empty words. Perhaps you should simply ask for her hand and let my father deal with her acceptance."

"Perhaps, but I have been made to understand that she is rather strong willed; and letting her believe that she has a choice in the matter may lead to an easier acceptance. Seeming to give your opponent room to maneuver is sometimes a very strategic move."

"And is my sister to be your opponent, sir?"

"I would say she is more of a partner in a complicated peace negotiation."

Elizabeth had to smile. "I believe you might do very well for my sister, Mr. Fret. I wish you all success in your negotiations."

"I thank you, madam."

When he had gone, Elizabeth looked at Darcy. "I cannot imagine how their marriage will work out, if they do wed. He seems every bit as determined in his ways as she is in hers. He could be either the best or the worst possible match for her, but I cannot help liking him for himself."

"If two people of decided opinions, such as us, can have a happy marriage, then I must believe that they may defy our worst expectations."

Late in the afternoon Elizabeth was sitting at the pianoforte, playing what was by now Darcy's favorite piece of music, when Mrs. Allen informed her that she had a female caller waiting in the parlor. "Did she give her name?" Elizabeth asked.

"She expressly stated that I was not to announce her, but I would be remiss in my duty if I did not warn you that it is Mr. Darcy's aunt, Lady Catherine."

"Lady Catherine!" Elizabeth said in surprise. "Whatever could she want here?"

"I take it you are already acquainted?"

"More than I would like, perhaps. Yet I will see her." Elizabeth knew that she must take on Lady Catherine alone; Darcy was meeting with his solicitor.

She entered the parlor and greeted her visitor cautiously, giving her the minimum courtesy required and requesting that Mrs. Allen have tea served for her noble guest. Mrs. Allen left the room and Lady Catherine addressed her, "You can have no doubt as to the purpose of my visit today, Mrs. Darcy."

"I may have various guesses, but I prefer not to use my imagination in cases such as this."

"I have come to offer my congratulations to you upon your marriage to my nephew."

"You can imagine my surprise, Lady Catherine, to receive such congratulations from you; but I thank you. How were you informed?"

"How was I informed? Darcy has made certain that all of society is informed. I read the announcement in the paper this morning, but word first came to my ears from several of my servants last night who heard it from some of the servants here. Darcy has no shame, it seems. It would appear that he is proud of his marriage."

"Would you rather have him ashamed, my lady?"

"I will be frank, Mrs. Darcy. You are not the one he should have married. That honor should have gone to my daughter. But you are married now and in the interest of avoiding further scandal it is best that we both make the best of it. You will hear no public disparagement from me."

"Further scandal, my lady?"

Lady Catherine flushed. "The scandal has been averted, thanks to Darcy's actions and my own. I assume your quick marriage was an effort to cut the rumors off before they had a chance to circulate widely, and I have done all in my power to eliminate them as well by dealing with Caroline Bingley. Until she makes the proper efforts to correct her slanderous comments to me she will not be welcome at any social function in the city. A word from me is enough to close the doors to any salon, as she will soon discover."

"But I thought you believed her charges!"

"I may have temporarily allowed my concern for my nephew to overcome my logical thought; but after speaking with Darcy at Pemberley, I came to realize how low Miss Bingley's state is in comparison to his, how inappropriate it was for her to dare to lay such charges at his door. Her father was in trade! She has forgotten her station, but she shall be made to feel it again."

Elizabeth paused to take in this remarkable change and Lady Catherine continued, "You may also thank Mr. Collins for our present understanding. He it was who reminded me that you are the daughter of a gentleman, and so I should not take the word of that woman over yours. Collins may have been put up to it by his wife, I think, but the point still stands. Though you are not equal to Darcy, you are at least superior to Caroline Bingley."

Lady Catherine then made inquiries as to Georgiana. "Miss Darcy is spending the day with Colonel Fitzwilliam, but I expect they will return shortly," Elizabeth told her.

"She is due to enter society next summer, as you probably know; and for that she will need a sponsor. As her sister that duty will probably fall to you. I expect it will be a rather overwhelming task for one of your background. When the time comes you will consult with me, and I shall assist you as she makes her debut. You will give me this honor, Mrs. Darcy; I absolutely insist upon it."

Elizabeth silently agreed that helping Georgiana make an

entrance into the Ton, where she herself had never been introduced, would probably necessitate her requesting someone's assistance; and since Lady Catherine was so determined to be useful she might as well take advantage of the opportunity. "Thank you, Lady Catherine. You are very gracious." They sat together for several more minutes before Lady Catherine took her leave.

"She wishes to make an advantageous marriage for Georgiana now that Darcy has made his choice," Elizabeth thought to herself, "and she knows that unless she mends fences with me, she will have no access to Georgiana at all. Well, it will certainly work to Georgiana's advantage to have such a sponsor; and if I have to put up with a few private disparagements now and then, I will gladly suffer them for her sake. But I almost begin to feel sorry for Caroline Bingley!"

Elizabeth and Darcy now began to make plans for a visit to Longbourn. "I should like to notify my mother of our marriage in person before she hears of it from other sources. It is certain to be a great surprise to all!"

"Yes, and it should be done soon in order to overcome talk of Lydia. Would you like to go there tomorrow?"

"Tomorrow is probably the day the announcements will be made in the paper there, is it not?"

"I believe so, according to what your uncle told me."

"Then, as enjoyable as it may be to shock them, we should probably plan to arrive before they have a chance to see the paper."

"Will your mother's nerves be able to withstand what you are about to do to them?"

"I am not certain whether her approval of your income will overcome her pointed dislike; but I can promise that whatever her reaction is, it will be highly entertaining."

CHAPTER TWENTY-SEVEN

Mrs. Bennet arose at her customary time the next day, which was generally well after the other ladies of the neighborhood had risen, and prepared for another day of delighted anguish over the disappearance of her dear Lydia. Not that she believed Lydia had run off; Lydia was too good a girl to do such a thing, when she had been raised so carefully. No, she knew beyond a doubt that Lydia had been kidnapped and that the kidnappers would shortly return to murder them all in their beds.

She was mildly disappointed upon realizing that nothing of the sort had happened overnight, but since there was nothing standing in the way of being the center of attention, she prepared to recite her daily litany of anxieties. Her routine was stopped before it had fairly begun, however, by the excited arrival of her sister Phillips, who had managed to make her presence known to Hill and then to storm Mrs. Bennet's bed chamber.

"You must stop such lies, dear Fannie; you must stop such lies at once! The paper is not what it used to be if it is allowed to print such silly jokes as if they were the truth!"

"What can have happened now, Sophia? What could the paper have done that is so very bad, when you know well that they refuse to print that Lydia has been kidnapped!"

"The paper says nothing of Lydia, dear sister--it speaks of Elizabeth and Mr. Darcy!"

"Mr. Darcy! What can it have to say of Mr. Darcy that is not true? Pray do not tease me, sister; for my heart is in palpitations already, thinking of what might happen to my dear girl! Indeed, what has undoubtedly already happened!"

Jane appeared behind her aunt Phillips with an expression that matched equal parts of surprise and delight. "Mama, it appears from the announcements in today's paper that Elizabeth has married Mr. Darcy!"

"Oh, and now you are tormenting me too! Is it not enough for you that I am on my deathbed with anxiety over your dear sister? And that your father has abandoned me; that he is running all over England instead of supporting me as he ought? Is there nobody who can have compassion on my poor nerves?"

Jane felt it was absolutely necessary to speak. "Indeed, I believe that it is true, Mama; for I had a letter from Elizabeth yesterday, and she said that she had accepted a proposal of marriage from Mr. Darcy!"

If she had detonated a small explosive in the house the effect could not have been much more dramatic than making this announcement. Mrs. Bennet, about to gasp out another complaint, stared at her with rounded eyes and a mouth left hanging open. Mrs. Phillips likewise stared; and Hill, in the process of pouring out a restorative for her mistress, left her hand in mid-air, the liquid inside pouring out, while she also stared at Jane.

"My dear girl!" Mrs. Bennet cried when she had regained her powers of speech. "Why did you not tell me this yesterday? Why would you not tell me this at once?"

"Forgive me, Mama, but you had said not to disturb you until we had news of Lydia." Mrs. Phillips finally remembered to close her mouth, and Hill remembered her hand and returned the bottle of restorative to vertical just in time to avoid disaster.

"Oh! Hang Lydia, she has nothing to do with this!" Mrs. Bennet exclaimed just as Kitty came rushing into her room.

"Mama, there is a carriage in front of the house with the Darcy arms on it, and Elizabeth has stepped out of it along with Mr. Darcy! What does it mean, Mama?"

Mrs. Bennet immediately got out of bed and rushed to the window in order to verify the remarkable event for herself. What she saw there made her immediately turn back to Hill and say, "Hill! Make me presentable at once! I must find my dressing gown and my morning dress, and you must help me with my hair this very instant! Somebody find my sprigged muslin, and somebody send Mary to the butcher's for a venison haunch!"

Jane and Elizabeth greeted each other with exclamations of utmost joy and delight, the one apologizing for such a hasty step, taken with no announcement to the family; and the other insisting that there was no reason for such apologies. "I know very well that you must have decided on this step for a good cause, Elizabeth. Nothing else would have induced you to such precipitous action. You can tell me what it is when we are at leisure."

"Gladly, Jane; but first let me introduce you to my husband, now your brother. We married just three days ago in town. And I have the best of news to give you of Lydia as well!"

In the general commotion of arrival and exclamations of surprise, and obsequious greetings from Mrs. Bennet to Darcy, they made their way indoors. Darcy and Elizabeth were greeted by all the members of the family and by Hill as well; while Mrs. Bennet endeavored to make up to Darcy now for all her slights of the past by asking what soup he favored with dinner, and if he entirely approved of the curtains in the drawing room.

"I have news of Lydia," Elizabeth announced as soon as she was able to be heard, preparing to recite what she and her father had rehearsed ahead of time. "Lydia was waiting in Uncle Gardiner's house in town when we arrived there a little early. She is safe, and she is now being courted by a friend of Mr. Darcy's. I expect we will hear soon about their marriage!"

"Oh, I am so glad that she is safe and soon to be married," Mrs. Bennet said, "for although she was very naughty for running away, I am sure it was not her fault. Depend upon it, she would never have run away if her father had allowed her to go to Brighton, as I pressed him many times! But I was overruled as I always am."

"I cannot entirely approve of the action of marrying without proper notice to our father," said Mary gravely, "but if you had our uncle's consent that was very nearly the same thing, and so I think I can give you my congratulations. Perhaps it will turn out all right in the end after all."

"Notice! Consent!" exclaimed her mother. "If Mr. Darcy wanted to be married immediately you may be sure we would have had no opposition, we could have said nothing against it. Elizabeth is to be praised for obeying my wishes for once!" Lydia was forgotten; Jane was set aside; Elizabeth was now beyond a doubt her favorite daughter, and she had always known that Elizabeth would make a most eligible match, for she was of all her daughters most beautiful. Darcy and Elizabeth bore with the effusiveness well enough until the arrival of Bingley gave them an opportunity to walk in the garden with him and Jane.

Much conversation was held between the four while they walked there, not the least of which concerned the changes in the lives of two of the group since the last time they had been together. Elizabeth and Darcy now had leisure to explain the real circumstances of Lydia's situation in London, and the threats from Lady Catherine, which had been the means of uniting them so quickly.

"Elizabeth, I cannot imagine how you felt, knowing the danger we were all in and knowing that your sudden marriage was the best way out of it. It was what you wanted, I know, but it was upon you so suddenly! How did you have the courage to do it?"

"I did not need courage, Jane; simply a few minutes to adjust to the changed circumstances."

"But it was so different than what you had planned and from what I think you might have hoped for."

Elizabeth exchanged a smile of remembrance with Darcy. "In some ways I had already faced that thought, Jane, when I knew that I loved William but did not like how everyone was pushing me towards him. Your letter convinced me that the present moment is the best moment for seizing happiness, and that I should not let external circumstances separate us unnecessarily. My decision to accept his hand was simply a prelude to the decision to marry quickly. Other than not having you there, I have no regrets."

"And what of Lydia's husband?" Jane asked. "Do you truly think he will be able to control her wild spirits?"

"If he cannot do it, I do not know who can," Elizabeth answered, and Darcy agreed with her. "She will be on a small estate in Newcastle, far from everyone she knows and forced to depend upon him; and he is a most determined man. I hope it will work out well; but if not, then Mr. Fret may be forced to send her to the Americas as well!"

"What of your marriage?" Darcy addressed Bingley. "Have you set a date yet? I can highly recommend the married state; you really ought to try it as soon as possible."

"Darcy! You are teasing me! Marriage has already changed you," Bingley said in astonishment. "Do not be so cruel as to torment me with visions of what cannot happen immediately, for I will not push my angel before she is ready."

"Jane, you really ought to take your own advice," Elizabeth advised her sister with a smile.

"I will not be pushed into a hasty marriage," Jane proclaimed with unusual spirit. Bingley attempted to soothe her.

"It is all right, my love; I will not pressure you."

"I absolutely will not be married before this coming s'ennight!"

Bingley stopped and turned, grasping both Jane's hands in his own. "Jane! Do you mean to say that you will marry me next week?"

"If that is the earliest you can arrange it then I suppose I shall have to be patient," Jane responded with a sweet smile at her intended, and Darcy and Elizabeth took the opportunity to discreetly disappear behind a hedge.

Bingley continued to stare at his fiancée in shock, still grasping her hands. "There is really no reason to wait, my love," Jane told him. "I had hoped to stand up with Lizzy, but since she is now married I see no reason to delay. My mother may wish to make a trip to town for the proper wedding clothes but that may be accomplished at any time, and there is no time like the present. I trust this is not against your wishes?"

Bingley began to laugh. "There is nothing that could be more in accordance with my wishes, unless we were to be married already! My sweetest angel, I cannot wait to take you as my own!"

CHAPTER TWENTY-EIGHT

Many comings and goings took place over the next week between Meryton and town. Georgiana arrived at Netherfield in time for Bingley's wedding, followed closely by the Gardiners, who had left Lydia under the careful supervision of Mrs. Annesley and several dedicated servants. Mr. Bennet refused his wife's request to travel to London with Jane in order to shop for wedding clothes. There was hardly time to have wedding clothes made before the ceremony, he told his wife by correspondence, and Jane had certainly had enough time already to arrange for whatever clothing she wanted. His real purpose, however, was to keep Mrs. Bennet separated from Lydia and not have opportunity to encourage her in her wildness, for Lydia was proving a challenge to the steady attentions of Mr. Fret. On the day before the wedding Mr. Bennet arrived to perform his duties as father of the bride.

"How goes Mr. Fret's courtship?" Elizabeth asked her father when they had greeted each other and had a chance to speak privately.

"Very frustratingly," Mr. Bennet replied, shaking his head. "Despite her earlier words, she is beginning to say that if she cannot have Wickham then she will have no one, and does not believe me when I say that he is gone."

"And he is well and truly gone? We shall not be troubled with him again?"

"I think not. I saw him flogged myself day before yesterday, and he could barely walk as they took him to his ship. He set sail hours later; unless he is a remarkable swimmer, we are not likely to see him in England after this."

"Shall you not show Lydia the letter Wickham sent to Mr. Darcy as proof of his perfidy?"

"I have offered to let her read it but she refuses to do so. As far as she is concerned, Wickham will come back for her and rescue her from marriage to such a 'disgusting old man' as Fret, as she says. I must say, his patience is extraordinary. It was helped along, I think, when I told him that Lydia's expected settlement of one hundred pounds per annum will be his upon their marriage. Although he did not ask for it, every little bit helps; and I do feel the need to support her in some way. I do not know whether to be more ashamed of her behavior or more disappointed in him, that he would take such a wife for so little money."

"It is not a small sum, Papa; five thousand pounds plus one hundred per annum is considerable."

"Perhaps, but I would not take Lydia for twice the amount! I do love a thrifty son-in-law almost as much as a rich one. You might have done much worse in picking a husband, Lizzy. We are all greatly indebted to your Mr. Darcy."

Elizabeth reminded her father good-naturedly of his confusion upon finding her at Darcy House the day after her wedding. "Papa, when you saw me there you said my presence was most inappropriate because I was engaged. But when we left you in Hertfordshire you knew that not to be the case. We had only begun to court. What did you mean by it?"

"Lizzy, did you really have any doubt what would happen when you went to Pemberley? I can assure you that I did not." Elizabeth wanted to argue the point, but in light of her rapid courtship and marriage thought it best not to say a word.

Happy for all her maternal feelings was the day upon which Mrs. Bennet witnessed the marriage of her eldest daughter, which had been her chief object since Jane had entered society at the age of sixteen. Only liberal applications of smelling salts kept her conscious at various points of the ceremony, as she anticipated the pin-money, and jewels, and the carriages that would now be at the disposal of both of her daughters. Longbourn, she knew, was nothing to the grandeur of Netherfield or especially of Pemberley; and she began to calculate with great interest the number of years Mr. Bennet might reasonably be expected to live, and how soon she might have to find a home with one of her daughters.

Jane and Bingley left directly after the ceremony, heading out on a tour of the continent as a wedding trip, and telling the Darcys and Bennets that they were free to use Netherfield as much as they desired in their absence. The Bennets took full opportunity of this generosity; but the Darcys returned to town two days after the Bingleys left so that Elizabeth could help convince Lydia of the necessity of accepting Mr. Fret's gracious offer.

She felt that her own efforts yielded but little in this regard. Lydia pouted and Fret remained immoveable. Lydia insulted Fret and he ignored her; and when she insisted she would marry none but Wickham, Fret informed her that, at her father's insistence, the banns had already been read. The die had already been cast, he said, and she would marry Fret or marry nobody at all; but he would allow her to choose any one of several dates at the end of three weeks in order to carry out the ceremony. This Lydia flatly refused to do until her father informed her that if she did not marry Fret, she would be free to live as she wished in the care of her cousin Collins. An active imagination did the trick, and Lydia agreed sullenly to the marriage her father wished. Upon the completion of three weeks, Lydia met her betrothed at the altar, exchanged the required words, and they were united in holy if not happy matrimony. After a cursory visit to Longbourn she left for the north with her new husband.

The day following Lydia's wedding, Elizabeth sat with Georgiana in the parlor at Darcy House when her husband entered the room looking remarkably pleased with himself.

"You look entirely too satisfied this morning, my love," Elizabeth said to him. "Have you been able to find rich husbands for either of my remaining sisters, or is there another miracle you have suddenly worked?"

"I will let you be the judge; but I will own that I have been pursuing one of your requests for some time, and now I can claim some success."

"A request of mine? I have made no requests, for I have you and Georgiana and need nothing else."

"But you did make a request of me, at Longbourn; or I should say two requests, which I am now quite happy to fulfill."

Elizabeth looked at him questioningly and he continued. "Your first request, if you recall, was to see the court of St. James. Perhaps you have forgotten that as my wife you are the niece of the Earl of Matlock, and as such you shall be presented to the court. Indeed, that step will be necessary if you are to sponsor Georgiana in her first season."

Elizabeth smiled in delight. "How Mama will gloat! To think that one of her daughters will be presented to royalty! Your attentions are sometimes too generous, my dear, but I shall do my best to endure this trial."

"Your second request is a bit more unusual, but it is still possible for me to fulfill."

"To have a maharajah appear in my parlor? I said it in jest, but I shall be even more impressed with you than I already am if you can truly cause such a thing to occur."

"Then prepare to be impressed. You and I have not spoken of a wedding trip, but I have been busily preparing one while you were dealing with your sister. Next Tuesday you and I will board the H.M.S. Alma and travel to India for our wedding tour, where we will take a house for two months; and where there will undoubtedly be maharajahs in abundance."

Elizabeth gasped in astonishment; then seeing that Darcy was in earnest she rose and accepted his warm embrace. "You do too much, my dear. This is not necessary."

"Indeed it is, for I am determined to grant any wish you might have."

"Then my only remaining wish is that you may always be assured of my affections for you."

The Darcys returned from their trip to India one month after the Bingley's return from their wedding tour of the continent; and when the two sisters saw each other again there was much to discuss, from the experiences, sights and sounds of their respective trips, to the prospects of impending motherhood for each one. Five months later Jane was able to present her husband with little Sophia, and just two weeks later young Fitzwilliam became the new heir to Pemberley.

The new grandchildren were able to draw Mr. and Mrs. Bennet from their home more often than anything else would have, and they delighted in arriving unexpectedly at both estates.

Miss Bingley did not return to society for quite some time after feeling the wrath of Lady Catherine descend upon her. Bingley, upon hearing of her malicious actions towards the Darcys, had seriously contemplated reducing her allowance or removing her to a cousin's estate in a distant county. But his efforts at curbing her tendencies were unnecessary. After being refused a voucher to Almack's and not given entrance to any salon of note for an entire season, she began to reconsider the wisdom of her actions toward all three of the Darcys. Further reflection compelled her to call on Elizabeth and atone for every arrear of civility, and only then did she find that Lady Catherine was at home to her when she called on her in town. Several months later she was finally able to resume her visits to her favorite salon. But although she was always civil to Elizabeth, Darcy, and Georgiana, she never fully forgave them.

Pemberley was now Georgiana's home, and the attachment

between the two sisters was exactly what Darcy had hoped to see. Elizabeth also had frequent visits from Mary and Kitty, who often stayed with them when they could not be at Netherfield. In the superior society enjoyed by Jane and Elizabeth, both sisters made great improvements in their manners and decorum, and by seeing Miss Darcy's behaviors they were able to model theirs on hers. In return they provided her with sisterly companionship and high spirits, and so great benefit was derived on both sides.

Jane and Bingley did not stay long at Netherfield, for such close proximity to her mother wore on both of their spirits; and within a year Bingley had purchased an estate in a neighboring county to Pemberley. In addition to every other source of happiness, the sisters were now within thirty miles of each other, and hardly a month passed without the carriages making the drive between the two homes.

Mr. and Mrs. Gardiner were frequent guests at Pemberley, most often staying for Christmas and the New Year, and the phaeton and ponies were certain to be used whenever they came. Darcy as well as Elizabeth truly loved them, and they were both conscious of the greatest gratitude towards the two who had, by bringing Elizabeth into Derbyshire, helped achieve the successful conclusion of Darcy's persistent pursuit.

The End

Thank you for taking the time to read Mr. Darcy's Persistent Pursuit. I hope you have enjoyed reading it as much as I enjoyed writing it!

You may be interested in following Lydia Bennet through her marriage to Jonathon Fret and her new home in Newcastle in Love's Fool: The Taming of Lydia Bennet.

Thank you to my ever-patient family as they listened, gave criticism, and encouraged me in this, my first foray into historical fiction.

And a big thank you to the fans and readers on Fanfiction.net, whose enthusiastic response inspired me to make this story available to a wider audience.

About the Author

Elaine Owen is the pen name of a married mother of two who enjoys reading, writing, martial arts, and music. She found her real life Mr. Darcy many years ago, but never stops enjoying reading and writing about the fictional version. Mr. Darcy's Persistent Pursuit is her first published work of fiction, and she is grateful that her critics seem to take more after Jane Bennet and less after Lady Catherine de Bourgh. You can contact her at ElaineOwen@writeme.com or catch up with her on www.elaineowenauthor.com.

Made in the USA
Middletown, DE
14 December 2018